Hunter and Morgan:

Gatecrasher

by H.K. Nightingale

Hunter & Morgan: Gatecrasher
First Published in 2019
by Happy Antlers Publications

ISBN: 978-1-9161775-0-5

For information contact:
Happy Antlers Publications,
Unit 10773, PO Box 4336
Manchester, M61 0BW

For my squee pack family, who always see me through.

Chapter One

One of the things Morgan loved about his job was that he never knew quite what to expect.

On one particularly dull day in June he found himself on a wet pavement in the centre-ish of Leeds, looking up at a drab and flaky sign. It said, 'Hunter Investigation Services' and was placed above a door that had been painted black quite some time ago. The address was right. The place was shabby, but otherwise as Pearl had described it.

Morgan knocked on the door. It rattled, as if one shove would put it clear off its hinges. Nothing else happened. Then Morgan noticed a button set into the wall to the left, marked 'press here'. So he did. There was a buzz, and an intercom hissed to life to emit a sort of barking noise. The lock clicked in a promising way, so Morgan clasped the tatty brass effect doorknob and pushed the door open.

There was a small vestibule, with stairs leading

straight up and a grubby white door to the left. The door had 'private, no entry' scrawled across it in marker pen, so Morgan headed up the stairs. At the top was another door. It had a window of frosted glass and creaked as Morgan swung it open and went through. Immediately inside there was a desk piled with papers and files and a thick layer of dust. To the right a cluttered coat stand, to the left a lopsided filing cabinet with a cycle helmet on top. Between the desk and the cabinet was a space just about big enough for Morgan to squash through.

He did so, trying not to touch anything; partly for fear of knocking over teetering piles of papers, and partly because of the dust, to which he was allergic. Beyond lay a larger desk, similarly cluttered but not to the same heights. And behind the desk stood a man.

The first thing Morgan noticed was his arms. He wore a smart white shirt with the sleeves rolled up to his elbows. He was tapping at his phone, and it made tendons shift in his forearms in an interesting sort of way.

"Yes? Who are you?" the man said. His accent was southern. London. Posh.

Morgan looked up. The guy would have had a handsome sort of a face if he hadn't looked so pissed off. It wasn't the smouldering sort of pissed off. It was more 'the milk's gone off and I put some in my coffee' sort of pissed off.

"I'm Morgan," Morgan said. "Morgan Kerry. The agency sent me."

"Oh." The man looked genuinely surprised. "The temp place?"

"'Oyster', yes."

"Right. I wasn't expecting a–"

Morgan raised an eyebrow.

"–person like you. Um." He coughed awkwardly and shoved his blonde, shiny hair out of his eyes.

"You mean you were expecting a woman."

"Only by statistics. I'm all for equal… Everything. Yep."

Morgan decided to be kind and let him off the hook. "It's all right. I get it all the time. Nobody expects a male secretary." He looked around at the piles and piles of papers. "Looks like you need some help, though."

"Yes. Well. The filing system's got a bit out of control."

"Hmm," said Morgan. "Where would you like me to start?"

"I guess you could file the invoices?"

"Great. Where are they?"

"Ah, well, if I knew that–"

"You wouldn't need help. Yep, I understand."

The man gave him a brisk half-smile and held out his hand. "I'm Hunter. Damian Hunter, but people generally just call me Hunter."

Morgan shook his hand. Nice firm grip. "Hello, Mr Hunter. Don't worry, we'll soon get everything tidied up and looking smart. It'll be much nicer for clients. First impressions and all that."

"I don't need it to look smart. I just need to be able to find things. My clients' first impressions are from the Internet. It's not the 1930s, Morgan. You don't get attractive young widows stumbling in here, dabbing at their tears with hankies and begging me to find out who murdered their husbands."

Morgan tried not to feel disappointed. "Well, I'd better get looking for these invoices, hadn't I?"

"Knock yourself out. Oh, but don't go in the bottom drawer of the filing cabinet on the right."

"Okay. Confidential files?"

Hunter had already gone back to fiddling with his phone. "Hmm?"

"The filing cabinet on the right. Confidential files? I imagine you must have a lot of those, in your line of work."

"Nah," said Hunter, barely glancing up. "The drawer sticks, is all. Oh, and that door over there, not the kitchen or the bathroom, the other one, I think it's a cupboard but I've never found a key for it. Let me know if you find one. Look, I need to go outside and make a call, the signal's crap in here. Will you be okay?"

He didn't wait for an answer, just swept from the office. The door rattled violently in his wake.

Morgan looked around at the piles of files and papers and God knows what, and sneezed.

Morgan touched the edges of the book as he did every night, a stroke along each side and a pat to each corner, to put the magical seals in place. The appearance of the book changed immediately. It lost its golden glow, its shimmer, the intricate designs etched on its leather bindings. It shrank. It appeared for all the world to be an ordinary book. Nice, but not the sort of thing you'd pick off a shelf. In fact, nobody would even think of taking it off a shelf, except for Morgan. The notion simply wouldn't occur to them, and within moments the book would be completely forgotten.

Morgan tucked it in its slot between Great Expectations and the B&Q guide to DIY on the bookshelf by his bed, and went to brush his teeth.

He kept thinking about Hunter.

Usually when people met Morgan they tended to like him. With one or two minor exceptions, he got on really well with people. He tried to be kind, and liked to listen to what others had to say. He seemed to have a natural charm, which his mother said came from his magic, and his uncle said came from his side of the family. Perhaps it was a little of both. Whatever the reason, Hunter's reaction had not been at all what Morgan expected. He'd seemed mostly irritated. Very strange.

Morgan brushed his teeth enthusiastically, half-singing, half-humming his way through a Kylie song, because it was how he timed it to make sure he brushed long enough. He rinsed and spat, and set his attention to his hair. He'd been growing it out, and it curled pleasingly around his ears and at the back of his neck. It was thick, dark and glossy. The problem was that it tended to stick up a bit on the top. The flatter he could make it lie down before he got into bed, the less chaotic it would be in the morning. Or at least, that was the theory.

Perhaps there was something else going on in Hunter's life that made him grumpy towards people, and Morgan had just stumbled into it. That seemed the most likely explanation. Pearl had mentioned he'd had quite a few temps lately. Perhaps they'd all let him down.

Or perhaps he'd pissed them all off.

It was only at that precise moment that Morgan realised that's what had happened. Hunter hadn't just been prickly or oddly unresponsive to Morgan's usual magnetic charms. He was actually a bit of a wanker.

Morgan shared his surprise with himself in the mirror. He replayed the whole conversation, from Hunter's opening 'you're not a woman' theme to his dismissive 'well, off you go, it's been an experience' followed by 'be here by nine tomorrow'. There hadn't been a lot in between except barked orders, heavy sighs of disappointment and the odd snap of arrogance. He hadn't once said please, or thank you.

Well then.

Morgan got into bed and pulled his paperback out from under the pillow. He was half way through 'Forbidden Blood': a particularly promising series about a vampire hunter and her werewolf sidekick, and had been convinced for three chapters now that this would be the volume when they finally got together. He'd just settled in when the front door banged.

"Only me!" yelled Caleb. "You asleep?"

"No," Morgan replied. He plumped up his pillow and went back to his book. A few minutes later there was a knock on the door.

Morgan sighed. "Come in, then."

The door opened a crack, and Caleb poked his head around it. Morgan patted the spot next to him on the bed.

Caleb came and sat. He smelt of pubs and stale aftershave. "You'll never guess who I saw."

"Idris Elba? Daniel Craig? That guy off the X-Factor?"

"No. None of them."

"Pity."

"Jennifer Lane."

"Who?"

"What d'you mean, 'who'? Jennifer Lane! From that first aid course we did when we were working at the solicitor's. The one who bandaged that guy from head to foot for trying to grab her arse."

Morgan grinned. "Oh, that Jennifer."

"Yeah, well, I saw her tonight in the pub, so I thought, right, seize the day. 'Cos that thought for the day thing on the calendar at work said that this morning. Carpe diem. So I went up and asked her to dance."

"She didn't bandage you, did she?"

"Au contraire, mon ami. She was very polite and agreed to dance with me, on but one condition."

Morgan waited expectantly. Caleb, who knew how

to tell a good story, paused until the tension had built just so, then said, "That her boyfriend could come too."

"Oh dear," said Morgan.

"No, no, no, you don't get it. Her boyfriend's bloody gorgeous!" Caleb giggled loudly and slapped the bed. "We had a three-way kiss in the car park and I'm going out to dinner with them next Thursday."

Morgan caught himself staring. He was as open minded as the next man, but still, he had not expected that. Not of Jennifer, anyway. Caleb always walked on the wild side. "Are you kidding?" he said.

"No! God, no, I couldn't make this shit up. You should see him, Morg, he's just the most gorgeous little twink you could ever imagine."

"I thought that was you."

They exchanged smirks. They'd agreed from the day Morgan moved in that there would be nothing more than friendship between them, because it was asking for trouble, shagging your room-mate. Caleb liked his life complicated. Morgan did not. Morgan's idea of a good date was curling up on the couch with a movie, or a whole Sunday morning spent alternately having sex and eating French toast. Caleb's idea of a good date was an orgy. With safe-words and a lot of feathers.

"So, how was your day?" asked Caleb, pulling the band out to free his hair from its man-bun.

"Oh, you know. Same as usual. So you're really going on this date?"

"Can you think of one good reason why I

shouldn't?"

"Won't it be weird, with two of them?"

Caleb gave him a squinty-eyed look of disbelief.

"It's just… How d'you know where to start? What if someone gets left out? Or feels jealous?"

"That's my Morgan. You'd be disappointed with a perfect sunset because you'd only see the dark coming."

"That's not true. I'm a very optimistic person."

"About everything except sex. Look, it's simple. The secret to a good threesome is communication, fair play and a bloody big bed. You should try it sometime."

"I think I'd just get confused."

Caleb laughed. "You didn't answer my question. What's the new place like?" He pulled his long legs up and sat cross-legged on Morgan's bed.

"It's okay. Apart from the boss."

"What's wrong with them?"

"His personality. He's arrogant. Demanding. Very annoying."

"Sounds like every boss I've ever known. Are you going back?"

"It's a week-long job. Maybe more."

"Ah, the lure of the long-term contract."

Caleb worked at the same agency as Morgan, but actively avoided any placements lasting longer than a week. It didn't do to get attached, he said.

"Or maybe you fancy him," Caleb said.

That earned him a thwack around the ears with 'Forbidden Blood'. "Did you miss the part where I said he was arrogant and demanding?"

"Ow! Arrogant and demanding can be a lot more attractive in bed than in the workplace."

"Not for me," said Morgan, firmly.

"You're so vanilla you may as well be custard."

"I am not custard. I just believe a relationship should be based on mutual respect and understanding."

Caleb sighed heavily. "And that, my friend, is why you are so very painfully celibate."

Morgan couldn't argue with that. But he told himself it didn't matter. If he was lonely - and he had to concede that sometimes he was - no number of one night stands would ever make him feel better. He'd tried it, the summer after he'd left college and split up with Henry. It had been a disaster.

He must have looked upset or something, because Caleb sighed again and gave him a hug. His skinny, wriggly body felt comforting pressed up against Morgan's, so Morgan hugged back.

"If he's horrible to you tomorrow, tell Pearl," said Caleb. He got off the bed and yawned.

Morgan rolled his eyes and shooed Caleb out of the room.

He could handle Hunter.

Chapter Two

At eleven the following morning, Morgan paused for a moment of celebration. He'd cleared a whole bookcase in Hunter's office. He'd even discovered some books in the process. A large, somewhat aged dictionary, Thompsons directories for the past six years and a dog-eared Jim Steinbeck novel. There were a few self-help books, too: *Quest for Success*; *Beat the Rest to Be the Best*; and *Crimes of Magic and the Men Who Solved Them* - the 1971 edition with the cheesy picture of the guy in a cape on the front. Morgan gave the bookshelves a good wash down and arranged the books on the middle shelf. He'd also exposed enough space on the floor to start sorting through the papers he'd removed from the bookshelf. He found a stack of slip files in a box in the corner and set about putting them to good use. He was getting a feel for the sort of material Hunter needed to file. The usual financials. Contracts. Case files.

The case files were confidential, of course, so Morgan tried hard not to read them. But they were all mixed up, so he had to at least notice names. He settled for trying to forget them as soon as he'd read them. His contract included a confidentiality clause but still, it was trusting of Hunter to let him loose on all this.

He heard the door downstairs open, letting the noise of the street in for a moment before it slammed shut again. Hunter's footsteps came running up the stairs. Hunter always ran up and down the stairs. He had a sense of restless energy and athleticism about him all the time. Morgan tried not to think about that.

"Morgan?" The interior door creaked as Hunter surged into the room. He looked a little flushed, as though the running had started before the stairs. "Oh, you found furniture. Congratulations!"

He stood in front of Morgan, a little out of breath, with a smile on his face. It made a refreshing change.

"I thought I'd file case notes by date opened," Morgan said. "Unless you'd prefer alphabetically by client? We didn't get a chance to go through things yesterday so I–"

"Ah. Yesterday." Hunter put his hands in his pockets. Somehow it gave him the look of a naughty school boy.

"Hmm," said Morgan, not at all sure where this was going.

"I was a bit of a grumpy prick with you yesterday, wasn't I?"

"Oh no, you–"

"I'm working on a case with some difficult people. Curse of the job, I'm afraid. And to be honest, I didn't expect Oyster to find someone as soon as they did. Not after they did a workplace visit for health and safety."

"It's very clean dust. And it's fine. Now, these case notes–"

"Never mind that for now. Do you have any plans for lunch?"

Morgan had a plastic tub of leftover pasta in his rucksack. That definitely didn't constitute plans.

Wait. Was Hunter inviting him to lunch?

"I'm flexible," said Morgan. He could have sworn that Hunter's eyebrow quirked itself at him. "I mean, no, no plans."

"Good. I'm meeting with a client. Come and take notes for me. It's always good to have a second pair of eyes."

Ah. Not a date. Well, that was good: Morgan did not need romantic complications in his life, and besides, only yesterday Hunter barely seemed able to tolerate him. But he would very much like to see Hunter at work. He gave Hunter a beaming smile. "I'd love to."

"Excellent. You might want to freshen up first. You've got a bit of…." Hunter touched his own hair at his temple. It was so fair and silky. Like spun gold. Morgan tried not to dwell on that and went to the bathroom adjacent to Hunter's office. The building was Victorian, and Morgan suspected the office had once been a bedroom. The bathroom would have been a dressing room. They were nice rooms: high ceilings with ornate mouldings; big windows that let in hefty streams of light in the late afternoon. He wondered, excitedly, whether there might be an original fireplace somewhere.

Morgan liked to find some kind of satisfaction in his work, however utilitarian his employers deemed it. He enjoyed pulling order from chaos, whether it was scanning a clutch of documents into one perfect pdf, or creating a filing system that lit up someone's' eyes because it actually made sense to them. Hunter needed all that Morgan had to offer in terms of filing and decluttering, but Morgan's end goal was grander: to leave Hunter with a beautiful work space. Somewhere spacious and airy where he could fit a proper computer. Morgan could imagine Hunter sitting at a big, real-wood desk, tapping at a sleek wireless keyboard. Stretching out his legs, muscles bunching in his thighs and-

"Morgan! Are you going to take all day?"

Morgan shook the thoughts out of his head, and a few dust bunnies fell out of his hair and landed in the sink.

He put the cold tap on full and stuck his head underneath it.

The venue for lunch was an artisan bakery two streets away from Hunter's office. It was called 'Sophie's Bakes'. Morgan had walked past it a few times and it always smelled good, but he hadn't realised that there was a cafe above the shop as well. It was surprisingly spacious: more than a dozen tables and plenty of space between them. The decor was simple, with scrubbed pine tables, white table linen and grey wicker chairs that matched the stylish wooden blinds at the windows. Hunter chose a table half way between the windows and the entrance. It was square, with a chair at each side. Morgan sat next to Hunter, rather than opposite, hoping it seemed less date-like.

A waitress skipped up to them with menus. Her hair was braided close to her head in four neat rows, finished with metal beads that clattered together when they moved.

She smiled at Hunter, and flicked a curious glance at Morgan. "Can I get you guys something to drink?"

"Some water for the table, please, Grace," said Hunter. "Three glasses, we're meeting a client. Morgan?"

"Water's fine," said Morgan.

"Three glasses, gotcha," said Grace and clattered her way through a swing door which presumably led to the kitchen.

"D'you come here a lot, then?" asked Morgan.

"It's very handy. And the staff are discreet."

Morgan felt a little thrill at the notion they were doing something secretive. He supposed it went with the territory for Hunter. "Is there anything I should know about whoever this is we're meeting?"

"His name is Osbourne White. Or so he claims."

"That seems an unlikely name."

"People are often wary about giving their real names. It doesn't make much difference to me so long as there's a non-bouncing cheque at the end of the deal."

"You get paid by cheque? Not many people do that anymore."

"It's a figure of speech, Morgan."

"Oh." Morgan fiddled with the corner of his napkin. "Anything else I need to know?"

"I would rather keep you innocent," said Hunter. The corner of his mouth twitched, as if he was trying not to smile. "Anyway, keep an open mind. See what you make of him. Ah, speak of the devil, here he is now."

Morgan looked eagerly towards the door, imagining someone tall and distinguished, perhaps with a trench coat and a shifty expression. But the person who came to shake Hunter's hand was short, with a bit of a paunch that threatened to pop the buttons on his stripy, pinkish shirt. He'd done that thing some men do when threatened by male-pattern baldness: he'd had his hair trimmed really close, almost shaved. As if trying to convince everyone that he'd lost his hair on purpose. But the overall effect was a salt-and-pepper shimmer that did nothing but highlight his smooth, shiny pate.

"This is my assistant," Hunter said. "Morgan Kerry."

"Pleased to meet you." Morgan shook hands and smiled his best customer service smile. "Mr White."

"Call me Ozzie," said Osbourne White. Maybe he

had used his real name after all. Morgan didn't suppose most people with false names thought up nicknames to go with them.

Ozzie sat to Morgan's left, opposite Hunter, and picked up the menu. "Any recommendations? I don't often get to this part of town."

"The falafel burgers are excellent," Hunter suggested. "Or the halloumi salad. If you're vegan, the quinoa–"

"Oh no, I eat anything," said Ozzie. "Burgers sounds good. Do they do fries?"

"I'm sure they do," said Hunter.

Grace returned with water and three glasses, each primed with ice and lemon, and pulled a pad out of her apron to take their order. Morgan chose a goats cheese and beetroot sandwich, with a side of olives. Hunter went with the halloumi salad and Ozzie was delighted to find that they did, indeed, have fries, even if they were sweet potato ones.

There was a wine list and although Morgan couldn't drink anyway, what with his allergy pills and his sense of professionalism, he was mildly surprised that Hunter didn't offer alcohol to his client. It might have put the guy at ease. Little beads of perspiration kept appearing on his bald brow, and he twisted his hands nervously in his lap, fiddling with his wedding ring. But instead of plying him with wine, Hunter switched on a cool but pleasant smile and said, "Please don't worry, Mr White. I'm sure we can help you."

Morgan wondered who the 'we' referred to. Was it

a 'corporate we', meaning Hunter's firm, or was he including Morgan? In which case, was there a chance his contract might be extended?

No. Of course not. He was getting ahead of himself. And anyway, Hunter had switched on the charm overnight. Who knew when he might switch it off again?

"I'm not worried," said Ozzie, against all appearances. "I know this is the right thing to do."

"Of course," purred Hunter. "So, what brought you to me today?"

"I found you on 'Trust PI'. You had five stars. Quite a lot of them from people with my sort of problem."

Hunter nodded, as if this was entirely to be expected. Morgan wanted to ask about Trust PI, but he was supposed to be observing. Nothing he couldn't look up later.

Hunter said, "You'll find my reputation is well deserved."

Ozzie nodded. Clearly whatever reservations he may have had, doubting Hunter wasn't one of them.

"So," Hunter said. "What can we do for you?"

Ozzie took a long drink from his water glass, and took a deep breath. "It's my daughter," he said.

"Yes?" said Hunter.

Ozzie's forehead wrinkled. His looked down at the lemon floating forlornly in his drink.

Morgan leaned forwards. He was fascinated. What was it about the guy's daughter? Was she in trouble? A custody battle, perhaps?

"She's my baby," Ozzie said, his voice cracking. "I can't bear to think of her out there all alone."

"Ozzie." Hunter's voice was soft. Sympathetic. Patient. Morgan didn't know he could even make that kind of noise. It was so different from yesterday's barks and sarcastic comebacks.

"She's been missing for three months," Ozzie said. "The police won't do anything because her mother told them she's okay."

"Do you think her mother's lying?"

"Put it this way. We have different ideas about what 'okay' might look like. It means she's alive, yes. But well? Happy? Doing her GCSE coursework? I doubt it." Tears welled and threatened to spill down Ozzie's cheeks.

"Is she living with her mother?"

"Her mother says so. Like I said. She has a very different idea of parental responsibility. That's a big part of why we split up."

But he was still wearing his wedding ring.

Grace arrived with their food. Ozzie withdrew into himself a bit, barely noticing the arrival of his burger and sweet potato fries. Hunter thanked Grace, turning his best smile on her, but he was keeping an eye on Ozzie too. Morgan followed suit.

They began to eat. Morgan's sandwich was delicious. Ozzie took a bite from his burger and chewed, but he had the look of a man who was eating for sustenance rather than pleasure.

Hunter didn't say anything, except to ask Morgan

if his lunch was okay. Morgan gave him an enthusiastic affirmative.

Eventually, Ozzie said, "She met someone."

The daughter or the wife? Again, Hunter didn't ask. He just created the space for Ozzie to talk.

"He's older than her. She's only fifteen."

Hunter paused, and rested his knife and fork gently on his plate.

Ozzie continued, his burger abandoned. "I've got to find her. I've just got to. Please."

"Mr White," said Hunter. "Before I take this case, I need to know everything. From the beginning. Please?"

He caught Ozzie's gaze. They looked at each other across the table for a long time. Morgan discretely got his notebook and pen out. And then Ozzie told them his story. He'd split up with his wife a year ago, but they weren't divorced. His wife was the one to leave, and at first his daughter, Poppy, stayed with him. It made sense: her school was local, her friends were nearby and she'd always been a bit of a daddy's girl. But over the past year she'd changed. Got in with the wrong crowd at school, dropped her old friends. She would stay out 'til all hours and come home smelling of smoke and alcohol. Then one afternoon, he came home early from work to find her having sex with a man on the living room sofa. Ozzie recognised the man. He was a teacher at the dance studio she went to for lessons. She wanted to be a choreographer. She was very talented. Destined for fame. She wanted to study Performing Arts at University. He showed them a video of a show she'd been in with her drama school. She was wearing leg warmers and a leotard, her hair pulled back into a severe bun. She was thin, tall, long-legged. Morgan could imagine her being a dancer.

Ozzie had been very angry to find her that afternoon. He'd shouted, she'd shouted back, the man had run away like the spineless coward he was. Ozzie had grounded her and sent her to her room.

When he went to check on her an hour or so later, she was gone. Her bedroom window was open and she'd taken her school rucksack and some clothes, a few toiletries. Not much, especially for a teenage girl who loved her make-up and fashion. He thought she'd be back by bedtime.

But she wasn't.

The following morning he called her mother, who told him Poppy would be living with her for a few weeks. That was three months ago.

He wanted Poppy to come home. He'd serve custody papers, if necessary. But he'd need evidence. He needed proof that her life was chaotic, that she was squandering her potential due to his wife's bohemian, permissive lifestyle.

He wanted to see his little girl again. Tell her he loved her. That she could put the past behind her and come home. Forgiven.

Hunter listened to all this very carefully, and his sympathy never wavered.

When Ozzie had finished talking, Hunter said, "It would be my privilege to help. If my terms are agreeable to you?"

Ozzie erupted with gratitude. He got up from his seat, clasped Hunter's hand in both of his and squeezed. Hunter murmured reassurances.

"I have some paperwork with me," Hunter said. "But please. Finish your lunch first. I'll start work on the case as soon as I can."

Once the floodgates had opened it seemed Ozzie had no idea how to stop them. He ate, enthusiastically, having apparently recovered his appetite. And as they ate, he showed them more photos of Poppy on his phone: kids birthday parties, dance recitals, first day at school, a holiday in Whitby. She looked like a happy kid, as far as Morgan could tell. It was hard to imagine the little girl in the tutu growing up into a stroppy teenager. But Morgan had worked in a lot of schools, and he'd grown up with six cousins, all younger than him. It happened to everyone: the rebellious phase; the narcissism; the moods. Even to him, if his mother was to be believed.

Ozzie ate, signed the contract without reading it, and left Hunter with another warm handshake. He gave Morgan a polite 'goodbye'.

Hunter ordered coffee. Morgan had peppermint tea. Grace cleared the table, smiled at Morgan when he thanked her, and put a mug of Americano in front of Hunter, and a steaming teapot, china cup and saucer and a little pot of honey in front of Morgan. The combined scent of rich coffee and light peppermint was surprisingly refreshing.

"Thoughts?" said Hunter, when Grace had left them alone again.

Morgan's first thought was 'God, you're magnificent'. What he said was, "He really misses his daughter." Which was too lame for words.

"That's a given."

"And she seems to like him. Or at least she used to. It's probably just a teenage strop."

"And the boyfriend?"

"Should know better."

Hunter nodded approvingly, as if Morgan had just passed some kind of test.

"But there's something off," Morgan said.

Hunter leaned forward. "Yeah?"

"Definitely something. But I don't know what."

"That's where I come in," Hunter said. "Watch and learn, Morgan. Watch and learn."

Morgan was humming to himself when he got back to the flat that evening. He'd had a very successful afternoon and cleared the whole north-eastern quadrant of Hunter's office. He'd hoped he'd get to discuss the ins and outs of Ozzie's case with Hunter, or at least offer some more of his observations, but Hunter had gone straight out again after lunch, given him a key and told him to lock up after himself. He'd barely been in the office long enough for Morgan to propose the beginnings of a filing system.

It didn't matter. No harm in firming up his theories about Poppy White before he offered them to Hunter.

He found Caleb in their living room, surrounded by what looked like the entire stock of a jumble sale. It was spread across both sofas, the coffee table and most of the carpet.

"I'm going to regret asking, I know," said Morgan. "But what are you doing, exactly?"

"Isn't it obvious?" Caleb's hair was escaping its ponytail to form a halo of unruly waves around his face. He shoved it out of his eyes. "I'm trying to find something to wear. And I have nothing. Nothing, Morgan."

"The dark grey jeans are nice."

"They're not. They make my knees look knobbly."

"Ah." Morgan began to pick his way through piles of t-shirts towards the kitchen. "What's the occasion?"

"I told you. I have a date with Jennifer and Dave."

"Oh. Your orgy."

"It's not an orgy. Just dinner."

"Would you like a cup of tea?"

"Of course I don't want a cup of tea. I want a bottle of vodka."

"That's probably not a good idea."

Caleb squealed his exasperation. Morgan put the kettle on.

"This was a terrible idea." Caleb leaned in the doorway of their tiny kitchen, pouting.

"So cancel."

"How's your stupid boss?"

"He took me to lunch."

Caleb made a stupid 'oo-er' noise.

"It was work. He needed help with a case."

"Seriously? That sounds exciting."

"It was really interesting. I don't suppose I should discuss it."

"Don't be boring, Morgan."

"It was a guy looking for his daughter."

"I hope you're sure it really is his daughter and not the victim of a really creepy stalker."

Morgan was sure Hunter had checked it all out.

Wasn't he?

The kettle boiled.

Caleb drifted back into the living room and his piles of clothes while Morgan made them both cups of tea. He picked up his iPad from the kitchen counter where it had been charging and tucked it under his arm. He gave Caleb a mug of tea and cleared a space on the sofa from the piles of abandoned shirts.

"Dinner is so complicated," Caleb said.

"I think it mostly involves food." Morgan fired up his iPad and took a sip of tea while it demanded his fingerprint. "At least you're not cooking."

"It would be so much easier if I was. The person who's cooking sets the rules. The guest has to negotiate a veritable minefield of social expectations."

"You're good at this stuff. You're the most expertly social person I've ever met."

"Every situation is different, Morgan. Fraught with niceties and conventions and the ever present Damoclean sword of inadvertent transgression."

"It's possible you're being a bit of a drama queen

about this."

Caleb snorted theatrically and threw a shirt across the room.

Morgan typed 'Trust PI' into Google and tapped return. "Grey jeans," he said. "Blue shirt. The one with the tiny doves on it. The thin belt with the buckle shaped like a Celtic knot and your clubbing shoes. The ones with the ridiculous pointy tips."

"I… Oh. Well, I could try that on, see what it looks like, I suppose."

Morgan didn't know anything about fashion. But he knew a lot about Caleb.

TrustPi.com was a website about Private Investigators, approved by the The Association of British Investigators - Hunter had the ABI logo at the bottom of his contracts, so presumably he was a member. Morgan bookmarked the site and swiftly scanned its contents, while Caleb went off to his bedroom to change. There were advice pages on topics from 'How to Choose and Investigator' to 'Why not go to the police?' and 'How to make a complaint'. There was a section on personal safety and links to agencies for just about anything, including missing persons, the AA and the Citizen's Advice Bureau. It left Morgan with the impression that there were all kinds of lost souls out there hoping, in moments of dark desperation, that someone like Hunter might solve all their problems.

Finally, he went to the tab marked 'Discussion' and found a forum. He tapped quickly on the topic called 'Reviews', and was faced with over three hundred pages. Then he realised they were organised alphabetically, with a thread for each PI company. A few taps and he'd found Hunter's reviews.

He'd expected the reviews to be a mixed bag, the Internet being as it was. But they were amazing. No score lower than four out of five, and the vast majority were five stars. He read the first few that appeared. Caring. Supportive. Meticulous. Fearless.

Those weren't words he'd have instantly associated with Hunter, although he suspected that 'fearless' could well be true; he just hadn't witnessed it yet. Caring? Supportive? Well, Hunter had treated Osbourne White that way, certainly. But meticulous? Morgan recalled the endless piles of dusty papers and shuddered.

"Okay, so you were right." Caleb returned, wearing exactly what Morgan had suggested and looking fabulous. He'd left his hair loose, just whispering over his shoulders, and he was wearing eyeliner. Caleb wasn't technically Morgan's type, but Hell, Jennifer and Dave were in for quite a night.

"You look amazing. Are you going to clear up all the stuff you're not wearing? Or should I put it in a charity bag for you?"

"God, Morgan. You're such a nag, you know?"

Morgan smiled to himself and sipped his tea.

Chapter Three

Morgan started his Wednesday by hoovering the Northwest quadrant within an inch of its life. The colours on the rug brightened up a fraction, but it would take more than a hoover to make it clean. Mental note: make list of carpet cleaning firms. Even if Hunter ignored it, or ripped it up, or used it to start off another pile of paper in the space Morgan had cleared, at least he'd have tried. The thought of Hunter undoing all Morgan's hard work the minute he'd left made him feel a bit sick. He needed to get the filing system worked out, fast.

The now-familiar thump of the front door opening dragged Morgan out of planning mode and was followed by footsteps taking the stairs two at a time. Hunter.

"Shit, what the…" Hunter's voice boomed through the half-open door to his office. "Oh, it's you. I thought we'd been burgled."

"Morning," said Morgan.

"You're early. God, you haven't been here all night, have you?"

"I'm supposed to start at nine."

"And it's ten to." Hunter didn't even have to look at his watch.

"So I thought I'd get the noisy part done before you got here. I hope that's all right. Only you did give me a key and—"

"Of course. Well, I can't fault your enthusiasm. But you're not a cleaner, Morgan."

"Perhaps you should hire one."

Hunter looked at the patch of bare carpet. "How are those invoices coming along?"

Morgan felt a prickle of failure. "Nothing yet. Just case files and newspaper clippings, mostly. Oh, and a box of computer parts."

"That was here when I arrived. I never really knew what to do with it."

"Shall I throw it out?"

Hunter gave Morgan one of his lopsided smirks. "Why not? I think that would be quite liberating."

Morgan grinned back. Or possibly mirrored the smirk. Hunter was wearing a black t-shirt, which stretched snugly across his chest and hugged his firm, rounded biceps. His eyes were twinkling.

Morgan cleared his throat. "I should get on. Unless you want to talk about the case, first?"

'Which case?"

"Osbourne White? From yesterday? I took notes

like you asked, and I've typed them up. Should I email them to your regular email address, or do you have a confidential one?"

"No need. I'll ask if I need to check anything." Hunter pulled out his phone.

"I had a few ideas, if you–"

Hunter put up a hand to shush him, held his phone to his ear and started talking, moving back towards the door. He shut it behind him and took the call at the top of the stairs.

Morgan felt a pinch of disappointment, but really, what did he expect? He knew nothing about PI work, and, thanks to his perusal of TrustPI.com, he was well aware of the dangers of amateurism. He wasn't here to detect anything other than invoices. So he put Osbourne White to the back of his mind and resolved to get started on the north west quadrant.

He stuck the hoover in the corner of the room and set to work. Morgan had (naturally) developed a system over the past two days. As he couldn't yet reach the filing cabinets, he had arranged a row of stacking boxes along the wall by the bookcase and roughed out a colour coding system for typical materials. Things that needed to be kept together, like case files, went in a clearly marked file. A lot of the stuff Hunter would need to go through himself, which gave Morgan a pang of anxiety every time he considered mentioning it to him. But even if he never got around to it, Morgan figured he could at least stack the lot of it in a corner marked 'archive' and put the filing cabinets into use for contemporary items.

Thankfully, Hunter wasn't adding to the mess as Morgan worked. There was no sign of a printer, and not one piece of paper mail had arrived since Morgan started. Perhaps what Hunter really needed was a curator.

And those invoices. Right.

Hunter stuck his head around the door. "I'm going out. Probably most of the day. Are you okay to lock up tonight?"

Morgan once again had to bite back a twinge of disappointment, but he put a grin on his face and said, "Actually, it'll go a lot faster without anyone getting under my feet." Which was absolutely moronic and so unprofessional Morgan shocked himself.

But Hunter gave one of his barky laughs and said, "Right you are."

His footsteps faded down the stairs, and Morgan was alone with the South West quadrant.

This area of the room contained the desk that had formed the initial obstacle to getting into the office. It was covered in old cardboard boxes and piles of papers, but Morgan could make out the outline of a rather nice curved reception desk underneath. Had Hunter had an assistant at some point? A receptionist? It seemed unlikely, if he didn't receive his clients here at all.

A distant pulse of drum and bass started up from the vintage clothes shop next door, and Morgan pulled the first pile off the desk to go through.

Most of the papers there were letters, including a

few from the bank that Morgan sneaked a proper look at. They were dated a few years ago and were moderately threatening. Apparently business hadn't been so good back then. He put them in the financials box, in date order. At least he didn't have to worry about Hunter paying him: the agency took care of all that. Anyway, more recent bank statements were much more promising. And Hunter could afford to take clients (and assistants) to lunch.

Like Osbourne White.

What had been the point of that? It had been so exciting, the idea that Hunter trusted him to really be part of his work after only a couple of days. To give him a little insight into his world of mystery and adventure. But that seemed to have fizzled to nothing overnight.

Unless… What if it was a test? What if he was leaving Morgan to his own devices to see what he was made of?

And if he was made of the right stuff, perhaps he'd get to stick around longer. With Hunter.

Morgan slumped against the edge of the desk. He couldn't afford to develop an attraction to Hunter. Hunter was his boss. He blew hot and cold worse than the heater in Caleb's car. And he didn't even like Morgan very much. Not like most people did. Unless…

What if he did like Morgan, and it was a problem? Because he was the boss. Perhaps he thought the agency frowned upon clients who seduced their temps. (They totally did: he could imagine the look on Pearl's face right now, complete with steam coming out of her ears.)

Wait.

If Osbourne White had found his 15-year-old daughter having sex with her dance instructor, why the hell hadn't he called the police?

Or had he?

Morgan pulled out his phone, opened his browser and started searching. News items, court appearances, dance schools. Poppy White, dancer. He found a Facebook page for a production of Grease that she'd been in just a few months ago, run by her dance school. Adrenaline started to rush through Morgan's body. He Googled 'Flash School of Performing Arts', found the site, clicked on staff... And there they were. Poppy's teachers.

And every single one of them female.

Morgan made a chirrupy noise of excitement and searched some more. Went back through dozens of photos of old productions, programmes, reports in the local press. There had never been a male teacher at that school, at least, not in Poppy's lifetime.

Osbourne White was lying.

Morgan tried his best to focus on the job at hand. He considered phoning Hunter to share his discovery, but he wanted to do it face to face. Was it even safe to be sharing case details over the phone? Certainly not in a text message. No. He'd wait until Hunter got back.

By six o'clock Morgan had revealed another quarter of carpet, a desk chair and two fully usable and mercifully empty filing cabinets. He'd worked an hour extra, but it was worth it. He hoovered the rug, polished the desk and stacked another two boxes with the rest by the bookcase. Finally he went to the bathroom and washed off the stickiness and dust of the afternoon as best he could. He didn't want to be the stinky person on the train nobody wanted to sit with. He wet his hands and ran them through his hair a few times. Six fifteen. And still no Hunter. It was disappointing not to be able to share his news, but Morgan had run out of excuses to wait.

He went back to the lovely, curved reception desk, now restored to its full glory. He sat for a moment while he popped his lunch box back inside his rucksack, and then he lingered for a moment longer to run his hand over the smooth wooden surface. Perhaps he should bring in a pot plant. A pen holder. Maybe an in tray of some kind…

The door swung open. Morgan had been so absorbed in his desk daydream he hadn't heard Hunter come up the stairs. And now here he was, staring at Morgan and the desk as if he thought he'd come into the wrong office.

"Fucking hell," said Hunter.

"Sorry," said Morgan, and stood up from the desk he needed to remember was not his.

"What for? This is brilliant!" Hunter cracked a smile that lit up his whole face, shifting from astonished to delighted in the blink of an eyes. "You've made serious progress, Morgan."

Morgan looked around him. "Well, yes. I haven't found the invoices yet, though. I've divided everything up by–"

"Do you fancy a drink?"

"I was about to–"

"Unless you have a train to catch, or…?"

Morgan processed what Hunter was saying to him. "No! I mean, not a specific one. Is this another meeting with a client?"

"No. Off the clock. I sometimes go to the Pig and Fig around the corner after work for a drink and something to eat. It beats the microwave, right?"

"Oh." Morgan's belly was all a-flutter. He had to remind himself, very firmly, that this was a work thing. Hunter was pleased with his performance, that's all. "Thanks. That would be great. There's something I wanted to talk to you about, anyway. If that's okay. I mean, a work thing."

"So long as it's not too tedious. I spent all day at HMP Doncaster."

"The prison?"

"Of course, the prison, Morgan. C'mon. If I'm going to tell you about my day I need a pint in my hand first."

The Pig and Fig was more of a bar than a pub, really. Its decor was colourful and there were a lot of mirrors. The menu was 'Mediterranean-Indian fusion', which was a bit strange, but Morgan wasn't averse to spiced aubergine so it worked out fine. He had a peach and strawberry mocktail, while Hunter had a glass of foggy, in-house micro-brewery beer called 'Pig-in-a-Poke'.

"So you've been in prison," said Morgan, unable to contain himself.

Hunter rolled his eyes. "Never overnight, I'm glad to say."

"Who were you visiting?"

"A very nasty man who is refusing to divorce his wife out of spite. Or, at least, he was." Hunter's half-smirk came out again. "I think he'll decide differently after today."

"How did you persuade him?"

"I tried common sense. Then I tried veiled threats. But he was as stubborn as a rock, so I had to pull out the pictures."

"You had pictures?" Morgan leaned in a little, fascinated.

Hunter nodded. "And a video, but I didn't have to go that far. People should be careful when they're going dogging, at least if they don't want to get found out."

"Dogging?"

Hunter paused with his glass half way to his mouth. "You do know what dogging is, don't you, Morgan?"

"You mean dogging as in…" Morgan's cheeks went hot. "Public sex?"

"Taking your pug for a trip round the park isn't exactly grounds for divorce, now, is it?"

"No, I mean I know, so… Dogging? Don't they wear masks? I mean, so I've seen. On documentaries.

And such." Morgan cleared his throat.

"On this occasion, they were dressed in full fur-suits. Dogs, zebras, minotaurs, the lot. Quite the party. And our naughty little puppy was taking it up the arse from a fox."

Morgan's brain short-circuited at the word 'arse'. He'd been trying very, very hard not to think of sex and Hunter at the same time, and as soon as Hunter said that word he failed spectacularly and imagined Hunter nailing him up against a tree. He scrambled himself back as fast as he could. He wasn't actually drooling, but his trousers were tight and Hunter was looking at him funny.

"A f-fox?" was all Morgan's poor brain could manage.

"With a big bushy brush."

Morgan was struggling his way around that mental image when the food arrived. He'd never been more grateful to be distracted by the smell of sweetly spiced vegetables.

Logic filtered back through Morgan's neural pathways and presented him with a conundrum. "If he was wearing a fur suit, how can you tell it's him?"

Hunter swallowed a piece of chicken and grinned. "That's the right question, Morgan. Two words: birthmark and Prince Albert."

Technically that was three words, but Morgan did not have the presence of mind to correct him. "On the, um, puppy?"

"Yep. Both very distinctive. Oh, and the car he was

getting fucked on was his, too, registration plate clearly on show. Very clumsy. Poor guy, he had no idea his mate had been snapping away while he was getting it on with Mr Foxy. Or that the minute he got himself locked up for carrying with intent to supply, his mate went round to console his wife. One thing led to another... And voila. Grounds for the divorce he didn't want."

"Did his wife know he's gay?"

"Even he doesn't know he's gay." Hunter's nose wrinkled up. "At least he claims he's not. Just a one-time thing."

"In a fur suit? In public? That's pretty specific for a bit of experimentation."

"Quite."

Morgan set down his knife and fork and took a gulp of peachy strawberry drink. Then he took a deep breath, ignored the heat in his cheeks and said, "I hate that straight guy bullshit. Big turn off for me. I refuse to be anyone's experiment."

He glanced at Hunter to get an idea of his reaction. Hunter held his gaze, nodded once and said. "Yes. Same."

A thrill went down Morgan's spine. He'd thought so. He'd felt a vibe. But magic didn't amp up your gaydar, and Hunter was one of those ambiguous sort of guys who didn't give out signals.

It shouldn't matter. Hunter was his boss.

Hunter. With the broad shoulders and the quirky smile and brilliant blue eyes, way bluer than eyes had any right to be.

"Another satisfied customer." Hunter raised his glass.

"What? Er, oh. Yes." Morgan clinked it with his own. "Speaking of customers, I did a bit of checking about Mr White."

"Ah, our missing daughter case. And?"

"I thought he was a bit relaxed about the man he found her with. Her dance teacher. Considering he was older and in a position of trust and everything. Only, it turns out there aren't any male dance teachers at that school. Not one, the whole time Poppy's been going there. So either her dad made a mistake or he made it up."

"Actually, it was a bit of both."

"Pardon?"

"The guy was a dancer, but not from the dance school. He was a fellow student from her A-Level Dance and Performance Class. Six months younger than she is. They'd been to dance practice the day Ozzie found them, so the guy had his dance kit with him, including a big bag with the dance school log on it. Osbourne put two and two together and came up with five. Then he embellished a few points to make himself look better and voila."

Morgan felt a bit disappointed. He'd thought he was so clever, doing all that research. But it turned out he had nothing Hunter didn't already know. Shit.

"So what d'you think?" Hunter said.

"What did he embellish?" Morgan said.

"Well, put it this way: would you risk having sex with your boyfriend in the middle of the living room when your Dad was due back from work any minute?"

"I don't… My Dad was never around."

"Semantics, Morgan."

"Oh, well, no. Even when Mum was away, I wouldn't." How were they talking about sex, again? Did all of Hunter's cases hinge on some specifics of an illicit sexual act? And did he have to look so smug (in a cute way, damnit) while he talked about it? As if he was testing Morgan's embarrassment circuits so he could tease him more effectively?

"Seriously?" Hunter said.

Morgan glared at him and bit down hard on a bit of mushroom. It was delicious. Everything here was delicious.

He was so screwed.

"My Dad was pretty strict," Hunter said. "And he wasn't entirely on board with what he called me being a 'friend of Dorothy'. Well, he said he was, because I don't think he wanted to seem like an arsehole. But he's always been twitchy about it." Hunter shrugged his shoulders and dragged a chip through his chicken gravy. "Point is, I don't think Ozzie saw nearly as much as he thought he saw. I think he saw his sweet little girl snogging a boy and lost his temper."

"The outcome was the same. She left because he was being over-protective."

"Ah, but it could be very important for him to face up to what really happened. He needs to let go of his little fantasy, because otherwise any custody mediator could simply point out to him that, according to him, his daughter's dance teacher assaulted her under his roof, and he didn't even report it. It's a good thing there isn't a bloke teaching at that school, or you could throw a libel suit into the mix."

Huh. Morgan hadn't thought of it that way, exactly. He'd been focused on what Ozzie had to hide, assuming he had a sinister motive. "Do clients often lie to you?"

"One way or another, yes. Human nature, I suppose. They assume I need winning over."

"And you don't?"

Hunter subjected Morgan to the full force of a twinkly-eyed smirk. "Not always."

Morgan resisted the urge to squirm in his seat and look away, and instead he grinned back. He'd been told he had a devastating smile. The way Hunter stared at it suggested he thought so too.

It was gone eight o'clock by the time they left the pub. The day was cooling off as it slipped into a pleasant, sunny evening. It turned out that Hunter was headed for the station, too, so they walked together, talking about movies (they both had a weakness for arty films and 1960s avant guarde) and music (Hunter liked classical, Morgan was more about obscure indie bands) and theatre (Hunter loved everything, Morgan had only ever been to the pantomime). Eventually they reached the station turnstiles, where they had to part for different platforms: Morgan for Burley Park and

Hunter for York. Hunter said, "Thanks, Morgan. You're doing a really good job with the office."

And Morgan was going to say, "No problem, it's a pleasure." But he didn't get the words out.

Because Hunter kissed him.

His mouth was incredibly soft. He touched the back of Morgan's head, so gently. It was over in a flash, leaving Morgan gasping, "Oh," as he registered that Hunter was moving away, towards the escalator to platform fifteen, but he was walking backwards so he could grin at Morgan and wave as he went. Morgan stood and watched him go all the way up, still grinning, until Hunter reached the top, turned and jogged over the bridge and out of sight.

Back at the turnstiles, Morgan stared at the departures board, then at the vending machine, and then at the blue sign that said 'Leeds' in big letters.

Then he said, "Well," to nobody in particular. And went to Platform 2.

After a short wait and a ten minute train ride, followed by a brief walk to Cardigan Road, Morgan opened his front door, walked up two flights to the top floor apartment he shared with Caleb, fumbled his key into the lock - funny, his hands were shaking - and went to the living room. Caleb sat on one of the two big leather sofas. The TV was on, volume low. There was a tray on the floor with dirty dishes from Caleb's dinner. The coffee table was covered in books and comics and controllers for the PS4 and remotes for the TV and the strawberry lip balm Morgan kept forgetting to put back in his pocket. Everything felt normal. Not at all unusual. You'd never know his mysterious, very handsome boss had kissed him or anything. He might have imagined it.

Caleb glanced up from the laptop he was balancing on his knees and frowned. "What's wrong?"

"Nothing," said Morgan.

Caleb gave him his 'what the fuck' face.

"I mean," Morgan said. "Maybe something."

"Uh-huh?" said Caleb.

"Can I ask you a question?"

"Absolutely anything. Nothing's off-limits to ol' Caleb, remember? TMI a speciality."

Morgan edged into the room and perched on the couch beside Caleb. His rucksack squashed against the cushions, so he took it off and dropped it on the floor.

"Well?" said Caleb.

"Have you ever, um, felt attracted to someone you shouldn't feel attracted to?"

Caleb laughed. "Only every other Thursday." He counted off on his fingers. "Gym teacher, best friend at school's mum, best friend at school, Ian McKellan - don't get me started, right? - that Mormon who knocked on the door the other week… I could go on all day. Why?"

"It's never happened to me before. No, wait, it has. I had a crush on Roger Federer like, God, I mean, but. Not someone real. And forbidden."

"Forbidden why? You don't have any restraining orders that I'm aware of."

"The boss."

"Pearl? Morgan, my boy, you are full of surprises."

"Stop it."

"Hunter," said Caleb, softly. Morgan liked how he said it, his northern accent deepening the 'u' and softening the 't'.

"Yes," said Morgan.

"Well, crushes can be fun. Innocent fantasies when he bends over the desk to pick up a stray paper clip, that sort of thing."

Morgan instantly imagined Hunter spread over the newly cleared desk back in the office, his perfectly rounded, firm, gorgeous arse stuck in the air. He groaned. When had he even noticed Hunter's arse?

Yesterday. When they went to lunch. Hunter had gone up the stairs ahead of him. "Caleb, what am I going to do?"

"You've only got another couple of days working there, right? You'll be fine. Perfect length of time to pine."

"And, um, what if I'm not pining, exactly?" Morgan gave Caleb a meaningful look on the word 'pining'.

"Ooooh. You mean he recognises the wonder that is Morgan Kerry? And he's gay?"

"Yes. Um. He kissed me. A bit."

"A bit?"

"Once. Tonight. At the station. Then he went to York, and I came here and now I have no idea what's going on or what it even means, or what the hell I'm supposed to do in the morning."

Caleb put a hand on Morgan's shoulder. "Listen to

me very carefully. It's simple. Tomorrow morning you get on the train and you go to work and you fuck him within an inch of his life on the photocopier."

Morgan shoved his hand away. "It's not funny."

Caleb laughed. "It is a bit."

"I don't laugh at your sexual disasters."

"I don't have sexual disasters. Merely triumphs."

Morgan flopped back on the couch. He could still taste Hunter's kiss. Or at least he imagined he could. Beer, mostly. A trace of lip balm. Watermelon flavour.

His mouth had been so damn soft.

"It's not the end of the world," said Caleb. "You're both consenting adults. If you want a bit of that, you take it. Think of it as a bonus. When your week's up, walk away. Or if you want more, well, then you'll be free to do what you want, right?"

Caleb made it sound so straightforward. Maybe Morgan was overthinking things. It might not even mean anything: maybe Hunter had done it on a whim, and all would be forgotten come the morning.

"I know what'll cheer you up." Caleb snapped his laptop shut and discarded it to the other end of the sofa. "Let me tell you all about my absolutely delightful dinner party with Jennifer and Dave."

"Can't wait," said Morgan.

Chapter Four

Morgan was in the office at eight thirty the following morning. Thursday morning. Only two days left.

The south-east quadrant awaited, with its coat stand and coy hint of a picture frame, and the infamous sticky filing cabinet. If Morgan could crack this one, people would be able to enter the room without shuffling sideways.

Nine am. No Hunter.

Morgan set to work.

Hunter still hadn't shown up by midday. Morgan went to Sophie's, but chickened out of going up to the cafe. Instead he spent far too long downstairs in the shop choosing a sandwich to go. But just as he was leaving Grace came down the stairs and said a friendly, "Hi."

"Hi," Morgan said back. "Is, um, have you seen

Hunter today?"

"Not today. Are you expecting him?"

"No. No, it's fine," said Morgan. "Bye." And he left before he could embarrass himself further.

He checked his phone for the millionth time, then took his sandwich back to the office and ate it with the slice of leftover quiche he'd brought from home.

Two pm. No Hunter. And something else was happening. Morgan wasn't making nearly as much progress as he'd expected to. He should have sailed through by now and filed away most, if not all of the papers. He'd done twice as much work the previous day. But he kept checking his phone. He'd find himself staring into space, going over half a dozen potential scenarios that ended up either with a phone call from Pearl to tell him Mr Hunter had put in a complaint and he was fired, or Hunter running up the stairs, into Morgan's arms and having his wicked way with him against the sticky filing cabinet.

Or perhaps Hunter would never come back at all, and Morgan would be left to sort out the filing, leave on Friday, hand the key back via the agency and that would be that.

Morgan slumped miserably on the shiny desk that had seemed so promising yesterday and stared at his phone. Willing it to ring and just as scared as to what might happen if it did.

And then, a phone did ring. In the office. But not his. No Taylor Swift ring tone: this was an old fashioned 'brring brring'. A landline.

Morgan hopped off the desk and looked around the office. He hadn't even known Hunter had a landline. All the publicity info, including his business card, just had his mobile.

And yet, it rang.

He finally located an old-style analogue phone under a pile of stuff under the window in the as yet untouched north-western quadrant. He picked it up, blew dust off the handset and, in his best telephone manner, said, "Hunter Private Investigations, how may I help you?"

"Hello?" It was a posh sort of hello, male voice.

"Good afternoon. How may I–"

"Is Dame there?"

"I beg your pardon?"

"Dame. Damian, I suppose."

Damian Hunter. Right. "I'm sorry, Mr Hunter is out of the office at the moment. May I take a message? Or I can give you his mobile number."

"He's not answering his mobile. I had a call from the hospital this morning but I was in a meeting."

Morgan went cold all over. The hospital? Oh shit. "I haven't heard anything." His voice sounded like a hollow, far away thing.

"Oh. I thought the hospital might have called his office but I guess they're only allowed to contact next of kin and he has me down as his partner, so–"

"What happened?"

"Sorry?"

"What happened to him? Why's he at the hospital?"

"Beats me. I'd better get down there and find out."

"Should I… I mean could you… Um… Can I take your name? In case he gets in touch."

"Oh, it's Peter. Peter Curtis. If he calls, tell him I'm on my way. Thanks."

There was a click, and then the insistent hum of the dialling tone. Morgan put the phone down and sat suddenly on the floor.

What the hell had happened to Hunter?

And if this Peter was his partner, what did that mean? Hunter didn't have a business partner. Which left… Boyfriend. Spouse.

Okay. Breathe, Morgan. Don't go jumping to conclusions.

He got out his own phone and Googled Peter Curtis. He got the answer straight away. Peter's Facebook was locked down but his mother's wasn't. And there was Peter: fair haired, brown-eyed and devastatingly handsome, with his paws all over Hunter. Family gatherings, a Pride march, some sort of award ceremony. Morgan looked at Peter clutching a Perspex trophy while Hunter looked at him with googly eyes, and tried to breathe.

It made a certain sick kind of sense, that was the thing. Like karma for wanting to have sex with his boss. Maybe Morgan was a revenge thing for Hunter. Or a spite thing. Maybe they had one of those relationships where it was okay to do other guys.

Whatever he was, it wasn't what he'd hoped, and just when he should be getting angry, he was actually terrified, because what the hell had happened to put Hunter in hospital? He could phone but that Peter guy was right. They wouldn't tell him anything: he was just an employee. Worse. A temp.

Shit.

What should he do now?

Face the facts. Hunter wasn't his boyfriend. Not even his friend, really. Hunter was a client, his boss until the end of Friday. They'd had a minor indiscretion. That was it. What he should do was perfectly straightforward.

He should finish the job.

Morgan ignored the squirrelly ache in his guts, picked up a fresh storage box and got to it.

Just as he was boarding the train home that afternoon, Morgan got a text from Hunter.

>Sorry, shit happened. OK now. See you tomorrow.

There were no seats free, so Morgan looped his arm around a pole and leaned against the luggage rack. He put his phone away as the train lurched on its way and breathed a small sigh of relief. Hunter was okay. One more day at Hunter PI and then Morgan would go wherever Pearl sent him next, Hunter and Peter could carry on their lives together and life would go back to normal.

Hard to believe that just twenty-four hours ago they'd been flirting over dinner and coming out to each other.

When he got home he found a note from Caleb pinned to the fridge (Out with J and D, back late, don't wait up Cxx) so Morgan shoved a frozen veggie bake into the microwave and made some tea. The flat was hot and stuffy, so he opened all the windows that actually opened. It didn't make much difference; the air remained still and thick. He took his dinner into the living room, turned on the TV and sank his conscious awareness into *Pointless* while he ate. After dinner he had a cool shower, which made the air feel marginally less stifling. He pulled on the soft cotton shorts that served as pyjama bottoms for the summer, sat cross-legged on his bed and got out his book of magic.

He traced his fingertips over the spine, the edges, the ridged stack of pages, until, with a soft whoosh of magic, the book transformed into its real form: a golden, sparkling, leather-bound tome. He flicked through the pages, each rich with brightly coloured manuscript, until he got to page seventy-three. He put his palm flat on the page, pulled his power into his chest and whispered: *Draconis.*

Magic glittered and swirled down his arm to his hand and from there to the page beneath. The air around Morgan went cool as he pulled energy through himself to fuel the spell. He slowly pulled his hand away from the book, and there sat a little gold dragon. No bigger than a bunny, with shimmering scales and a feathery mane; soft, iridescent wings which it lazily spread and flapped, as if it was waking from a long sleep. Which, in a way, it was. Morgan hadn't summoned it for several weeks, restricting himself to just the magical exercises he needed to do each day for control and wellbeing. That's what Ms Rosero said they were for, anyway. It certainly hadn't helped much with either over the past week.

"Are you going to be whiny?" said Aiyeda. She spoke in a husky Spanish accent, nothing like Morgan's blend of London and Yorkshire English. Her golden scales took on a hint of grey-blue at the tips. "I hate when you're whiny."

"I don't want to talk about it. Just… Come here."

Aiyeda waddled off the book and up onto his knee, then hopped into the hollow formed by Morgan's crossed legs. He gently stroked the dragon behind her ears and the little horns that sat between them and she made a rumbly noise. Aiyeda's claws weren't particularly gentle where she clung to his ankles, but she couldn't physically hurt him. She wasn't, exactly, real. She was a manifestation of Morgan's magic, an avatar of that part of his psyche. Most majos called them familiars, but Morgan was deeply averse to cliché. When Aiyeda had first manifested to his teenage self he'd rolled his eyes at the fact she (or he: gender was fluid for magical manifestations, apparently) was a dragon. He'd wanted an echidna or a wombat. A llama. Something cool but totally not what you'd expect to be magic. Ms Rosero had snorted and told him that a dragon was a perfect reflection of him, because he was so flamboyant and dramatic.

Ms Rosero had a lot of opinions, but she was also a

saviour as far as Morgan was concerned. She'd arrived mysteriously at his primary school at the end of year six, for special lessons with him and a girl called Hannah. Morgan had always known he could do things most other people couldn't. Little things, at first. He could make candle flames wave about a bit. Create ripples in a glass of water. The other children always seemed to like him. He was instinctively careful with it, but it didn't mean much more to him than, say, if he'd been really good at maths like Chantelle, or been able to turn his eyelids inside out like Sanjay did. Then one day Ms Rosero turned up and explained to Morgan and Hannah that she'd be taking them for extra lessons in elemental control. Which sounded suspiciously like chemistry but, it turned out, wasn't. It was what most people called magic. Hannah was way ahead of Morgan: she'd visited her grandmother in Jamaica last summer and had learned how to make little fireworks spring from her fingertips.

Mostly what Ms Rosero taught them, however, was control. Because a lot of people didn't like magic, majos had to be regulated, licensed and regularly counselled and monitored. Once a month from the age of twelve, Morgan had to go to meetings with other local majos. He used to call it 'MA' because it felt a fuck of a lot like a meeting for addicts and losers. People who couldn't deal with their own abilities. And Morgan could deal fine, thank you very much.

Until the day he burned down a warehouse.

It was Ms Rosero he'd called from the police

station. Most people might turn to a solicitor, or their parents - he was only just eighteen - but Morgan knew nobody would believe this was a case of teenage high-spirits, a dropped cigarette or even an expression of vandalism inspired by his frustration at being brought up without a father figure in his life (that had never bothered him, despite what the social workers said). It was, in fact, accidental arson, inspired by his own stupid desire to show off to a boy he'd fancied. It had backfired horribly. The boy could have been killed or maimed, if he hadn't been a really fast runner.

Somehow, Ms Rosero convinced the police that it was an accident. The experience of being arrested was more than enough of a wake up call for Morgan. She wouldn't explain how she did it, but Morgan had his suspicions. People generally liked him, in a vague, friendly sort of way, at least until he did something really annoying to burst the bubble. But Ms Rosero seemed to get her own way more often than not, which was a whole step higher up the scale.

From that day he went to meetings of the local coven every month; he meditated every day; he did his control exercises; and he treated magic with every ounce of the respect it deserved. He didn't use his power to light candles, or make ice cubes, or make extra fireworks for bonfire night. He tried to charm people with who he was, not the power he held coiled within him. He deferred his offer to study elementalism at university until it expired, and signed up to Pearl's agency as a temp. Temping was ideal: nobody could get too close. It worked.

It had worked.

Morgan curled up on his bed and tried very hard not to think about Hunter, while his magic curled up in his lap, rested her head on one knee, and purred to comfort him.

Morgan awoke with a start as his bedroom door opened. He was instantly alert, heart pounding - until he recognised Caleb's familiar face peeping around the door. The room had got dark, but there was no missing Caleb's profile: the slightly hooked nose, angular jaw, the wavy hair brushing his shoulders.

"Morgan?" Caleb whispered. "You okay?"

Morgan flicked on the bedside lamp and blinked at him. "I was asleep."

"Sorry, man. Sorry. It was just you didn't do the washing up and the TV was on."

Caleb never did any washing up unless he was asked and spread chaos wherever he went, so it seemed unfair, to say the least, that he should wake Morgan up to complain about a dirty plate. Morgan sat up and tried to make sense of things.

"Can I come in?" asked Caleb.

"Sure." Morgan glanced down to the bed. Aiyeda had faded while he'd been asleep. "What time is it?"

"About two." Caleb sat next to him.

"Is something wrong?"

"I didn't mean to wake you."

"No problem. What is it?"

"I just feel… We had sex. Me and Jennifer. And Dave. At least, sort of, but… I dunno, man. They're married."

"What, like, an open marriage?"

"Obviously. There was a photo by the bed. She's in a white floofy dress and everything, and there were bridesmaids. So I asked and they said, yeah, but that was between them and whatever they did with anyone else was separate. It killed the mood a bit, for me at least. I left as soon as I could. I felt kinda used. Does that make sense?"

He sounded small and fragile. Morgan put an arm around him. "Of course it makes sense."

Caleb's propped his chin on Morgan's shoulder. "I don't want to be someone's boy toy, you know? It changes the whole power thing. Like they're a unit and they could gang up on me. I don't know. I'm probably being a total prat."

"You're not a prat."

"And it plays up to the pansexual stereotype. Will fuck anything. Not satisfied with one gender, must have them all. Like Pokémon. Oh shit, I'm not even making sense to myself anymore. I'm sorry, Mor, I shouldn't have woken you up."

"It's okay." Morgan hugged him.

"I wasn't sure you'd be back tonight. Thought you might have sailed off into the sunset with wonder boss."

"He's not a wonder boss. He's a bit of an arse, actually. That and I'm incredibly naive."

"Do I need to punch him?"

'I don't think that'll be necessary. Besides, he's been in hospital most of today."

"Did you punch him?"

Morgan laughed. "No, Caleb. I did not punch him. I'm pretty sure he works out an actual gym. Punching him would be foolish."

"It's not about strength. It's about intent. Or something. What did he do?"

"His boyfriend called the office while he was out."

Caleb pulled back a bit so he could make eye contact. "Seriously?"

"Yep."

"God, we shouldn't be let out. The world is full of bastards and we are just two innocent twinks with 'prey' written on our foreheads."

Morgan couldn't argue with that.

They sat there for a little while, nestled up to each other. Then Caleb sighed.

"Want some hot chocolate, twink?" said Caleb.

"With whipped cream on," said Morgan. "Twink.

Chapter Five

The door to the office was open when Morgan arrived for his last day, and he could see Hunter's silhouette through the frosted glass. Morgan cleared his throat, as if he expected Hunter to be in the middle of something he wouldn't want him to know about.

He opened the door. Hunter stood by his desk, with his phone in one hand. The other arm was in a sling.

"Are you all right?" asked Morgan, with a lot more concern than he'd planned.

"I'm sorry about yesterday. You've made great progress here."

Morgan glanced at the relative calm that was the South-West quadrant: its sticky filing cabinet, rather lovely print of a Caribbean island and acres of freshly hoovered carpet. "Thanks. I should be able to get the rest finished today. I still haven't found those invoices. What happened to you?"

"I had a run in with an old client. Nothing to worry about."

"Oh. Good." He wanted to ask about Peter, and the hospital, and what was wrong with Hunter's arm, but he stopped himself. It wasn't any of his business. "So. Um, I'd better get on."

Hunter frowned at him. "I have to go out for a while." He sounded reluctant, for some reason. "Would you like to join me for lunch?"

"With a client?"

"Well, no. Just the two of us."

"I'm sorry. I'm already meeting someone." Amazing how lies could just fly out of Morgan's mouth when he was angry. Whoosh, just like that. Normally he was terrible at it. But he'd gone through shocked and sad and disappointed and now here he was. Furious.

"Oh. Well, some other time, yeah?"

Morgan smiled politely. There wouldn't be another time. After today he never intended seeing Hunter ever again.

"Right," said Hunter, with a confused sort of smile. It obviously hadn't even occurred to him that Morgan could have found out about Peter. "Well, I'm going to see Poppy White's boyfriend now. You could come along if–"

"I'd better not. As it's my last day. And, you know. Invoices."

"Right," said Hunter, again. Now he looked defeated. Good. Served him right.

It was only when Hunter had gone, and Morgan

was alone with his storage boxes and files, that he realised how much he would have loved to meet Poppy White's boyfriend. Not to be with Hunter. But because he'd encountered a mystery, and Morgan yearned with every fibre in his being to solve it.

Just before lunch, Morgan found the invoices. They were in a pile on top of Hunter's desk, covered by a mountain of old Time Out magazines and some take out leaflets. Morgan dropped the invoices in Hunter's freshly discovered and cleaned in tray. Job done. Now he just needed to devise a filing system that Hunter might actually use in the future and he could leave with the knowledge of a job well done.

Not that it mattered whether Hunter used the filing system or not when it was done. That wasn't Morgan's concern. At all.

There was a buzzing sound. It took Morgan a moment to place it as the buzzer for the office: there hadn't been a single visitor all week. He hurried over to the button by the door and pressed it. "Hunter Private Investigations. Can I help you?"

"Well, I could do with investigating." Caleb's voice came through the speaker, all deep and sultry.

"What do you want, Caleb?" said Morgan.

"Thought you might like lunch. Unless you're otherwise engaged?"

"No. I mean. Yes. Lunch is fine. I'll be down in a sec."

He grabbed his rucksack, locked the door behind

him and jogged downstairs. Caleb was waiting for him out on the street.

They went to Costa, because Caleb was fussy about his cinnamon lattes. Morgan glanced at Sophie's on the way past, then firmly looked the other way. Costa was busy and noisy as usual, but at least they got a table away from the counter so they could hear themselves think over the squeal of the coffee machine.

"So I was wondering." Caleb picked at his chicken and Caesar wrap. "Maybe I should give Dave and Jennifer another chance. And then I thought, don't be stupid, Caleb. I mean, didn't it hurt enough the first time? Right?"

"Right."

"And after that I thought, well, who's fault is that? They're not mind readers. They weren't to know I'd feel weird about them being married."

"They lied to you."

Caleb scowled. He'd probably been trying to ignore that part.

"By omission, admittedly," Morgan added. "But it was a pretty important thing to omit."

"What about your boss? Has he paid for his crimes yet?"

"I don't know. He did something to his arm. It doesn't matter, anyway. Four more hours and I'm done. Pearl's already lined me up with some work at an estate agents for next week. Are you really thinking about getting in touch with Jennifer and Dave again?"

Caleb sighed. "I don't know. I know I shouldn't. But

then I remember how good it was before we got to the bedroom and I saw that stupid photo. The anticipation, the flirting…"

"Yeah."

"And then, heartbreak. Maybe it's best to give the whole thing a rest for a while."

Morgan bumped his cup of tea against Caleb's latte. "I'll drink to that. Stay strong, Caleb."

"Yeah. You too."

Caleb walked back with Morgan after lunch, as he was done for the day and it was on the way to the station. They were deep in conversation about potential co-ownership of a small air-con unit for the flat when they arrived at Hunter PI. Only to find that Hunter himself was standing there, pulling his keys out of his pocket.

"Hi," said Morgan. "Here, let me." He put his own key, that he'd had out and ready since they turned the corner into the street, into the lock and opened the door.

"Thanks," said Hunter. But he made no move to go inside. He was too busy cruising Caleb. Or at least, giving him a curious glance. Bastard.

"Aren't you going to introduce us?" Hunter said.

"This is my flatmate, Caleb," said Morgan. "Caleb, this is Hunter. My boss-for-the-week this week."

"Hi," said Caleb. He wasn't looking at Hunter with quite the measure of hostility Morgan would have preferred. But that was Caleb for you.

"Flatmate, eh?" said Hunter. "Well."

"We just had lunch," said Morgan. See, he could even back up his lie now.

"We did indeed," said Caleb. "And now he's all yours for the rest of the afternoon."

Hunter's smirk appeared. Morgan tried not to look at it. "Best get back to it." He nodded at Caleb. "See you later."

"Absolutely," said Caleb, and winked at him.

Okay, that was a bit strange.

"Right," said Hunter. "Nice to meet you."

He shook Caleb's hand, which was a surprise to both of them, and then Caleb strode off down the sheet, hands in pockets, whistling the Ghostbusters theme. It was one of the few things Caleb could actually whistle.

Morgan gave Hunter a platonic, professional flash of a smile and led the way upstairs.

Hunter paused in the doorway to his office, his eyes wide with wonder.

"All right?" said Morgan. "I found the invoices."

"You found the desk," said Hunter. "And a whole carpet. And a floor lamp. Did I always have the floor lamp?"

"Yes. I left a pot of wax in the top drawer. You should polish the desk once a month or so. Especially when it gets colder again. It's real oak."

"It is?" Hunter looked at the desk as if he'd never seen it before. It was truly magnificent: so big it dominated the room, with sturdy legs carved into lions paws at the bottom. There was a secret compartment under the built-in leather blotter, and another one in the top right hand drawer, which had a false bottom. The locks and handles were brass, gleaming now that Morgan had polished them up. It was a work of art. The battered leather office chair Hunter had been using looked better just for being next to it. As if the batteredness was somehow manly and deliberate. It could do with a desk lamp and a few tasteful accessories. And not the giant PC screen Morgan had initially imagined. No, that was far too modern. Just a discrete laptop. A MacBook Pro. Timeless and stylish.

"I feel like I've had a makeover," Hunter said. "Thanks so much."

"Just doing my job."

"I thought you were an office temp. Not an interior designer."

"Absolutely. I was just looking for those invoices, after all."

Hunter did one of his trademark bark-laughs.

"I've got a system in mind for the filing. Can I run it by you? Then if you agree I'll be able to get everything put away before I leave tonight."

"Oh, right. It's your last day."

"That's right."

"I was wondering if you'd like to stay on a bit."

"Sorry. I've already got my next assignment. But I'm sure Pearl can find someone else for you. Now, that system…?"

Hunter ran his fingers along the edge of his desk. "Right. Yes, of course. Whatever you say, Morgan, I'm sure it'll be fine."

Morgan insisted on explaining it anyway. Hunter wasn't really listening most of the time, but he nodded and agreed. It was a bit disappointing - normally Morgan went out of his way to match the system to the client, but Hunter hadn't been around enough for him to get much of an idea as to how he worked. Other than that he was clever, charming (when he wanted to be) and a fucking liar who lied about his relationship status.

System explained and approved, Morgan set to clearing out the storage files and loading up the filing cabinets. Hunter sat at his big, impressive desk and got out a notebook and pencil. He doodled for a while and then said, "Can I ask your opinion on something?"

On what, exactly? Fidelity? Open relationships? Kissing people and running away? "Of course."

"Poppy White's boyfriend confirmed what we thought." (Morgan noted the use of 'we'.) "They weren't having sex, even, just snogging, so he says. Although he thought he might have had his hand up her shirt." (Morgan had a sudden, visceral imagining of sliding his hand up under Hunter's shirt, because his imagination was a traitor with no moral compass.) "Poppy's dad went ballistic, got into a big fight with Poppy and chucked the boyfriend out of the house. Threatened to call the cops if he ever came near the place again. A bit extreme, right?"

"Yes."

"Funny thing, though, Poppy hasn't been in touch with this guy since. And that was the first time she'd let him near her. She'd come on to him out of nowhere in dance class, practically dragged him back to her place. And she must have known there was a good chance she'd get caught, because her father usually got home around that time."

"She was spoiling for a fight?"

"Looks like it. But, why? And why did it have to involve a guy like that?"

Morgan thoughtfully slipped papers into their newly-labelled files. "I'm assuming that whole 'goading people into having heart attacks' is just a TV thing?"

"Pretty much."

"What if she wanted an excuse to run away?"

Hunter raised an eyebrow.

Morgan continued, filing more rapidly as his mind worked at the problem. "She was a big Daddy's girl, but for some reason she wanted to go live with her mum. So she picked the one thing she knew he'd lose his temper over, lit the blue touch paper and stepped back. Boom! Daddy goes off on one, she fights back, runs to her mum and says she has to live with her now because her dad had a jealous fit over her boyfriend."

"Heh." Hunter leaned back in his chair and grinned at him. "You're good at this."

"Did I get it right?"

"I won't know for sure, not without talking to her or her mum. The so-called boyfriend wouldn't know, and I don't want to challenge Ozzie's view of things until I'm certain. Thing is, I can't get too close. Obviously Ozzie doesn't want either of them to know he hired me to find dirt on them."

'Tricky," said Morgan. He introduced another case file to its new home: Cold (blue tab) > Divorce > Client dropped.

"Stay another week, Morgan. You're not a known PI. You could go in undercover. Ask a bunch of innocent questions."

A thrill of excitement fizzed in Morgan's belly, but he couldn't indulge it. How could he solve the case - or whatever it was - if it meant being in close quarters with a man who'd lied to him, just as all these poor pillocks in the divorce cases had been lied to? A man whose kiss Morgan could still remember. Still wanted.

Yeah, sorry Ozzy. No can do.

"I told you. I'm already assigned. Sorry. I really hope you find out what happened."

Hunter's face fell. A tiny muscle in his cheek twitched. "Yeah. Okay. Not to worry. I'll work something out."

"It's for the best," said Morgan, firmly. He might have said it to convince himself as much as Hunter, but it was also the closest he'd come to saying, 'keep your kisses to yourself, you philandering git', so it was important.

Hunter's phone rang. Predictably, after a brief and one-sided conversation which Morgan had come to realise was typical of Hunter's introductory call with a new client, Hunter said he had to go out. Presumably to meet the client. It might take him a while to realise he had a perfectly serviceable office to meet people in now.

The filing cabinets filled up fast; faster than Morgan had expected, in fact. There was a lot of stuff. By the time he reached the last storage box (not even including the archive) the only drawer left was the bottom one in the filing cabinet by the door.

The sticky one.

Morgan gave it a tug. It was the only thing left in the whole office that didn't work as it should. He wasn't sure he could have left it even if he hadn't had a whole stack of files all labelled up with nowhere to go.

It didn't budge.

He tried to pry it open with a ruler. A letter opener. A screwdriver. (He'd found some truly fascinating and useful things in the drawers of Hunter's desk.)

It still didn't budge.

Dammit. Morgan really wanted to finish the job. And he really wanted to open this fucking drawer.

There was one way.

He reached out his hand.

Morgan's magic wasn't about spells or magic words. His magic book wasn't really a book of spells. It was a conduit, an enchanted object that helped him to channel his magic safely.

Much like the necklace he pulled out from under his shirt, where it usually lay. Nothing remarkable: a narrow but sturdy strip of leather thonging from which dangled a small, flat, polished stone with a stylised tree of life etched on it; but it helped Morgan to focus his magic when intricacy was more important than power. Morgan held the tree, reached for the cabinet and called to the metal of the battered old filing cabinet.

There. A snag of steel, bent out of shape when it had taken a boot to the lock. A long time ago now: rust was moving in and eating away at the folded metal.

Morgan curled his fingers in the air and sculpted steel. Slowly, with a soft groan, the filing cabinet straightened and flattened and tucked its way back into its original shape. Morgan formed a fist and pulled in, towards himself.

The drawer opened.

Morgan shook out his hand, releasing the last little fragments of power he hadn't used. He was good, these days, at taking just what he needed, bit by bit. No surges.

Inside the drawer was a shoebox. Nothing else. Morgan took it out and lay it on the carpet in front of him. He took off the lid. It was full of keepsakes, notebooks, journals. Instinctively he knew he shouldn't be looking; the whole collection of stuff screamed 'private' at him. But he did pick up the topmost photograph. An old photographic print, fading with age. There was a woman in the photograph, with a baby in her arms. She was standing in the porch of a pretty substantial-looking house. She had long blonde hair and wore a dress with hefty shoulder pads that screamed '80s'.

The door downstairs thumped open, and Morgan had the photo back in the box and the lid on in a single breath. What should he do? Put it back in the cabinet and pretend he'd never opened it? No. Hunter would notice. Okay. Honesty. Always the best policy.

He put the shoebox on Hunter's desk and scrambled back to the box of filing, taking out the first folder just as the office door opened.

"Hi," he said, not looking up. "Nearly done."

"You got that open," Hunter said. Morgan thought there was… something, in his voice. But he wasn't sure what. He glanced up; Hunter was already on his way to his desk, and the shoebox.

"Yeah. I have a knack with filing cabinets. That looked personal, so I left it for you to take care of."

Hunter ran his fingertips over the lid of the shoebox. He didn't open it. "Thanks. I'll–"

"There's plenty of room in the desk drawers. They're all lockable."

"Right. Thank you. Morgan–"

"And voila." Morgan shut the no-longer sticky drawer and brandished his empty archive box. "All done." He glanced at the big, old fashioned clock he'd found and put up over Hunter's desk. "Five oh five."

"I was wondering–"

"I'll be off, if that's okay." Morgan put the archive box in the stack with the others and picked up his rucksack. On a whim, he went back to Hunter and firmly held out his hand. "It's been a pleasure. Good luck with Poppy and Ozzie. I know you'll figure it out."

Hunter opened his mouth, shut it again, and shook his hand.

"Um, thanks," he said.

And that was that.

Chapter Six

Move-U occupied a small shopfront on Headingley High Street. It used to be an off license, but now it was a state of the art estate agents. It had an interactive display unit in the front window which allowed customers to flick through a stream of tempting properties. It was one of Morgan's duties to clean the display each morning after it had been mauled by local drunks.

By Friday he had come to really hate the drunks of Headingley. Not only were there bodily fluids smeared freely over the window, but someone had decided to write 'my new crib' under the display unit with a Sharpie, along with a drawing of a spurting cock and balls. And when he finally managed to get the ink off, it became apparent that they'd scratched their delightful design into the glass with something sharp before they'd coloured it in. Morgan poured his bucket of soapy water down the drain, stuck the alcohol spray into his apron pocket and traipsed inside the shop, peeling off his rubber gloves. "Wendy, we'll need to get someone out to get the scratches out of the window. Do you have anyone on the books?"

"No, Morgan. We don't have a French polisher or an animal behaviour consultant on the books either." Wendy thought she was really good at sarcasm. She wasn't. She was irritating and dismissive and God, Morgan hated this gig.

"Well, I've done the best I can," he said. "I'll get on with the rental applications, shall I?"

"Well, d'uh," said Wendy, with a savage tap of her mouse. The printer started whirring in the corner.

Morgan put his cleaning stuff away, washed his hands in the tiny break room and snuck to his desk before Wendy could try to stun him with her wit again.

Only seven hours, and he could go home, go to bed and never come out again.

The door swooshed open and a woman came in. She was dressed in a skirt (short but smart) and jacket, with a white blouse. Her hair was a warm blonde, straight and glossy, brushing her shoulders. She wore sandals with an impressive heel and cute straps around the ankle. Her nails were very red. Expensive-looking glasses perched on her nose, narrow with thin gold frames.

She ignored Wendy's, 'Hello, can I interest you in any of our lovely properties?' and headed straight for Morgan's desk.

He'd seen her somewhere before. Couldn't quite place where.

"Hello," he said. "Can I–"

"It's Morgan, isn't it?" she said.

"He's just admin," said Wendy. "But I can–"

"We met on a first aid course," the woman said and thrust out her hand. "Jennifer Lane."

Oh, okay. Caleb's friend.

Morgan shook her hand. "Um, hello."

"How are you?"

'Fine. You?"

"Fine. I've been trying to get hold of your friend Caleb."

"Really?"

"He's your flat mate, I believe?"

"That's right."

"Is his mobile phone working?"

For those of us who aren't blocked. "As far as I know."

"Oh." She looked crestfallen.

Morgan glanced at Wendy, who had her eyes fixed on her computer screen but was listening so hard he was surprised her ears weren't bleeding with the effort. "I could ask him to call you, if you like?"

She looked at him over the top of her glasses. "So you think his phone's working fine calling out, hm?"

Morgan shrugged. "I don't know. But I can ask him. If you want."

"Has he, um, said anything about us? I mean, me?"

Wendy got up to walk to the printer, giving Morgan

a hard stare on the way.

"The thing with Caleb is, he's big on honesty. He's had some bad experiences in the past. You might not think it, with that whole bad boy thing he has going on, but he's surprisingly vulnerable. With that in mind, shall I ask him to call you?"

She bit her lower lip and nodded. "Thanks. I'd appreciate it."

"Now, you'd better go before you get me fired," he whispered. "I'm in for a bollocking as it is."

Jennifer glanced at Wendy as if she'd forgotten she was even there. Her dom-lipsticked mouth curled up in a snarly sort of grin. "No you're not, sweetie," she whispered back. "Leave her to me." Then in a louder voice she said, "Thank you, Mr Kerry. I'll speak to your colleague."

Half an hour later she left with an armful of information about the upcoming executive office development and left a dreamy-eyed Wendy calculating a future commission that would never happen.

Morgan could see why Caleb liked Jennifer.

After the longest day in Morgan's working life (and considering he'd worked in call centres, that was saying something), he dragged himself up to the hot, stuffy living room in the flat and threw himself face down on the sofa. He groaned. His back ached from the very unergonomic chair; his legs ached from hours spent at the photocopier; and his head ached from being in Wendy's company all day. At least Mark would be back on Monday. It wasn't so bad when Wendy had two targets to throw her crass, unfunny comebacks at.

Caleb got home an hour later, as his current assignment was at the University of Huddersfield. lucky bastard. Uni gigs were always a walk in the park: they didn't have time to train you in their labyrinthine systems, so you got all the easy work; they understood the importance of good coffee and everyone was on flexi-time so no-one expected you there before nine. Caleb stood by the sofa with his hands on his hips, considering him.

"Stop with the judgy face," said Morgan. He'd managed to roll on his side and turn the TV on to watch *Pointless*, but nothing else.

"You don't have to go back next week, you know. Just tell Pearl they're taking advantage."

"It's not so bad," said Morgan. He muted the TV and closed his eyes.

"Yeah, right. Obviously. Honestly, you're hopeless." Caleb stomped off to the kitchen. "Tea?" he yelled.

"Thank you," Morgan yelled back.

Caleb returned with two mugs and a bag of Thornton's chocolates. Morgan hauled himself upright to make room for him on the sofa. Caleb sat, opened the bag and offered Morgan one. "Dorota's birthday," he said. "Everyone in the office got chocs."

"Seriously?"

"Yup. I think she has the hots for me. I got a muffin as well."

"That reminds me. Jennifer came into the office today."

"Jennifer?"

Morgan bit into his chocolate with a snap; his mouth filled with salted caramel. It was the nicest thing that had happened to his mouth since… well, for a long time. "She wants to talk to you. I think maybe even apologise. I said I'd pass on the message."

Caleb's eyebrows scrunched up into a scowl.

"You don't have to," said Morgan.

Caleb offered him another chocolate. Strawberry cream this time. God, if Caleb would just spend the rest of their lives feeding him chocolates, maybe they'd make a great couple after all.

"Here's the deal," said Caleb. "I make us omelettes and oven chips, you go and run yourself under a cold shower 'til you're awake, and then we'll go out."

"Go out?" whined Morgan. "Why would I do that?"

"Because you've been moping all week and it's not healthy."

Morgan grunted.

"Also, I just offered to make you an omelette, and my omelettes are fabulous." That was actually true. "And I shared my chocolates with you."

"I still don't want to go out."

"And yet, you are going to go anyway. It's okay. I won't take you clubbing. It's drag quiz night at The Bridge."

"Why must you be like this?"

"Get in the shower, and you can have another

chocolate."

Morgan's eyes narrowed. "I hate you."

But he got in the shower anyway.

The Bridge was unequivocally gay, unapologetically camp and unavoidably loud. Caleb was wearing a clingy purple skirt and false eyelashes, along with glittery purple nail polish, an old black and grey Black Sabbath t-shirt and a pair of sparkly silver Converse. It was enough that he counted as drag, which got them in half price, but muted enough that he just looked like a damn pretty boy. Morgan hadn't done drag since that one time at college. It didn't really appeal to him: he'd felt clumsy, all elbows and knees and stompy platform boots. Caleb just looked gorgeous and as at ease as he ever did. They found seats at a table with a couple Caleb knew from somewhere or other, and Morgan supposed it might not be a bad night after all.

"This is Morgan," said Caleb, as they sat down.

"Oooh, your flatmate," said one of the pair; his skin was like polished mahogany, his eyes huge, deep brown, with an appealing innocence. He had a wicked smile, too. He was wearing something with sequins that Morgan was pretty sure was a full-length evening dress. "Welcome, Morgan. I'm Darius, and this is Harlequin."

"Hi." Harlequin looked small, a bit fragile next to Darius' broad-shouldered bulk, but there was something fierce about him, an intensity to his eyes and the set of his mouth. His hair was half blue, half white - a soft white, not harsh bleached-blond - and he had one blue eye, one purple. Presumably contact lenses. Disconcerting. He wore a crisp white shirt, rolled neatly half way up his forearms, and a waistcoat.

"Hi," Morgan said. "Nice to meet you."

"Male pronouns tonight," Harlequin said to Caleb.

"Gotcha," said Caleb. "Drinks, everyone?"

Harlequin asked for vodka, and Darius said he'd help Caleb at the bar. Morgan asked for an orange and soda.

"Driving?" asked Harlequin, when the others had gone to the bar. Morgan wondered how the hell Darius could walk on those heels. He was tall to start with, but Morgan guessed they'd add at least four inches.

"I don't drink much." Never, in fact.

"Fair enough." He was well spoken but there was a definite twang to his voice from the other side of the Pennines.

"I'm majos." For some reason it was easier to own up to that than have Harlequin wondering whether he was a recovering alcoholic or something. Morgan got the sense that he wasn't the type of guy to judge anyone.

"Oh, I see. Darius is, too. I once saw him move a beer mat right up to the other end of the bar." He tapped the side of his head to indicate that Darius hadn't been using conventional methods to do so.

"I haven't seen him at Coven."

"Oh, Darius doesn't bother with all that bullshit."

Morgan glanced over his shoulder. Darius and Caleb were standing together at the bar, shoulder to shoulder. Caleb's arse looked amazing in that skirt, but

Darius was something else.

"I'm a lucky boy," said Harlequin.

"Oh, I wasn't–" Wasn't what? Checking out Harlequin's boyfriend? He totally had been. "You been together long?"

"Year and a half. I met him here, first term at Uni. He's local, I'm from Manchester." That explained the accent. "So, one year and nine months. You and Caleb?"

"Four or five years? But we're not–"

Harlequin's thin lips stretched into a smile. "Oh, honey, I know you're not."

To Morgan's relief, the drinks arrived then.

Caleb had bought him a mocktail full of watermelon and strawberries that was actually quite nice, although he could have done without the sparkling umbrella that nearly poked him in the eye. A queen arrived shortly afterwards with quiz sheets and glittery pens with unicorn horns on the end.

It was a weird kind of evening: every round of the quiz ended with a drag act on the tiny but well-lit corner stage. The winning team of each round got a prize from whatever act was on: a round of drinks; a lap dance; being hauled up on stage as a stooge for a magic act. Morgan was relieved at the end of every round they didn't win.

And then they did.

He glared accusingly at Caleb, who was by that time full of mimosas and clapping his hands in delight at the prospect of Morgan's imminent public humiliation. Morgan was considering whether he had time to escape to the toilets when Harlequin put his hand on Morgan's arm and said, "Just leave it to Caleb."

The next queen to take to the stage wore a twinkly, knee-length tube dress with a sequin union jack on the front. She had a huge, ginger wig. Ah. Ginger Spice. So…

Oh God, there were four of them in 'Team Rainbow' as Caleb had dubbed their team. Plus one of her. Five Spice Girls. Morgan's stomach churned with panic and possibly an overdose of strawberries.

"The back of the stage is dark," Harlequin said. "Leave Caleb in the spotlight. Follow my lead."

Numb with terror, Morgan let Harlequin take one hand, Darius the other, and next thing he knew he was on the stage, behind Ginger Spice. But Harlequin was right. The back of the stage was out of the spotlight.

The spotlight that Caleb was standing right in the middle of.

"Just sway and snap, honey," said Darius, with a grin.

The music started, Morgan took his cue from Darius, imagined he was someone else and began to sway and snap.

"Yo, I'll tell you what I want, what I really really want," sang Ginger Queen.

"So tell me what you want, what you really really want," Caleb sang back.

The crowd went wild.

Caleb's singing was a lot better than his whistling and, exhibitionist that he was, he blossomed in the spotlight. Morgan was so transfixed by his performance that he barely remembered to die of embarrassment when it came to his turn to sing.

Later, when they'd received their applause and left the stage, Caleb decided Morgan was probably Sporty Spice and thus destined for a career in the doldrums, making meaningful Northern Soul albums and finding happiness in ordinary life. Apparently Caleb was Posh. He'd shack up with David Beckham and live a life of fashion and glamour.

Then Caleb went off with Ginger Spice to drink more mimosas at the bar.

"Don't think too badly of him for abandoning you," Harlequin said. "He's had a tough time of it lately."

"You mean the thing with the married couple?" Morgan said. He could tell instantly, from the way Harlequin's brow arched, that he'd said the wrong thing. Shit.

"I was thinking more about his mam," said Harlequin.

Caleb didn't have a mother. Not anymore. She'd kicked him out when she'd found out he was gay. It was about the time of the warehouse incident. One of the things that Caleb and Morgan bonded over, both of them rejected because of who they were, one way or another. Caleb by his mother, and Morgan by just about anyone who was scared of magic. Which was most people, when faced with magic like his. "What d'you mean?" Morgan asked Harlequin.

"Shit, man, not my place to tell you. I thought you knew."

"She found him," Darius said, and then, to Harlequin, "Don't kick me under the table, sweetie, I think he should know."

'It's not for us to say."

"So you think. I think our boy needs all the help he can get."

Morgan glanced over at the bar, where Caleb and Ginger Spice had their tongues down each other's throats.

"Really?" Morgan said.

Harlequin and Darius nodded in unison.

Chapter Seven

Morgan got a cab back from the Bridge and arrived home around one. Caleb stumbled in at three. Morgan heard the bathroom door slam, followed by loud retching noises.

Great.

He got out of bed and went to check on him. Caleb was slumped on the floor by the toilet, looking miserable.

"I'll get some water," Morgan said. "See you in the living room when you're ready."

A little while later Caleb joined him on the sofa. He was wearing plaid shorts and a shirt Morgan was pretty sure had belonged to his last boyfriend. His face was scrubbed and his hair tied up.

"Wasn't sure you were going to make it back," said Morgan. "You seemed to have scored with Ginger."

"We had creative differences," said Caleb. He sipped at the water Morgan had got him. "Shit, I feel terrible."

"You'll be okay."

"I'm sorry I ditched you for a drag queen, Morg."

"I'm a grown up. I can get home on my own."

Caleb shrugged. "I wanted to cheer you up."

Morgan considered that for a moment. He supposed he did feel marginally better. He'd liked Harlequin and Darius. And the memory of Caleb singing *Wannabe* with that rich, clear voice was really rather grand. He felt proud.

"You did," he said and gave Caleb's arm a little rub. "What about you? Before the creative differences, I mean."

Caleb gave him a wry grin "It was okay, I guess."

Morgan desperately wanted to ask about his mother. But now wasn't the time. Maybe it wasn't up to him to ask. It's not like Caleb was slow to share when he wanted to. He'd tell Morgan, when the time was right for him. But still it stung hard that he'd been struggling with something so big and hadn't come to Morgan with it.

"I think I might call Jennifer tomorrow," Caleb said. "D'you think that would be completely disastrous?"

"It might be good to have a conversation. Get everything out in the open. Closure, I guess?"

"Hmm," said Caleb. Morgan guessed he was thinking about a lot more than closure, but now wasn't the time for him to argue about that either.

"Just make sure it's what you want," he said

diplomatically.

"Who knows what I want?" Caleb slumped against Morgan's shoulder and waved his glass of water, sloshing a fair bit of it on the sofa. "Who knows?"

Fair comment, thought Morgan.

Monday morning dawned with its usual quiet inevitability. Morgan showered and dressed, noting that he'd forgotten to do laundry over the weekend. It probably wouldn't have been worth trying: Caleb had spent most of Saturday looking wan on the couch and would not have welcomed the whine of the spin cycle. Sunday had been hot enough to shove them both off the couch to go and sit in the Folk Café for the afternoon. The music was a bit depressing, but the air conditioning was fabulous.

He stuck a load of shirts and underwear into the washing machine and set out for work. Move-U was still there, sadly not visited by bailiffs or stolen by fairies over the weekend. Mark and Wendy were sitting at their desks, talking about Mark's long weekend at a friend's wedding. This time next week the woman Morgan was providing cover for would be here instead of him, and they'd all be talking about her holidays.

"Usual drill, Morgan," said Wendy. "Clean the window first."

A please wouldn't have gone amiss.

"Fair warning," Mark said. "It's gruesome."

Morgan filled his bucket with water and detergent with a sense of dread. What would it be this time?

Homophobia? Racism? Chewing gum?

He sighed, snagged the alcohol spray and headed out to the window display.

The stench hit him before he took in what he was seeing. There was a stream of cocktail-stained vomit mostly dried on to the window and below it a puddle of piss. It must be recent, probably the early hours of Monday morning, not to have evaporated by now.

Morgan stood there for a moment, fighting his body's urge to add his own breakfast to the whole mess. As the nausea waned, pure, white-hot anger surged up in its place. The kind that came with power. Fast and elemental. Dangerous. Morgan put his bucket and spray down with shaking hands and walked up the street, away from Move-U and the mess and the stink. He found a patch of grass with a couple of benches on it by some kind of war memorial and sat there. He closed his eyes. If he could just breathe, connect with the deepest part of himself, the part that just went on breathing and living whatever else was happening, the part that could see emotion and magic and humiliation come and go and come and go without stopping - if he could do that, he'd be okay.

Morgan's breaths lengthened, his heartbeat slowed and his magic subsided. He was still angry. But he was in control.

He took another couple of minutes to make sure everything was stable, and then he went back to the shop. He took his bucket and spray and walked past Wendy and Mark to the cleaning cupboard. He emptied the bucket, dried it, and set it back on the shelf. He took off his apron and hung it up on the hook. He didn't listen to the sniggering that was going on in the office.

He went to his desk, aware they were watching his every move, and took out the few personal items that he'd kept there: a Kit-Kat, a packet of paracetamol, a clothes repair kit, his own personal stapler with his name on it, and a spare phone charger. He put them in his rucksack, hitched it on his shoulder, and went to Wendy's desk. He put his keycard for the photocopier on the top of her overflowing in tray. "It's been a pleasure," he said. He nodded to Wendy and to Mark. "All the best."

"You can't just go," said Wendy.

"Yes. I can."

"Your contract—"

"Does not include cleaning."

"It's part of the job. We all do it."

"Great. You won't miss me, then. I must have taken everyone's turn over the past week."

"It's not the same for you. You could just…" Wendy mimed what Morgan presumed, to his horror, was supposed to be someone casting a spell. "Magic it clean."

How the hell did she know he was majos?

"Well?" said Wendy. "Why don't you? What's the point of having it if you don't use it?"

Morgan left Move-U before she got a first hand demonstration.

Over the walk from Move-U to the station, Morgan focused on not thinking of anything. He caught a train straight away to the centre of town, where Pearl's agency was. He felt deliciously, dangerously calm. He held the (very clean) glass door to Oyster Recruitment open for a tall man in a grey suit who was on his way out. He smiled politely at him and got a beaming smile in return. And a lingering glance.

He walked through the enquiries area, which was thronging with potential recruits, past the break area and the toilets to the office at the back. The wall was half-glass and the blinds were up so he could see Pearl was alone. He knocked once and went right in.

Pearl looked up from her desk. Her generous curves were poured into a blue, white and orange dress that somehow gave an air of no-nonsense professionalism. Her hair was relaxed, glossy, caught at the neck in a large mother-of-pearl barrette, smoothed and polished within an inch of its life. She wore no make-up other than a smooth swipe of purple over each eyelid. There was something motherly about Pearl: perhaps her ample bosom, or her loud, joyous laugh. But people underestimated her at their peril. There was steel in those big, dark eyes. And she was directing them at Morgan right now.

"How the fuck did Move-U know I'm majos?" Morgan said. It wasn't what he'd intended to say; he'd spent the whole journey here persuading himself it wasn't the most productive thing to lead with. But it just slipped out anyway.

"Well, good morning to you, too, Mr Kerry. Will you take a seat?"

Pearl indicated the seat in front of her desk, and without even thinking about it, Morgan sat.

"Now, young man, if you would like to start from the beginning?"

One 'Mr Kerry' and a 'young man' and he'd only said one sentence. This was not going the way he planned.

"I think I'm within my rights to ask." Morgan muttered.

"I have no idea how they discovered that. I can assure you, it did not come from me. However, it is becoming very common these days for HR departments to run their own background checks."

Oh. Oh, shit. Of course.

"It's not illegal," she said. "But you know, if it's not in your contract, you don't have to use your talent as part of your job."

"I know. It's just…" Morgan sighed. "They made me clean the window."

It sounded so pathetic, once he said it out loud. Petty and ridiculous.

He could feel Pearl's eyes burning into him.

"They did whatnow, boy?"

He told her, in accurate and humiliating detail, what had happened. It sounded more pathetic with every word he uttered. He'd dealt with worse, after all. The real reason he'd quit - the only reason - was that he'd been scared witless that one petty incident had aroused his magic so fast, so powerfully that he'd almost lost control. He finished, "I'll take the penalty for non-completion."

"Wait one moment."

Morgan waited with a sense of growing dread as Pearl picked up the phone. Her large, gold hoop earrings glinted at him.

She dialled. He heard the ringing, a click, a sing-song 'Move-U HR department, how may I-'

And then Pearl laid into them. Morgan sat there, eyes going wider and wider as she released a string of invective so powerful, so deadly calm and professional that he quaked on behalf of the person at the other end. There were words like 'degrading', 'unsanitary' and 'breach of client trust'. She ended with a devastating, 'Oyster Recruitment will be unable to provide you with staff in the future without a reassurance in writing that this will not be repeated,' and set the phone back in its cradle.

"Oh," said Morgan. "Thank you."

Pearl sighed. "You should have come to me earlier, child."

Great. He'd gone from 'young man' to 'boy' to 'child' in the space of ten minutes. But on the whole, he'd rather Pearl feel sorry for him than be mad at him.

"I didn't want to make a fuss," Morgan said.

"Fortunately for you, I love making a fuss. Administrators are not cleaners. Now, what are we gonna do with you for the rest of the week, huh?"

"I meant it. I'll take the penalty."

"Ah, stop it with the martyr face, Morgan. As it happens I have one client who has been begging for a repeat visit. Won't have anybody else."

Morgan frowned. He was pretty good at his job, but then so was everyone else at Oyster. Pearl wouldn't have it any other way. Who had he impressed so much they'd want him back? The bank from last month? That had been pretty sweet. Or the solicitors? Or… Oh. Oh no.

Pearl tapped a key on her keyboard and the printer made a discreet 'beep' and started to smoothly roll out a letter-headed document. A contract.

"Hunter," Morgan said, dully.

"The very same. You impressed him."

"I checked the not preferred box."

"And I just got you out of washing sick off a window."

"But the job was done. And, just so you know, that was mostly cleaning, too. His office was a wreck."

She went very still. Oh no.

"He hired you for office clear out and organisation. Did he not?"

"Yes, Pearl."

"Was there any sick?"

"No, Pearl."

"Pee?"

"No."

"Other unsanitary human or animal fluids?"

"No. I'm sorry. I'm just… Upset. I'll do data entry,

call centre, anything. Please. He probably forgot how the system worked, I did tell him and—"

"Enough, Morgan. He doesn't want you for filing. He wants you as a PA. He paid on time and you impressed him so much he wants to give you a three month contract. Sign here. And stop feeling sorry for yourself. It's not very attractive."

It was on the tip of Morgan's tongue to say that the guy he'd held the door open for earlier had thought otherwise, but he kept quiet. There would be no talking Pearl out of this without a lie, and Morgan was rubbish at lying. Besides, Hunter might have been a dirty cheater but he wasn't a bad employer. He didn't deserve the chewing out Pearl had just given Move-U. Except possibly by his boyfriend.

There was only one thing for it. He'd have to talk to Hunter and explain why he didn't want to work there or have anything to do with him ever again. Then Hunter would cancel the contract, Pearl would put Morgan on call centres for the rest of his life, and he could just crawl into a ditch and die.

"Sorry. Thanks," Morgan said and signed.

Chapter Eight

Morgan got to Hunter PI to find the downstairs door ajar. A workman was peering into the guts of the buzzer mechanism. Morgan jogged up the stairs to the top and knocked on the glass-panelled door before opening it.

Hunter was sitting at his huge, gorgeous desk, looking into a shoebox. He didn't have the sling anymore.

Morgan rapped on the door again, and this time Hunter looked up.

He smiled, broadly, eyes sparkling, and got to his feet. "Morgan! Pearl said you were working at some Estate Agents."

"I was. I'm not anymore."

He moved into the room, trailing his index finger along the curved reception desk inside the door. The office was just as he'd left it. Clean and tidy. There were a few more things on Hunter's desk: a laptop (MacBook

Pro), a coffee cup on a coaster. A leather desk-tidy. All perfect and tasteful, and just what Morgan had imagined.

"It's good to see you again." Hunter held out his hand.

Morgan shook it. It was warm and strong and sent tingles up his arm. Oh dear. He'd been telling himself he was over Hunter by now. Clearly he'd been a bit optimistic about that.

"I take it that the fact that you're here means you're willing to accept my offer," Hunter said.

"Pearl said you wanted a PA. For three months."

"Yes. I've been subcontracted by West Yorkshire Police to help out with a project. It's highly confidential. Not pretty. And it's a lot more work, on top of the caseload I already had. I need someone who can hit the ground running and understand what the work is. You showed a lot of promise, you know, in the short time you were here."

Morgan felt a little glow of pride. "You mean, you want me to help you with investigations?"

"Yes. Don't get me wrong, there will be a ton of paperwork to deal with. I was a police officer for nearly a decade; I can tell you the bureaucracy is a nightmare. But it would be great to have a fresh pair of eyes, someone to talk things over with. And there's tasks I could delegate." He smirked. "The boring stuff, you know. Desk research. Endless Googling. Reading through phone records - believe me, they're never as juicy as you expect."

Morgan let himself imagine it. Working here. Investigating. Helping people. Solving mysteries.

"So, will you?" Hunter asked. His voice and expression had lost all of their edge: his eyes were practically begging him. Morgan imagined them begging for him to do something else, and sighed.

"There's one thing I need to clear up first," Morgan said. Because okay, yes, he was going to take the job. Not for Hunter, not for Pearl, but for the little thrill of excitement he'd got at the thought of helping with detective work. Apparently he'd discovered a soft spot for a vocation he'd never even considered before. But he couldn't cope with anymore misunderstandings between them. "What happened at the train station that night."

"Ah," said Hunter. "That."

"I know it was one of those impulsive, spur of the moment things," Morgan said. "And that you didn't mean anything by it—"

"Actually—"

"— and I enjoyed it. I did."

"You did? But—"

"Of course I did. You're very… But there's some things I won't go along with, and cheating is one of them. My therapist says I have impossibly high standards of loyalty and a shit ton of abandonment issues because my father left my mother for another woman. I don't know, my therapist says a lot of things. But. Anyway. I don't do cheating. So you're off limits. And honestly, that's probably for the best, if we're going to be working together for a while, anyway, because you're very... I did like you. And Pearl is quite insistent on the no fraternisation clause."

"Is that why you got all stroppy with me? Because you had a boyfriend? Is it Caleb?"

"Caleb? No! No, not me. You." Morgan licked suddenly-dry lips. "You and Peter."

"My ex, Peter?"

"Your... Ex. Oh."

"How on earth did you get the idea I... How do you even know about him?"

"He rang. The day you were hurt. He said he was your next of kin."

"Jesus wept. No, Morgan. I haven't been with Peter for a year and a half. I just don't keep my records up to date. They went onto my phone while I was unconscious, to see who to contact. He's a friend, but that's all. He was fucking annoyed with me, if you must know. I'm free. Single. And I thought maybe..."

Morgan blinked a few times, letting the newly-arranged world settle into place around him. The world in which Hunter hadn't cheated on anyone. Where they had, in fact, both been free to do whatever they pleased with each other.

But they hadn't. Because Morgan was a complete and utter idiot. For fuck's sake. The chance had slipped through his open, stupid fingers. Yeah. Attachment issues. Ms Rosero would have a field day with this.

Hunter got up and came around the desk in slow, prowly steps. "This thing about Pearl," he said. "How strict?"

"You've read the contract," said Morgan, a thread of mournful regret seeping into his voice unbidden. "What d'you think?"

Hunter scrunched his nose up and tilted his head. "When you say read…"

"Oh. So you haven't read it?"

Hunter shook his head. He had one of those eye-twinkling, filthy smirks on his face. Morgan was in serious trouble.

Hunter took another step, which brought him right up in Morgan's personal space.

Oh God.

"You said you like me." Hunter spoke softly. He didn't have to speak very loudly because he was so close Morgan could feel the whisper of his breath over his cheek. And then his ear, as Hunter leaned right in and whispered, "I like you, too. I was thinking about that kiss all night."

"Were you?" Morgan's voice came out as an unmanly sort of squeak.

"I bet you were, too."

"Can't say I remember," said Morgan.

Hunter saw the tease for what it was and chuckled. He threaded his fingers through Morgan's.

"She's really serious about fraternisation," Morgan said.

"Don't worry about it," Hunter said.

"But—"

"I haven't signed the contract yet."

Oh. Oh, but…

Then Hunter's mouth was on his and Morgan's brain shorted out.

It was soft at first, sort of innocent. But then the tip of Hunter's tongue teased at Morgan's lower lip, and of course Morgan opened his mouth, just a little but it was enough to invite Hunter in, and Hunter didn't need asking twice. He slid his arms around Morgan's waist, pulled him in close, and it was so easy for Morgan to let him, to put his own hands flat on that broad back, feel the muscles shift and ripple as Hunter moved. There were reasons that this was a bad idea: the Pearl thing, the don't-shag-the-boss thing, the fact that Hunter could be really grumpy, especially in the mornings or if he couldn't work things out. But he tasted so good (hints of coffee and peppermint) and he smelled so good (some kind of subtle, clean-smelling aftershave, citrussy shampoo) and he felt absolutely fucking amazing. Hunter was holding him so close there was no way he could ignore Morgan's hard-on as it jabbed him in the hip, mirroring the press of Hunter's own cock against Morgan's thigh. The kiss went deep; Morgan popped the button on Hunter's trousers and slipped his hand inside.

Hunter gasped.

"Just once," Morgan whispered. "Before you sign."

"Are you serious?" Hunter's voice sounded thin and needy, and okay, Morgan had his hand on his cock - and oh, God, it felt warm and thick and Morgan wanted it in his mouth - but, really Hunter's lips were quivering at Morgan's neck. "Just once," he repeated. "Let's make it good, eh?"

"Oh God," Hunter whined, and fumbled with Morgan's fly. "After the three months, we can talk. Okay?"

"Can I blow you now?"

"Yeah. Fuck, yeah."

Morgan grappled with Hunter's underwear and trousers as he shoved him back against his desk. He managed to free his cock more through luck than judgement, but that didn't matter. All that mattered was that he could see it. Touch it. His mouth watered. He dropped to his knees. Hunter's cock was a good fist full, the head plump and already wet at the tip. Morgan's heart pounded. He looked up at Hunter as he stuck out his tongue and licked from root to tip in one slow, broad swipe. Hunter grabbed a handful of Morgan's hair.

Morgan took Hunter's cock in his mouth, and let everything else go. All that mattered was the salty warmth of Hunter's skin, the long, low moan he dragged out of Hunter's throat as he sank down. And down. And down.

"Fuck," said Hunter, as Morgan's lips brushed the root of his cock. Morgan sucked, cradling Hunter's balls in his palm. He kept eye contact, Hunter's gaze brilliant blue, intense, as if he couldn't quite believe this was happening. Morgan pulled back far enough that he could swirl his tongue around; he tasted every inch of Hunter's cock, licked every ridge. When Hunter's cheeks were flushed and his hips were straining with the effort of not fucking himself into Morgan's throat, Morgan took him all the way down again. He paused, breathing hard through his nose, and when he came up again he wrapped his fingers around the root of Hunter's shaft so he could pay proper attention to the head. He flicked his tongue at the slit, tasting precome. Then he hollowed his cheeks, tightened his lips around Hunter's cock and started to fuck him with his mouth. Hunter whimpered, running his thumb adoringly along Morgan's cheekbone. Morgan kept going, merciless, relentless, his tongue flat along the underside of Hunter's dick, while his mouth kept everything hot and wet, matching the rhythm with his fist.

"Morgan, wait, I'm close."

Morgan just looked up at him and winked. He didn't stop. He stroked behind Hunter's balls with his forefinger. He wanted to turn him around. Eat his arse until he begged to be fucked. He'd bet Hunter was usually a top. But Morgan would show him all the pleasures of taking a cock up the arse. And then he'd let Hunter fuck him because fair's fair and this thick, hard cock would feel so good slipping inside him and, oh fuck.

Morgan came. Hard. In his underwear. He must have made some kind of noise or something around Hunter's cock, because Hunter's eyes went wide with recognition and then he threw his head back and filled Morgan's mouth with salty-bitter-slick jizz.

Well. Well.

He rested his forehead on Hunter's firm, tight belly,

and gently sucked him through the aftershocks.

Footsteps.

There were footsteps on the stairs.

"Quick," Morgan said, jumping to his feet. He fumbled with Hunter's trousers, trying to pull them up. "Someone's coming."

Hunter batted his hands away and took over, and somehow they were both dressed and not touching by the time the guy who'd been fixing the buzzer came in. Not touching but breathing hard, and Morgan guessed his face was as flushed as Hunter's. He turned away and shuffled the invoices in Hunter's in tray.

"All done, mate," said the buzzer-man. "The micro camera feeds straight to the Internet, and has its own storage of up to four hours should the connection fail. There's all the info you need here to fix up the app on your phone." He passed over an instruction booklet. Morgan glanced at it: the cover bore the message 'Congratulations on your purchase of '*Micro-Visual*'.

"Right," said Hunter. "Er, thanks. Thank you."

Common sense jolted Morgan back into the real world. The world where he wished he didn't have sticky underwear; where he wanted to crawl right under Hunter's desk and disappear. Hunter signed a piece of paper to confirm that the workman had indeed installed a buzzer/camera or whatever it was for him. Morgan squirmed with embarrassment and stickiness. And then the man left, and Hunter turned to Morgan and shit, the man was so beautiful Morgan didn't know what to do with himself.

"That was–" Hunter started

"Pretty close, eh? I don't think he saw anything, though."

"I was going to say, amazing."

"Oh. Um, thank you."

Hunter took the invoice from Morgan's hand and put it back on the pile. He gently tugged Morgan towards him, and Morgan couldn't help but go. Hunter gave him a soft, lingering kiss, and hugged him.

"Um," said Morgan, but it was the best he could do. This shouldn't be happening. But it was so nice. He had no idea what he was supposed to do now.

"I didn't plan this, you know," Hunter said. "I was just going to suggest dinner." He kissed him again. "Or a movie."

"Yeah. Me too. I don't usually…" Oh God, Hunter probably thought he was a giant slut. "Not on the first, or, I. Um."

"I'm glad you did," purred Hunter.

"We should stop," said Morgan. He sounded unconvincing, even to himself.

"We could go for dinner."

"It's a bit early for dinner, don't you think? I only just got here."

Hunter' picked him up and plonked him on the edge of the desk. Morgan squeaked; he'd nearly sat on something. He retrieved the shoebox lid that he'd almost squished and handed it to Hunter.

Hunter took it from him and picked up a photo from the desk. As he dropped the photo back in the box

Morgan recognised it as the one he'd seen when he cleaned out the filing cabinet. The pretty blonde woman with the baby in her arms.

"Someone special?" Morgan blurted out, curiosity getting the better of him.

"My mother," said Hunter, softly. He put the lid on the box and put it back in the desk drawer.

"Oh." Morgan shifted awkwardly. "Is she, um…"

"I haven't seen her since I was a child. She left me and Dad to go off and study magic. Or at least, that's what she said."

"Your mother is majos?"

"Yes. It didn't materialise until she had me."

That happened to women sometimes: the big ol' kick of pregnancy hormones started what adolescent hormones hadn't quite managed to spark. It often caused complications, be they medical, emotional or magical. "I'm sorry," Morgan said. "Must have been hard."

"You could say that. She struggled on for a few years, had another baby, but eventually it was clear the magic meant more than anything else. So she left. Went to live in a commune of majos in California. Never looked back. She wrote to my father once a year to let him know she was still alive and send money for us, when we were kids. But that's all we got. it was easier for her to cut me and my sister off completely, no letters, no phone calls. So that's what happened. I'm told magic often breaks up families, one way or another."

"That's not strictly–"

Hunter looked at him with his serious, no-nonsense expression, all vivid blue eyes and grim mouth. "It broke up mine."

"I'm sorry," Morgan repeated.

"Nothing to be sorry for. Just take my advice, Morgan. Stay well away from majos. Life's easier without."

Oh. Well. At least Morgan knew Hunter hadn't been digging up every bit of his past like Move-U had. And it offered Morgan an easy way out. He could confess that he had magic right now. Then Hunter wouldn't want to employ him at all. He could go back to Pearl and get reassigned without disappointing her - or enraging her - and forget Hunter ever existed. Again.

Because that worked so well the first time.

"Anyway, where were we?" Hunter said, shoving the shoe box away and pulling Morgan in close again. "That's right. You'd just agreed to come to lunch with me."

And maybe if it wasn't for the magic and Hunter's mother and the fact Hunter would hate him if he knew he was majos, maybe if it was just Pearl and her fraternisation clause, Morgan would have gone for it. But he couldn't. It would be hard enough for Hunter to reject him as an employee. If he let himself get involved...

Morgan slid off the table. He felt lightheaded, powerless as everything that had seemed so promising a moment ago slipped away. "Sorry. One time only, remember?"

"You were serious? About the fraternisation bullshit?"

"Sorry." Why did he keep apologising? "Yes. It's a big deal."

"Well." Hunter skimmed his hand over Morgan's arse. "I still haven't signed the contract. What happens if I forget to sign it at all?"

"You'll get a very polite, very convincing phone call from Pearl. And I'll get a very sarcastic, very angry phone call from Pearl. And then I'll get fired. Probably. I've been a lot of trouble today."

"And if I do sign it? How'd she ever know?"

"Pearl? You can't keep anything from Pearl. Caleb swapped shifts in a call centre once with another guy. Call centre people didn't notice. But she knew. We never worked out how. Believe me, she'd know." Hunter didn't look convinced. So Morgan had to bring out the big guns. "Besides. I'd have to lie to Caleb, but he'd guess, because he's my best friend. And I'm a rubbish liar. And then he'd have to lie to Pearl, and that wouldn't be fair."

If they ever got together - which they never would, because apparently Hunter hated everything Morgan was - he could never hide him. He'd want to tell everybody. He'd want to show him off.

"You're serious about this," Hunter said.

"Yes. It's for the best."

Hunter sighed. "Oh Morgan."

Yeah. Oh Morgan.

Hunter kissed him on the forehead, then stepped

back and shook his hand.

"I'd better sign that contract, then. Welcome back, Morgan."

Somehow, Morgan managed to shake his hand and smile.

Morgan got home to find Caleb lying on the sofa, with his hair in a towel, green mush on his face and a slice of cucumber on each eye. Morgan was sorely tempted to take a photo so he could threaten Caleb with Instagram-exposure if he needed to blackmail him at some point. But Morgan's head was a blur of emotion that whirled around the twin thoughts 'what the hell just happened?' and 'Oh God, Hunter'. So he just said, "You want tea?"

Caleb nodded and gave him the thumbs-up.

Morgan ditched his rucksack by the sofa and went into the kitchen. The washing machine was flashing a green light rather aggressively at him to tell him his laundry was done, so he put the kettle on and took an armful of damp clothes outside. The kitchen door opened out onto a tiny flat space nestled amid the sloping tiles of the roof. There was just enough room for two garden chairs and a small picnic table. The washing line spanned from the kitchen door to the edge of next door's roof. A strange quirk of architecture from whoever did the loft conversion that created Morgan and Caleb's flat, but it was nice to have an outdoors and it allowed for windows that let in sunshine to the living room.

He pegged out his clothes in a nice orderly row, from socks at one end to jeans at the other, and then he made some tea. He put Caleb's mug down on the coffee table near his head, and took his to the other end of the sofa, where he sat, after tickling Caleb's bare feet to get him to move them.

"You're late," Caleb said.

"It's been a long day."

"I thought Move-U closed at five."

"Yeah, well, I left at nine, so I wouldn't know."

Caleb raised his head, plucking the cucumber off his eyes.

"Tell me everything," he said.

"I quit," Morgan said. It felt like such a long time ago.

"Okay." Caleb sat up properly, towel falling off his head. "From the beginning."

So Morgan told him all of it, even about the magic part (kind of, only he played down the turmoil) right up to the part where Pearl offered him the job with Hunter.

Caleb stared at him with rapt attention.

"So," Morgan said. "I went to his office."

"And," said Caleb. "Is he still gorgeous?"

Morgan couldn't answer that straight away.

"Oh my God," said Caleb. "He's still gorgeous. Did you fuck him?"

The words 'don't be ridiculous' were on the tip of Morgan's tongue, but this was Caleb. So he said, "Yes."

Caleb's jaw dropped.

"Kind of. I mean, he didn't bend me over the desk

or anything, it was more…" Desperate. Urgent. "It was a one-time thing. It won't happen again."

"Why not?"

"Fraternisation. You know the rules."

Caleb snorted to show exactly what he thought of the rules. "You just have to not get caught."

Morgan could have argued that point, too, like he had with Hunter. But he knew Caleb would see right through him. "Okay, it's not just that. He's got a bit of a thing about magic. His mother was majos and she abandoned him for some kind of commune in California."

"Oh shit. I'm sorry, man. You think you can spot them a mile off, don't you? But there's always one in the pack that just squeaks through seeming like a perfectly normal human being."

Everything caught up at the back of Morgan's throat, and for one horrible moment he thought he might cry. "I really like him."

"Morgan, sweetie."

Morgan stared very hard at the mug of tea cradled in his hands, and sank his teeth into his lower lip. "It would have b-been easier if he'd had a fucking boyfriend."

"You're sure you believe him?"

Morgan nodded.

"If you told Pearl he's a card-carrying majophobe she'd get you out of there so fast the ink on the contract wouldn't have time to dry."

"That's the problem. I don't want to leave. It's not

like he's going on rallies or daubing graffiti everywhere. He's just a person who's had a bad experience. A very bad experience."

"I don't have an issue with him hating his mother. I'm not all that fond of mine, either. But it's not your fault. I mean, say she had dark hair–"

"She's blonde. Like him."

"Whatever, okay, so she's blonde. Does he hate all blonde people because they remind him of her? What if she was gay?"

It wasn't the same thing at all, but Caleb liked to stand up for minorities, even ones he wasn't part of, so Morgan didn't challenge it. It was nice to feel defended, even if it was for something he didn't care about. The stuff that had happened at Move-U was way worse than Hunter being wary of something that had actually hurt him.

Although, it wasn't magic that had hurt him, was it?

It was all so difficult.

"I just really like him," he told Caleb.

"It must have been a really good fuck."

Morgan nodded. It had been. But this wasn't about sex, not really. He didn't have the words to explain that the kiss afterwards had been even sweeter. The look in Hunter's eyes, the way he'd brightened up when he'd seen Morgan standing there in his office. How kind he was. The way his cock had stretched Morgan's mouth, just enough to give an ache.

Okay, so some of it was about the sex.

"Don't tell me you're really going through with it?"

Caleb asked. "Three whole months of celibacy and moping and him being afraid of your magic?"

Morgan looked down at his mug. "He doesn't know about my magic."

"What?"

"He never asked, I guess. It didn't come up. So he doesn't know."

"Yet. What if he finds out?"

"Why would he? I'm there to do paperwork. I don't do magic in the workplace."

"You don't usually fuck in the workplace either."

"And I shouldn't have this time. It won't happen again. It'll just be work." Morgan took a deep, shuddering breath.

A glob of green mush fell from Caleb's face to splat on the carpet.

"Avocado?" said Morgan

"Yeah."

"Nice."

"I've got to look my best. I'm going out to dinner with Jennifer and Dave tomorrow night. Fresh start."

"And you're okay with that?"

Caleb lay back and put the cucumbers back over his eyes. "Sometimes honesty is a work in progress, Morgan."

No kidding.

Chapter Nine

Morgan turned up at Hunter's office the next day to find a piece of card on the reception desk, folded lengthwise into an inverted V shape, so it stood up. It had 'Morgan Kerry' printed on it in big, black letters.

Hunter grinned a lopsided grin at him.

"Labelling me?" Morgan hoped the lame joke would cover how thrilled he was. He straightened the sign up so it was exactly parallel to the edge of the desk.

"You know where everything is," Hunter said. "Oh, and I got you this." He put a mug on the desk. It had 'Keep Calm and Investigate' written on it. "Just bring in whatever tea you want. I get milk on the way in. Do you drink ordinary milk? I couldn't remember if you were vegetarian or vegan?"

"Cow's milk is fine," said Morgan. "Thanks."

"I want you to feel comfortable."

"I do."

He really didn't. But not because of the office, or the mug, or the milk.

"You'll need a computer. Do you prefer Mac or Windows?"

"I'm only here for three months."

"You'll need it though."

"I have a laptop I could use."

"You don't have to do that."

"It's no trouble."

"Morgan, what's wrong?"

Morgan stroked the handle of the mug. "I'm fine."

He wasn't. He wanted to run away. He could feel Hunter's eyes boring into him.

"Shit," said Hunter.

"It's awkward, okay?" Morgan forced himself to turn and face Hunter, to look right into those bright, bluer-than-blue eyes and be honest. Well. Sort of honest. "After yesterday, when we… and you're being so kind, it all feels weird."

"Would you rather I was a bastard about it?"

"Of course not. I just want it to be… Ordinary. For you to treat me like a temp. Because that's what I am. For as long as you want my help. Tell me what to do and I'll get on and do it. As a professional."

He watched that sink in a bit. Hunter seemed to get it. He nodded and went back to his own desk. He shuffled a few papers. Morgan cautiously leaned his rucksack against the modesty panel under the - his - desk and sat. He scooted his chair to the sweep of the curved L that faced into the room. To his right was

Hunter's desk, under the big windows. To his left was the door; behind him were three filing cabinets. It was a snug, protective sort of space. He put his mug to his right hand side, and thought about getting some plants to go on top of the filing cabinet.

A painful silence fell over the office. Morgan stuck it out until his skin was crawling with the need to do something, anything. And then he said, "Shall I make some coffee?"

"Okay," said Hunter. "Then we can get started."

That sounded like music to Morgan's ears.

As he waited for the kettle to boil, he watched Hunter out of the corner of his eye. He was tapping at his phone. The papers on the desk had the West Yorkshire police crest on them. He wondered what they were.

He made coffee for Hunter. There was a selection of herbal teas on the tray as well. He picked out a vanilla green tea. It smelled delicious as he poured the hot water over it.

"Pull up a chair," said Hunter, as Morgan gave him his coffee.

There was only one other chair in the room apart from the battered leather one Hunter was sitting in, and that was the weird, wooden chair on wheels that Morgan had used to move boxes of files around on last time he was here, and which now sat behind his desk. He pulled it across the office, wondering whether Poundland would have any more of those comfy red cushions Caleb had got for his room.

Hunter rolled his shoulder. The one that had been in a sling.

"What happened?" Morgan asked. "You never said. The day you were in hospital. If it's not too personal."

There was something odd about the phrase 'too personal' when applied to someone whose cock had been in his mouth, but hospital visits could be sensitive things. Hunter might have some horrible degenerative condition, or-

"A man came to see me about a dog," he said.

"Sorry?"

"The furry gentleman my client wants to divorce, who I visited in prison? His friend, a certain thug by the name of Paul Bates, he who took the video, had a sudden attack of guilt. He decided to pay me a visit and tell me, in no uncertain terms, that I should lay off. Bad timing for him, because it was all done and dusted by the time he found me." He must have noticed disapproval in Morgan's eyes, because quickly he added, "Not that it would have made any difference."

"But he hurt you anyway?"

"He took me off guard. Grabbed my arm and shoved me against the wall. Dislocated my shoulder. It happens, sometimes, if it gets pulled a certain way. Injury I picked up on the force. Worst part is it hurts like fuck and for some reason makes me pass out when it happens. He panicked and ran away. Someone walked past and saw me. Called an ambulance. I woke up in A&E feeling really stupid. Then Peter gave me a

hard time for not changing the emergency contact on my phone. It wasn't the best day, I'll be honest."

"But it's okay now?"

"Just a bit stiff."

The word 'stiff' went straight to Morgan's groin, where his cock mistook it for an instruction. "That's why you've got the camera for the entryway now," he said, shifting in his chair and hoping Hunter wouldn't notice.

"Well, you know. Better safe than sorry." Hunter's eyes were on his again, sparkling. Teasing.

"Great," said Morgan. "So, what's the project?"

"Ah." Hunter took a slurp of his coffee. "Two projects, to be exact. One you already know about."

"Ozzie White?"

"The very same. I checked out the school, and we're probably onto a winner there. Her old school were told she'd moved out of the local authority area, but no new school has asked for her records yet."

"Yay?" said Morgan.

"Hmm. So the next job is to talk to her mother, see if we can find out anything from her. The mother still lives in Hebden Bridge, the address Ozzie gave us. No job as far as I can tell, but she volunteers at an art gallery once a week, helping out with craft sessions for school kids. I want to go there this afternoon and see if she's there. My contact says she's usually there on Tuesdays."

"You have a contact at an art gallery in Hebden Bridge?"

"I have contacts everywhere, Morgan. It goes with the territory."

Morgan tried to pretend he wasn't impressed.

"That's where you come in," Hunter said. "I don't want to make myself conspicuous just yet. But you can go along, turn on the charm, see what you can find out. Meanwhile I'll take a poke about the town. It's an interesting sort of place, have you ever been?"

Morgan shook his head.

"It's hippie central. Everyone knows everyone. All ex teachers and ex social workers. If Poppy's been moping about like a teenage disaster waiting to happen, someone will have spotted her with professional concern."

"What should I ask Mrs White?" asked Morgan.

"Nothing too obvious. Follow your instincts. And I wouldn't call her Mrs White, if I were you - remember she was the one to walk out of the marriage. Her first name's Alice. My guess is she's ditched her married name by now."

"What if I don't have instincts?" The project was getting a bit panic-worthy. It felt important and the last thing Morgan wanted to do was mess up.

"Trust me, Morgan." Hunter grinned at him, a warm, sexy grin. Which was unnecessary, frankly. "Your instincts are excellent."

Morgan was consumed by the need to impress and the fear that he wouldn't, so they were on the train to Hebden Bridge before he realised Hunter hadn't told him about the other project. The police one, presumably. The train was busy and they were sitting at a table directly opposite a young mum and her kids. It didn't seem right to ask about it in public, so Morgan kept his mouth shut and looked out of the window while Hunter tapped away at his phone. The younger child opposite, no more than a toddler, was asleep on his mum's lap. The older one watched Peppa Pig on an iPad. Thankfully, he was wearing headphones.

Hebden Bridge was everything Hunter had promised. One of many old mill towns along the rivers and canals of West Yorkshire, it nestled cosily into the green-backed Pennines. Industry had long since fled, replaced by tourism and what the town's website called 'a haven for creativity'. The shops sold pots, books, art, tourist trinkets and a lot of things made out of felt.

The gallery where Alice volunteered was one of a dozen units on the ground floor of an old mill. Apart from the vastness of the industrial architecture and old brick walls it had little of its heritage on show. The floors were solid wood, and the various shops and exhibition spaces sparkled: clean, well-lit units behind plate glass doors. Hunter went to the cafe space upstairs, leaving Morgan to find Alice.

The gallery was called The Bell Jar, presumably in tribute to Sylvia Plath. It wasn't the earnest, poetical space he'd expected. It was full of pottery and glass, ceramics and textiles including (inevitably) felt. The walls were white with a frieze of the words 'I am, I am, I am' in gold italics all the way around.

There was a sleek white counter just inside the door with a cash register on it along with baskets of badges and polished glass chips with feminist symbols on them. A woman sat behind the counter, knitting a huge spidery shawl in metallic rainbow colours. She was at the late end of middle-aged, greyish-blonde hair with lilac highlights coaxed into a relaxed bun at the back of her head. She wore a peasant top in which her breasts bounced happily, unrestrained by any hint of restrictive underwear, as she clicked her needles together. She looked up, met Morgan's gaze and said a warm, "Hello."

"Hi." Morgan smiled at her. "Is it okay if I take a look around?"

"Of course. Would you like a leaflet? There's a workshop on in the art room, but it's children on Tuesdays."

He took the home-printed sheet of paper she offered him. Underneath 'The Bell Jar' logo it explained that the gallery was a place of self-discovery for women. A feminist haven of creativity.

Well, she hadn't thrown him out or looked at him funny, so presumably he was welcome to look around.

He fumbled a pound coin out of the change in his trouser pocket and dropped it in the Women's Aid charity box. She smiled at him again, then returned to her knitting.

Morgan moved slowly through the various exhibits. There were a few women wandering around, but they took no notice of him - or each other, come to that - all absorbed in an appreciation of the art on show.

Movement at the end of the gallery drew his eye.

There was another glass door there, with the words 'Art Room' etched on it. He sidled up to a collage of a suffragette march in felt and patchwork nearby and glanced through the door. Three young children sat around one of the half a dozen tables in the room. They were cutting up old rags under the supervision of a willowy woman with long, red hair contained in a plait that ran right down her back. She had to be Alice: the likeness to Poppy was unmistakable, right down to the long dancer's legs and slender body. She squatted down at the table to help a little boy who was having trouble making headway with his round-ended safety scissors. She showed him how to tear the fabric instead, and her eyes lit up when he squealed in delight.

There was no way he could talk to her in there, and it would look suspicious if he hung around the gallery until closing. Then he saw a list of workshops on the wall next to the room. This one ended in ten minutes, then there was a break of fifteen before the next one started. He wondered if Hunter had known that and steered him here at exactly the right time.

Probably not. But Morgan wouldn't have been surprised if he had.

There was a selection of books for sale in an alcove near the art room, so Morgan stationed himself there. It was easy to burn ten minutes dipping in and out of angry feminist poetry by angry local poets.

The door to the art room opened a few minutes after the stated time, releasing the sound of yoga-style relaxation music. A couple of the other patrons went to claim their children as they spilled out; by the time they'd all gone, the gallery was empty apart from Morgan, the knitting-woman and Alice. Alice was relieving cramped back muscles with a long, sinuous stretch. It must be wearing for someone so tall to be curling herself up to be on a level with small people.

Morgan caught her eye and smiled. She did this thing that most people did when they met Morgan for the first time: she flickered a perfectly normal stranger-greeting half-smile at him, looked away, and then she did a micro double-take, as if registering something amazing she'd just seen. She looked back and this time her smile was full-on, and she was taking a half-step towards him.

"Hello," Morgan said.

"Hi." She glanced around the gallery. "Are you a parent, or…?"

"Just came to take a look around. A friend recommended the place."

"It's fabulous, isn't it? So much talent. Did you see the Holdsworth vulvas?"

Morgan swallowed, hard. "Um…"

"Here. Let me show you."

She led him down a short corridor he hadn't noticed at the back of the gallery, past a set of stairs with a 'staff only' barrier across them and into a small, square, white room. A hand-written information plate on the wall just inside the door said, 'Vulvas in Mixed Media: a show of shared femininity by Julia Holdsworth'. There was a biography of Julia

Holdsworth underneath, but Alice filled him in on the details as they approached the first piece.

"Julia wanted to show the variety of womanhood throughout the world."

To say Morgan felt out of his depth was an understatement. But he needed to create a rapport with Alice, and if she was passionate about this, well, he'd just have to do his best. He stood in front of the first exhibit and tried to look intelligent.

He'd never seen a photograph of a woman's private parts quite so close up. Maybe the odd glance when he was surfing porn. She'd done something with the colours and the texture. It looked like an undersea creature, all pink and furry. Not unattractive, just weird. He wasn't sure what the point was. He'd never done much art at school.

He decided not to share any of this with Alice. Instead he made a 'hmm', noise and tilted his head a little in what he hoped looked like a gesture of artistic contemplation.

"This one's my favourite."

Alice's favourite was made with fragments of highly glazed ceramic in shades of blue and purple. It looked like an exotic flower unfurling. Morgan glanced at Alice; she gazed at the piece in adoration, her eyes shining in the gallery-muted light. And, okay, he saw her point.

"It's beautiful," he said, and he wasn't lying. He could see why she liked it.

She led him around the rest of the pieces, pointing

out details here and there while Morgan thought more about female genitalia than he had in his entire life up to that point. The art showed vulvas that were bald, furry, abstract, so realistic it felt inappropriate to look at them, natural, mutilated; and then one that had been created by surgery, a miracle for a person born with the wrong body. He lingered there for a while. He'd often wondered about trans post op bodies, but it felt disrespectful to go Googling for them. The vulva in front of him was a furled mystery, no more or less than any of the others in the exhibition. Unique, feminine, perfectly different.

"I'm guessing you're not straight," said Alice. She was smirking at him. He wondered if it had been some kind of test of loyalty to the feminist cause, bringing him in here.

"No," said Morgan. "Why?"

"You seem very relaxed and politely interested. Most straight men find the exhibition challenging. They're either fighting an erection all the way round or they're thinking of their mothers and sisters. Even the ones who can cope with all that don't get it. Maybe intellectually, but they don't feel it. You do, don't you?"

Morgan glanced back at the human-created, post-op vulva, with its plump, wrinkle-hooded clit and lips like rose petals. He remembered a friend from college who's been trans and found it so impossible she tried to take her own life. "Yes," he said.

"Well done," said Alice. Her eyes were shining. She looked proud. But not of Morgan, whom, after all, she'd only just met.

"Are you the artist?" he asked.

Alice laughed. "No. She's my girlfriend."

Ah. Well, that explained a few things.

"Do you have time for a cup of tea?" he asked. "I'd love to know more about her."

"Well, it so happens I do," said Alice, beaming at him.

Chapter Ten

When Alice returned to the Bell Jar for her next workshop, Morgan made his way to the other end of the huge cafe, where Hunter sat with his laptop. Morgan took the seat opposite him and waited, trying not to grin his head off.

Hunter raised an eyebrow at him over the top of his laptop screen.

Morgan's grin burst free. "You'll never guess."

Hunter closed his laptop and leaned forwards. "Tell me."

"Well, put it this way. Ozzie isn't going to get his wife back." He paused for effect. He was enjoying this far too much. "She's a lesbian."

Hunter leaned back, eyes wide. Surprised. Genuinely surprised. Morgan had finally managed to tell him something he didn't know.

"She's in a committed relationship with an artist," Morgan said. "She came from a religious family. Grew up thinking her sexuality was evil, blah blah blah. Married Ozzie, a nice boy from her church, to prove to her parents she could overcome it all and be a normal housewife. She realised it wasn't going to work almost straight away, but she fell pregnant on honeymoon. So she stayed married to Ozzie because she didn't want Poppy to grow up in a broken home, and Oz realised that, exploited it. Bullied her a bit, I think. And then she met Julia at a quilting class. They've been together for five years. Oz can't accept it. He thinks one day the devil will leave her and she'll come back to him."

"Shit," said Hunter.

"I know, right? But there you go. That's what happened." It was all Morgan could do to keep from bouncing in his seat with the excitement of it.

"And Poppy?"

"Alice wanted her to make up her own mind, and Poppy was angry with her at first so she chose to stay. But Ozzie was really strict and Poppy hated it. Eventually it got too much, so Poppy got herself thrown out of the house so she could come and join her mother."

"And is she in school?"

"No. Not yet. Alice wants to give her space. She's looking into home-schooling."

"Free to come and go as she pleases?"

"Well, yes." Morgan's excitement deflated a bit. Hunter had a hawk-like look about him.

"Dance class?"

Morgan's heart sank. This wasn't going at all as he'd

imagined. "She said Poppy's taking a break from dancing to work out if it's really what she wants. But that's a good thing, isn't it? She's been through so much, growing up with all that restriction, her mother not able to be who she really was—"

"Morgan, stop."

Morgan closed his mouth, snapping his teeth together.

"We were hired to show that Alice is an unfit mother. We're looking for evidence that Poppy isn't being properly supervised, so that Ozzie can get her back." Hunter's voice dropped a bit, edged with sympathy. "It's not up to us to decide whether it's okay or not."

Morgan slumped back in his chair, all the joy seeping out of him. "No. You can't."

"I'm sorry." It sounded as if he might be. But not enough, clearly. "It's a job, Morgan. I'm a detective, not a family therapist."

"You would send Poppy back there? To be told that her mother's going to hell for being gay, that she has to dance whether she wants to or not because to do otherwise would be to betray her God-given talent, and that she can only marry someone else inside their stupid, bigoted religion, which means she'll marry someone just like her fucking father. Just to repeat the whole cycle all over again? Are you serious? "

"Morgan. Keep your voice down."

"No!" Morgan got to his feet. "Not about this. Never about this. If this is what you do for a living, do it by yourself. I quit."

Magic flared up Morgan's spine like fire. It made it easy to storm out. He ran down the stairs, out of the mill and down to the canal, breathing hard, using all the control he could summon to keep his power from erupting. There was a bench there, but he couldn't sit. He stood and stared at the water, imagined diving into it and letting it soothe the fire away. He imagined his magic soft and gentle, tiny, foam-filled waves.

He let out a breath he hadn't even realised he was holding, and sank down on the bench.

Well. That was that, then.

He wanted to cry. He'd never quit an assignment in all the time he'd worked for Pearl, and here he was quitting two in as many days. But worse than that, how could he have been so wrong? He'd thought Hunter was a good person. But maybe he'd just wanted him to be, because he was so fucking attractive. Shit.

"Morgan." Morgan glanced over his shoulder to see Hunter standing behind him, his messenger bag over one shoulder, Morgan's rucksack over the other. "You left your bag behind."

"Thanks." Morgan looked back at the canal.

Hunter sat next to him and sighed. Morgan pressed his lips together, fighting to keep the tears at bay. The last thing he needed now was to let Hunter see him cry.

"You're right," said Hunter.

A little flame of hope flickered inside Morgan. He tried his best not to take any notice of it.

"It's a horrible situation," Hunter continued. "But

it's not for us to make judgements. We have to deal with the facts."

Morgan looked at him. He must have looked grim, because Hunter pulled himself up tall and edged back a little, as if expecting a smack to the face. "Here's a fact for you," Morgan said. "That woman grew up thinking she was evil incarnate. I suggest you attempt to deal with that."

It hurt him, too. Morgan could see it in his eyes. But Hunter didn't back down. "Here's another fact. Poppy is only fifteen. She's not old enough to be running around unsupervised."

"Fifteen year olds can be very mature." When Morgan was fifteen he used to do the shopping, the laundry and all the household paperwork, because his mother worked two jobs.

"It's her GCSE year. If she fails, what then?"

"She might not fail," said Morgan, stubbornly. But a little bit of doubt poked at him.

"What if she goes to a party and takes the wrong kind of drug?"

"Alice says she's very responsible."

"Well, she would. Wouldn't she? She doesn't want to lose her any more than Ozzie does."

"You don't get it. Alice really cares about her. She does."

"So does Ozzie."

"Yes, but–"

"You're seeing him through Alice's eyes. And only Alice's."

"He's a bigot! He told her—"

"No, you don't get what I'm saying. We have two points of view here, at polar opposites. But who really matters here?"

Morgan opened his mouth. Closed it again.

"Poppy," he said.

"Yes," replied Hunter, softly. "The law is there to protect her, Morgan. We have to trust it, if nothing else."

"The law's on his side," Morgan realised.

"Only if Poppy doesn't get her act together."

Morgan was quiet for a few moments, mulling things over. He tried to find a loophole in Hunter's argument, something he could throw in Hunter's face with a loud yell of 'ha! I'm right, you're wrong, sucker!' But nothing came to mind. Then something else popped up.

"What matters most to you?" he asked. "That things end up the right way, or that you get paid?"

A muscle in Hunter's cheek twitched.

"If Poppy wants to stay," Morgan continued, "and we can find a way to make it happen, would you do it? Even if it means telling Ozzy to keep his money?"

Hunter looked away, up the canal towards the bridge. His shoulders were rigid with tension.

"Do you really think so little of me?" Hunter asked.

Well. That wasn't what Morgan had expected.

Hunter turned around. "Do you?"

"I've only worked for you for seven working days," Morgan pointed out. "And you weren't around for a lot of that. I barely know you."

"You only knew Poppy's mother for an hour and you believed her."

That was a fair point, but Morgan wasn't about to admit it.

Hunter said, "Where does Poppy hang out? Any idea where she goes in the evenings?"

"I know where she'll be tonight. She's going to a talk about feminist art with Alice and Julia. Alice was very excited about it."

"You know where that is?"

"At the Bell Jar."

"Right. We're going."

"You're kidding."

"Nope."

"And what do we do when we get there?"

"You'll see." Hunter checked his phone. "Let's get some food. Could end up being a long day."

To Morgan's relief, they weren't the only men at the Bell Jar that evening. Of the thirty or so people there, about a quarter looked to be boyfriends or husbands, and there were one or two solo males too. The knitting-lady was there, and he spotted Alice sitting in the front row with a dark-haired woman he presumed to be Julia, and, much to his relief, Poppy, who looked much younger in person.

Hunter didn't seem phased by the event, even when the first slide appearing on the big screen at the front of the room was one of Julia's most graphic vulvas. He listened carefully with an intelligent look on his face and watched everything. Morgan tried to concentrate on the talk, but he kept finding himself sneaking looks at Hunter's profile.

The theme of the talk was women's crafts through the ages and how they'd never been taken seriously as arts because they were considered women's activities. Apart from a (female) heckler who claimed Tracy Emin's work in appliqué was largely 'sensationalist crap', the talk was well received and followed by a lively Q and A. Then there was wine and nibbles and mingling.

As agreed, Morgan took Hunter over to meet Alice, Julia and Poppy.

"Morgan!" Alice seemed really pleased to see him. "You came after all. Is this your partner?"

Poppy hissed, "Mum!" at her. Morgan blushed and floundered, which was not at all helpful. It was just that this part of him that really liked Hunter and thought all the 'no sex with people at work who have a bad opinion of majos' rules were bollocks, really, really wanted to be Hunter's boyfriend.

Hunter shook Alice's hand and said, "Damian Hunter. Nice to meet you. Morgan was very impressed with the gallery. I must say I agree. Fantastic place."

"Isn't it?" said Alice, warmly. "Oh, this is my partner Julia, and my daughter Poppy."

Poppy gave a brief, disinterested smile-and-wave. Julia shook hands with both of them. She looked less like an artist than anyone else in the room. Her hair was pulled back into a neat, glossy bun and she wore a business-like skirt and silk blouse. She had the same kind of makeup as the girls in Pearl's office did: muted, stylish, professional.

"I saw your exhibition today," Morgan said. "It's great."

"Thank you," said Julia. Thankfully she didn't seem keen to enter into an in-depth discussion about vulvas. But she did seem pleased.

He noticed Poppy drifting off towards the table where drinks and nibbles were set out.

"I'll go and get some wine," Hunter said. "Who wants what?"

He took orders for Alice (red), Julia (white) and Morgan (orange juice) and followed Poppy. Smooth.

"What do you do for a living, Morgan?" Julia asked. Her eyes were sharp, but her hand was folded around Alice's, her thumb smoothing at her knuckles.

"I'm just an office temp."

"And Damian?"

"Same." The cover identity Hunter had offered up was basically Caleb. Possibly because he thought that way Morgan might actually remember it. "We met through work. How about you?"

"Julia was running a workshop," said Alice.

"Alice was an exceptional student," said Julia. She was very well spoken, positively posh, with just a hint of a northern accent. Lancashire, not Yorkshire.

They were so loved-up it warmed Morgan's heart. He glanced at the drinks table. Hunter was listening to

Poppy, who was talking fast, waving her hands around in an animated sort of way. Like she'd been waiting a long time to say whatever she was saying, and now it was all coming out in a rush.

"So," he said to Julia, before she or Alice could register that Hunter was taking a while with the drinks. "Are you working on a new project?"

"Nothing focused yet. I'm looking at a series of portraits based on wedding photos. I'm still doing research, though, so I'm working as a wedding photographer."

"Julia specialises in same-sex weddings," said Alice. "You should take her card."

"Oh, no, we're not, I mean… We haven't been together that long." Morgan laughed nervously and then blurted out. "What about you?"

"What about us indeed," Julia muttered.

Alice shot her a cross look and said, "I'm waiting for a divorce."

"I'm sorry," said Morgan. "Oh, look. Drinks!"

Hunter and Poppy arrived carrying wine and orange juice as ordered. Poppy had ended up with something that looked like pop but smelled a lot like one of those flavoured ciders. Morgan raised an eyebrow at Hunter, who gave him a bland, innocent look in return.

"I was telling Damian about school," Poppy said, excitedly. "He thinks Hebden School's a great idea."

"Well," Hunter said. "I should declare a bias. I went to a progressive school myself."

"Did you?" asked Alice.

Morgan had the same question on his lips. Was this true, or was it part of an elaborate attempt to extract information?

"The Olive Tree, in Staffordshire," Hunter said. "It suited myself and my sister very well."

"Really? We've been looking at options for Poppy for a while, but it's hard to know what to do. She has her heart set on Hebden School, but honestly, when she's been in the system so long, and she'll probably need to retake this year—"

"What Alice means is that Poppy's father wouldn't approve," said Julia, pointedly. "And unfortunately he still has a say."

"He can fucking put up with it," Poppy said. "I'm sick of him. I've done what he wanted all this time—"

"Not here," said Alice.

"Don't fucking stifle my self-expression!"

Julia sighed. "See?" she said to Alice. "Switch your grounds to adultery. Cite me as co-respondent. Get rid of him. Look after your daughter."

Alice looked desperate, caught between her lover, her daughter, and her control-freak husband. Morgan didn't see a laid back bohemian in her at all. He saw someone who in some ways was just as new as Poppy, a butterfly straight out of her cocoon, beautiful and fragile, and just a bit lost. He wondered if that was patronising of him. He hoped not.

"Well," Hunter said. "It's been lovely to meet you. Unfortunately, we need to catch a train, so…"

Everyone pulled themselves together in a very

English sort of way, all drama swept aside for a flurry of 'goodbye' and 'nice to meet you' and 'I hope the trains are running on time', and 'please, have my card, don't hesitate to call'. Morgan engaged professional mode for his goodbyes, until he came to Alice. Impulsively he gave her a hug and whispered in her ear, "It'll work out, I'm sure." She squeezed him in return.

Then, to Morgan's astonishment, Hunter took his hand - actually took his hand, like they were proper boyfriends - and led him out of the Bell Jar, tossing a wave to Poppy over his shoulder as they went.

They walked out of the old mill, down the road, and they'd got to the canal before Morgan said, his voice thick with regret, "Ozzie's going to eat them alive in court."

They stopped. It was nearly dark. A houseboat moored nearby was decked in fairy lights that made the surface of the water glow in warm reds and greens and golds.

"I don't think so," Hunter said.

"He isn't?"

"Not if Alice really trusts her girlfriend. I checked up on Julia while you were looking in that crystal shop earlier. D'you know what she did before she gave it all up for art?"

"No?"

The victory-smirk appeared on Hunter's face. "Divorce lawyer."

"Seriously?"

"Seriously. If we let Ozzie go to court it would be

like throwing him to the sharks. She was really good. Made an absolute fortune. Plenty to send Poppy to the hippie school and keep Alice in lentils while she finds herself."

His turn of phrase could be kinder, but Morgan found himself beaming all over his face just the same.

Hunter continued, "We'll go back and tell our client that things are complicated, unfortunately, and dearie me, it was a pity he didn't tell us everything, but if he wants to see Poppy, the best way is to play nicely. Hopefully, he'll still pay us. If not, well." Hunter shrugged. "We've still got the police contract. And we had a nice day trip. Didn't we?"

Apart from the blazing (nearly literally) row, more vulvas than Morgan had expected to see in a lifetime and the fleeting belief that Hunter was a complete money-grabbing git… Yes. It had been an amazing day. It really had. He'd really got a taste for investigating.

And Hunter was still holding his hand.

"It was okay," said Morgan, fighting to keep his grin at sub-luminous levels.

"Just okay, eh?" Hunter's eyebrow went up, but the smirk stayed. Morgan wanted to kiss that stupid-sexy smirk right off his face.

So he did.

"More than okay," he admitted, pressing his lips to Hunter's. Warm, soft, lingering. Hunter wrapped his arms around Morgan but he didn't push anything; he just let Morgan flutter kisses at the corners of his mouth, then the middle, then press a little harder, until Hunter conceded and let his mouth open, allowing Morgan's tongue to slip inside and flirt with his. Morgan felt the cool night air flutter through his hair; the warmth of Hunter's body; the strength of his arms. He let it build to a point where he had to either stop or throw Hunter down on the ground and have his way with him. As they were standing on a public tow path within sight of several over-the-shop flats and a couple of houseboats, he stopped. He wasn't sure even Hebden Bridge was that progressive.

He rested his forehead on Hunter's, and buried his fingers in his thick, silky hair.

Hunter 'mmm'd and swayed his hips a little, like they were dancing. Morgan kissed him again, just three quick pecks.

"I—" Hunter started.

"Don't," said Morgan.

Hunter didn't.

Morgan breathed it all in: the working-water smell of the canal in the background and the dewy dampness of the air were a backdrop to the fresh scent of Hunter. Clean skin, clean citrus cologne, clean clothes, and under it all something deep and rich, like leather.

Hunter kissed his neck, and Morgan's breath fluttered out of him with a noise somewhere between a whimper and a sigh.

"You are one continual surprise, Morgan Kerry," Hunter whispered against his skin.

Morgan smiled.

Chapter Eleven

The flat was in darkness, presumed empty. It wasn't far shy of midnight, and Caleb was out with Jennifer and Dave. Morgan crept in on tiptoe just in case, navigating the living room by the moonlight that poured through the bare windows. He went to the kitchen, turned on the counter-top lights, and poured himself a glass of water.

He'd said goodbye to Hunter on the train, when he had to get off at Leeds, leaving Hunter to carry on to York. All the way back they'd sat close, but not touching, just talking. He'd asked Hunter whether he'd really been to a progressive school, and it turned out he had. He'd hated it. But he had a lot of stories about camping in the woods and building tree forts and the time the school democratically decided that there should be a total ban on wearing socks, for reasons Hunter could no longer remember.

It was surprisingly easy to imagine him as a

boisterous, sandy-haired boy, rebelling against the lack of authority. No wonder he'd ended up in the police force.

Morgan had traded a few school stories of his own, focusing on the 'gifted and talented scholarship' and carefully leaving out the one third of the curriculum that had fallen under the remit of Ms Rosero.

Then they'd arrived at Leeds, and he'd picked up his rucksack and Hunter had got up to let him past, but at the last minute he pulled him close and kissed him, and as the train had shuddered to a halt at the platform Morgan stumbled, and Hunter caught him and sent him on his way with a soft, "See you tomorrow, Morgan."

Morgan looked out of the kitchen window at the moonlight and the laundry he'd forgotten to bring in and realised something important. He wasn't planning to give Hunter the 'we can't do this' talk tomorrow. He wasn't planning to call Pearl and say he'd have to leave for any of the number of perfectly valid reasons he could give her, either. He didn't care about magic, or fraternisation clauses or Hunter's ex. All he cared about was Hunter. He was planning to go into the office and pick up with Hunter precisely where they'd left off on the train.

The front door crashed open and Caleb staggered in, turning all the lights on by bumping his shoulder at the switch.

"Morgan!" he said, drunk-loud, pink-cheeked. "Guess what?"

"Um," said Morgan, blinking at the sudden light.

"I've just been to a sex party! An actual sex party!"

And then he wilted like a poppy on a dry day and passed out cold on the couch.

When Morgan got up the next morning to go to work, Caleb was still on the couch, wrapped up in the blanket Morgan had fetched for him. He had panda eyes from his eyeliner and he was snoring into a cushion. The bucket Morgan had left by the couch just in case was mercifully empty.

Morgan ate a bowl of cereal in the kitchen, then got his washing in and folded it neatly on the kitchen counter into two separate piles for ironing and putting away respectively. He balled his socks up in pairs, thinking about Hunter, and caught his reflection in the window. He was grinning his head off.

Caleb slept on. Morgan went back to his room to do his morning meditation.

After meditation he came back to find Caleb sitting up, blanket pooled over his legs, yawning.

"Morning," said Morgan, chirpily.

"Morning, what... What the fuck?"

"Eh?"

"Your dragon's right there! On your shoulder!"

Morgan glanced at Aiyeda, who preened her golden scales at him. She looked a little smug. And, seeing as she was a manifestation of his magic, more or less, that meant he was a little smug. Well, why not?

"Just burning off a bit extra," Morgan said. "Say

hello to Caleb, Aiyeda."

Aiyeda snorted at Caleb. A wisp of steam came out of her nose.

Caleb made a squeaking noise.

"Don't be a baby," said Morgan. "She won't hurt you. Are you okay?"

"Surprisingly so, which probably means I'm still drunk. Or high. One of those things."

"Do you have work today?"

"I'm not a moron, Morgan. I wouldn't get wasted the night before a job."

Morgan snorted.

"Damn, it was a wild night, though."

Morgan budged Caleb up the sofa so he could sit down. Aiyeda hopped off his shoulder and started nosing about on the coffee table.

"So," said Morgan. "Sex parties, eh?"

Caleb blanched. "What about you? Don't you have to be at work yourself?"

"Not for another hour, no."

The TV came on in a blaze of noise. Caleb yelped and clamped his hands over his ears. Aiyeda looked over her shoulder with an expression of total innocence on her face and her paw on the TV remote.

Morgan got up and took the remote from her. He turned off the TV. "Be good," he said to her. "I'm having a conversation."

Caleb groaned.

"I like to keep up on current affairs, Guapo," said Aiyeda, snootily.

"No you don't. You were looking for cartoons."

Aiyeda huffed smoke and padded off to the other end of the coffee table. She started to flick through a magazine, taking an exaggerated moment to lick a single, sharp claw before using it to turn each page. It was testament to her control that she didn't rip the thing to shreds.

"So," said Morgan to Caleb. "You had a wild night?"

Caleb rolled his eyes. "You're not going to let it go, are you? Even after your dragon just made my head explode?"

Morgan smiled beneficently.

"Oh, all right then. We went for a nice dinner, and then we had a few drinks at this burlesque club called 'Bubble'. Dave's a member. Jennifer scored something interesting, and please turn your judgy face off right now, it was safe. Essence. None of your street drugs for our Jennifer."

"Oh, Caleb, you didn't."

"It was just a little buzz."

"A magic buzz."

"Would you rather I was snorting coke or popping Ecstasy cut with rat poison?"

"I'd rather you were sticking to vodka."

"Morgan, you are such a prude sometimes."

Aiyeda snort-hissed. "Tell me about it. You should see his dirty dreams." He looked over his shoulder, eyes narrowed at Morgan. "Pathetic."

"You know nothing about my dreams," said

Morgan. "You're just pissed off I won't let you watch cartoons."

"Bah!" said Aiyeda, and went back to his magazine.

"You have no idea where the magic came from," Morgan pointed out to Caleb. "Or that it would do what it claims to do. Or how powerful it is. Some peoples' magic is weaker and degrades much faster than others."

"Yeah, well, maybe you missed your vocation?" said Caleb, with a pointed look in Aiyeda's direction.

Morgan sighed. "Okay, so they fed you, got you drunk and gave you questionable mood-affecting magic. Where did the sex party come into all this?"

"It wasn't questionable. It came from an old friend of theirs."

"Whatever."

"Okay, okay. So we were watching this burlesque show, enjoying a nice high. Dave had his hand on my thigh, and Jennifer was whispering some very naughty things in my ear. And then this guy came to our table. He was wearing a tux with no jacket, white gloves and a white pompom on his backside, like a bunny tail. No ears, though. He was carrying this silver tray with a big, old-fashioned looking key on it, and three masks, like, masquerade masks, you know? All black lace and feathers. So he goes and pops the tray on our table and says, 'With the compliments of Mr Appleford.' Turns out, every night the guy who owns the club selects any of the guests he fancies to come and join a private party downstairs. Jennifer and Dave were really excited, because they'd wanted to get in for ages, but never got picked. So we put on the masks, and the bunny-tail waiter guided us downstairs to a big door, like on a dungeon, you know? All iron hinges and this big metal keyhole. We popped on the masks, Dave stuck the key in the keyhole, and in we went. Only, not a dungeon inside. Thank fuck, because you have to be careful who you play with, right?"

Morgan nodded. He was so drawn into Caleb's story he'd almost forgotten he actually knew where it ended up.

"Not a dungeon at all. Just a big room with the hugest four poster you could bloody imagine in the middle, and the floor was all covered in big cushions and expensive looking blankets and silk sheets. We were there for hours. There was champagne and, yeah, okay, more magic, but I only took that one Essence from Jen. After a bit you forget to be shy or worry about who's touching you. It's just sex. Wherever you look. Gorgeous people having sex and wanting to draw you into it. I swear, Morgan, I edged for hours and hours, just touching, being touched, like floating on this big cloud of pleasure."

Morgan glanced at Aiyeda. The little dragon was sitting on its haunches, staring at Caleb, round eyed, slack jawed. Morgan had never seen it look shocked before.

Morgan was pretty shocked himself. Maybe Caleb had been right about him. Maybe he was… Well, not a prude. Innocent, perhaps?

Well, not that, either, considering some of the things he'd imagined doing to Hunter last night. And yet still, shocked.

God. Caleb.

"Are you okay?" he said. "I mean, now you've come down, or you're coming down… Really, are you okay?"

"I'm fine." Caleb fell against the back of the couch, arms flung wide. "Seriously, beyond fine. I feel amazing. Well, apart from the hangover."

"You don't feel…" Morgan searched for the right word. 'Used' felt a bit moralistic. 'Taken advantage of' sounded patronising. "Upset?"

"No. Why would I?"

Morgan and Aiyeda exchanged glances. Caleb did seem all right. Perhaps this was just one of those 'your mileage may vary' things. Morgan didn't want to kink-shame, or behave like a maiden aunt with an attack of the vapours. It was just so far from what he thought a good time might look like. And what would happen now? Would Jennifer and Dave make a habit of taking him to clubs because he'd attract the attention of the next depraved sex-party host they wanted to impress?

"It's just sex, Morgan," said Caleb. "Sometimes you just have to throw caution to the wind and say, 'fuck it!', you know? Just… Fuck it. Life's short. Live while you can."

Okay, that made some kind of sense. "Carpe diem, right?"

"Carpe diem, Morgan. Exactly. Now fuck off to work, and take your dragon with you. I have a lot of sex and drugs to sleep off."

Given Hunter's opinions about magic, Morgan knew it would never be 'bring your dragon to work day', so he took a few moments to call his magic back inside of him, where it settled as a warm glow somewhere around his centre. Then he caught the train to the city centre and walked to Hunter's office. The front door was open, so he gave a quick buzz and let himself in. Jogged up the stairs and opened the door, to find himself looking at the unmistakable aluminium back of an iMac. There was a wireless keyboard on the desk, too, and a mouse and trackpad. And a sleek, white iPhone box.

Morgan looked from all the expensive toys over to Hunter, who was leaning against his desk, arms folded across his chest. Smirking, naturally.

"Well." Morgan popped his rucksack under his desk.

"I hope you feel suitably well-equipped," said Hunter.

Morgan strode across the room, got right up in Hunter's space and kissed him. "A clapped out old laptop would've been fine."

"Rubbish. I have standards to maintain." Hunter unfolded his arms and rested his hands on Morgan's hips.

A delighted little laugh escaped from Morgan. "I absolutely love it. How did you know I have a hard on for shiny tech?"

"Oh, now, let me see." Hunter shifted his hips and

pulled Morgan in a bit tighter. "Yep, there it is."

"That might just be for you," murmured Morgan.

Hunter chuckled. Then he took a slow breath in, quite possibly sniffing Morgan's shampoo. "I thought you might have changed your mind again."

"We should take it slow," said Morgan. "But we should take it."

Hunter breathed in again, this time a big, unashamed huff of Morgan. It was very hot. "Yeah. Let's."

"We'll have to make sure Pearl doesn't find out. And please tell me you didn't get me a computer so I'd have sex with you."

"No! I ordered it yesterday, before any of that. I'm honestly hurt you'd think such a thing, Morgan."

He didn't sound hurt at all. He sounded how Morgan felt: light and giddy, like laughter could come bubbling out any moment.

"We'd better get to work, Mr Hunter," Morgan said.

Hunter lightly smacked Morgan's arse. "Off you go then, Mr Kerry. Be sure to get your equipment ready."

"I'll have you know my equipment is always ready, Mr Hunter."

Hunter giggle-snorted and smacked his arse again.

Morgan was in danger of volunteering for a full-on spanking session when Hunter's phone rang. Hunter wasn't in the habit of missing calls, so it gave Morgan a moment to run back to his desk and fire up his new computer. He popped his new Poundland cushion onto his chair before he sat.

"Okay," Hunter said to whoever it was on the phone. "We'll be there at ten thirty. Yeah, I'll check. Bye."

"New case?" Morgan asked. The computer sang a sweet little tune to him as it came to life.

"Could be. Um, I know you told me, but I've had a lot on my mind. Where might I find the missing person's files?"

"Right of the book case, top two drawers. Alphabetical by surname."

"Wow. That really is efficient."

Morgan beamed at him. "It's what I do."

"Among other things," murmured Hunter, and he started rifling through his filing cabinet.

Morgan hadn't been in a police station since the warehouse incident, and he didn't remember much about that one, except that it had smelled of antibacterial spray, like hospitals, and none of the rooms he'd been in had windows. This police station was different. For one thing, it had no majos facilities, it was just an old-fashioned police station. The interview room he and Hunter were shown to had windows, carpet and curtains. It did smell of antibacterial spray, though.

They'd had time to do no more than sit down before the door opened again and two people came in. One was a woman, with sharp, clicky heels and long, black hair that swung in a ponytail down her back. The other was a slender young guy wearing a crisp, white shirt and an earnest expression. His thick eyebrows were scrunched up, giving the impression that he was about to pay excruciating attention to everything that happened and hoped to hell he didn't get anything wrong.

The woman said a curt "hello," to Hunter, then shook Morgan's hand and smiled. Her lipstick was the colour of a ripe cherry, combining with her dark hair to make her skin look ultra-pale. It was very dramatic, might even have been scary if it wasn't for the warmth of her smile. "I'm DS Shaw," she said. "And this is DC Goswami."

Morgan greeted both of them politely. Hunter shook hands with Goswami, but just nodded at DS Shaw. Well. That was all very weird. Hunter's manners were usually impeccable.

They all sat down, business cards changed hands and Detective Shaw said, "So. What've you got for us?"

Hunter gave her a quick look, the meaning of which Morgan couldn't fathom, and said, "I think we've found a misper that matches your description."

There was something about the way Hunter casually threw detective jargon into the conversation that sent a very pleasant shiver down Morgan's spine.

"Reginald Klyne," Hunter said, taking a picture out of the folder where Morgan had very carefully filed it. "Aged forty nine, Customer Experience Assistant at William Hill's bookmakers in Leeds. So passionate about the industry that he follows his own tips, but not with reputable bookies. A debt management company came to me to help track him down. He owes them thirty grand."

DI Shaw's immaculate eyebrows shot up. "Did he, now?"

"Ah," said Hunter. "He's in the past tense now, is he?"

"Put it this way, your employers won't be getting their money back any time soon."

"Clients," said Hunter. Detective Shaw ignored him.

"How long's he been missing?" asked Detective Goswami.

"His landlord was the last one to see him," said Hunter. "December the twenty second last year."

"Nearly six months ago."

"I wasn't contacted until April," said Hunter. "The trail was already cold."

"Well, you can close your file," Detective Shaw said.

"What happened to him?"

"I'm not at liberty to disclose that."

"Jess, come on."

Detective Shaw's eyes narrowed, but Hunter didn't back down, holding eye contact.

Morgan and Detective Goswami exchanged a 'what the fuck' sort of look.

"Thank you for your help, Mr Hunter," Detective Shaw said. "Please submit your invoice through the usual channels. I'm sorry it won't be quite as lucrative as your original employer would have offered."

"Client." Hunter clicked his tongue on the 'C' and the 'T'.

Detective Shaw smiled with no humour whatsoever and got to her feet. Another round of handshakes, Detective Shaw missing out Hunter again, as if she felt he didn't deserve it. Morgan bristled a bit.

"Please don't hesitate to get in touch if we can be of any further help," said Hunter, smoothly.

"Someone will be along to show you out soon." Detective Shaw put the picture in her own file. It was a lot thicker than Hunter's. Then she swooshed out of the room, with the same intent sense of purpose as she'd swept in. Detective Goswami threw an apologetic smile over his shoulder at Morgan.

"Was it just me," Morgan said, "or was she a bit rude?"

"She's always rude, Morgan." Hunter sighed heavily. "She's my sister."

Chapter Twelve

Morgan waited until they were back out on the street before he said, "So. Your sister."

Hunter was fuming, unrestrained now from any need to hang on to the moral high ground. "Yes. My bloody sister. She thinks she's so smart and clever, just because she's still on the Force. She has no–"

"So you both went into the Police. After school."

"She got her degree first. Fast tracked her skinny little arse right past me."

"You weren't a Sergeant?"

"No, Morgan. I was not. We both went for promotion. She got it, I didn't. But that does not mean she's better than me. Understand?"

Morgan decided it was best to nod. He had no idea how police ranking or promotions worked, only that police detectives on TV seemed a lot more old and grizzled than Hunter or his sister.

"I'm guessing she's married, then, what with the different surname?"

"Was."

"She must have married young."

"She's only a year younger than me. But she moves fast. Married, had a kid and divorced, all before she was thirty."

"Oh, so you're an uncle?" Morgan had always wanted to be an uncle. He loved kids.

"Yes," said Hunter. A soft tone had intruded on his otherwise grumpy voice. "Liam. He's three in September."

"Aww," said Morgan.

"I don't get to see him very often. You saw what she's like."

Morgan's main impression had been that she seemed very professional. Beautiful, too, and now he knew that she and Hunter were related he could recognise similarities around the bone structure and their boundless confidence. And she'd seemed very pissed off with Hunter which, well, that didn't seem so unimaginable. Only yesterday he'd wanted to throw Hunter into a canal himself. He kept these observations to himself, though, and just answered with a non-committal sort of 'mmm'.

"I want you to get in touch with her sidekick," said Hunter. "Find out what happened to Reginald Klyne."

"I think we know that. He's dead."

"Well, of course he's dead, Morgan. I what to know why. How. When."

"You think the debt collectors will want to know?"

"Of course not. *I* want to know."

Morgan grinned at him and was gratified to notice the grimness of Hunter's expression diminished significantly. "Good," he said. "So do I."

They went to a coffee shop for lunch. It was the other side of the city to the office, but everyone seemed to know Hunter, just like they did at Sophie's. They were shown to a table in the walled garden at the back, where there were only four tables, none of which were occupied. Morgan watched the way Hunter's eyes flitted over the menu, darting around from item to item like a bird scanning for a juicy worm.

"Burger, I think," Hunter said, a few moments later, and suddenly Morgan realised he ought to choose his own lunch too.

He opted for avocado salad and an iced tea.

Once the waitress had taken their order, Morgan got out his brand-new work iPhone and tapped in Detective Goswami's number from his business card. He glanced up; Hunter was busy scrolling through his own phone, so Morgan quickly tapped in Detective Shaw's details too.

Then he called Goswami. It rang three times before he answered. There was a lot of clattering in the background; probably a canteen, or maybe Jess took her sidekick out to lunch too.

"Hello, Detective Goswami. Morgan Kerry here. We met this morning."

"Hello," said DC Goswami. "Is everything all right,

Sir?"

"I'm fine. Please, call me Morgan. I like to think we're associates, aren't we?"

"Can I help you with something?"

"The thing is, I'm new to all this, and Mr Hunter's asked me to write up the report for our clients. I'm not sure what I'm allowed to say and what I'm not?"

"Nothing about the case is public knowledge as of yet."

"Ah, I see. Well, I'd be grateful if you could tell me more when you can."

"Um, yes."

"And if you need anything else from us, please don't hesitate to ask. Obviously I don't know the particulars, but if Mr Klyne's gambling had anything to do with his death…"

"It's possible," said Goswami. "I'm sure Detective Shaw–"

"That's great. I'll be sure to tell you if there's any developments at our end, of course."

"Thank you, I'll… Hang on a minute please."

Morgan waited. Hunter was watching him.

"Um," said Goswami, after a minute or two. His voice was low, almost a whisper. "There is something. Do you know where Mr Klyne worked up his debts? I've got to go through it all from scratch and it would save a lot of time if you could…"

"I'll check our records as soon as we get back to the office," Morgan said. "Anything else you'd like me to look for?"

"Not yet. Our investigation is in its early stages so we don't want to discount anything."

"I'll see what I can do about those bookies," said Morgan. "Thanks, Detective."

"Call me Sahil. Bye for now."

Morgan ended the call and looked up at Hunter.

"Not a bad start," said Hunter.

"I didn't get anything out of him."

"You got an information request," Hunter said. "It's more than Jess gave us. The fact is, they need us as much as we need them. It'll just take her a while to catch on."

Just then the food arrived, cutting off their conversation. It would be easy to point out that if Hunter dropped his attitude towards his sister, she might let her guard down a bit too. Morgan was tempted. But he didn't think Hunter was likely to listen, so he kept his thoughts to himself.

"So, what next?" Morgan asked when the waitress had gone. His tea smelled amazing.

"We go back to the office and find out as much about Reginald Klyne as we possibly can," said Hunter. "Then we have currency."

Hunter's files on Klyne were sparse. He'd lived in a terraced house in Harehills, near the bookmakers where he'd worked. His only known associates were co-workers. Hunter had interviewed as many of them as he could find, and they all said the same thing: Klyne kept himself to himself, lived alone and was chronically single, as far as anyone knew. He knew everything there was to know about greyhound racing - except which dog to back. He was a prolific gambler. Online, betting shops, trackside - if someone was offering odds, he'd take them.

Hunter's conclusion, when he'd exhausted all available leads back in April, was that suicide was the most likely outcome, especially considering how much Klyne owed. The debt collectors had accepted it, at least as a working theory, but asked him to keep looking.

There was one thing that didn't seem to fit the picture. Klyne had a Facebook account, most of which was public. The last post, dated 23rd March, featured a picture of a door in a cluster of heavenly clouds and said simply, 'What a way to go.' There was an aubergine emoji and a smiley face next to it.

Morgan scrolled down. Nobody had commented on the post. Nobody had commented on any of his posts. He'd only had ten Facebook friends, all of them gamblers or bookies from the look of it, but he'd posted nearly every day, with racing tips or pictures of greyhound sanctuaries or with annoying shares of whatever was trending at the time.

It was all very sad, really.

"So, that aubergine emoji makes it look like whatever he planned, sex was involved," Morgan said. "Who with, do you think?"

"I don't know. The only woman he knew was the branch manager at William Hills. She's married with three children, and they were on holiday when he disappeared."

"Maybe a prostitute," said Morgan.

"Or maybe he likes aubergines. Or maybe it's some kind of emoji shorthand."

"Penis smile?"

"What?"

"That's how it would read. If it was literal."

"Nobody says 'penis smile,' Morgan. I mean, wow. There's something really creepy about that. Penises don't smile."

"Maybe you're not treating yours right," said Morgan, blandly.

Hunter snort-laughed.

"Maybe he just wanted moussaka for dinner." Morgan sighed. It felt grubby, somehow, piecing together all the bits of this man's life. Things he'd probably been really ashamed of when he was alive.

He glanced up from his computer to find Hunter looking at him.

"What?" said Morgan.

"Nothing."

"What??"

"Just looking."

"Oh, really? And do you like what you see?"

"Possibly."

Morgan turned back to his screen, trying to repress a smug grin.

"D'you want to go for a drink after work?" Hunter asked.

Morgan was about to say something along the lines

of 'fuck, yeah', and then he remembered.

"Sorry, I've got to go somewhere at six."

"We could finish early if you like."

"I thought you hired me because of your immense workload."

"Fuck, Morgan, you drive a hard bargain."

"After work tomorrow, for sure."

"Oh. Good."

"What d'you want me to do with our betting friend? I take it if I send what I've found so far over to the police you'd sack me."

"They probably know a fair bit of it already. Keep it all to hand, just in case. Forget about him for now. I've got some addresses for you to run. See if any of them actually exist."

Well, that sounded like fun.

Of the first ten pages of addresses, only one existed as far as Morgan could find out. Hunter seemed pleased, but he didn't say what it was all about. Or, rather, when Morgan asked he said, "Just a hunch," in a tone that Morgan was coming to understand meant that he wasn't about to say anything else. Then Hunter's phone rang. Morgan heard him arrange to meet someone in Sophie's.

"Don't wait up," Hunter said, as he hunted around in his desk drawer. "I might be a while."

Morgan flipped through the thick stack of addresses he still had to check. Plenty to keep him going 'til home time. Probably half of tomorrow morning, too.

Hunter pulled some keys out of his drawer. He

stuck one set in his pocket. On his way out of the room he dropped the spare set on Morgan's desk.

Then he paused at the door, came back and leaned over the desk to give Morgan a kiss on the cheek. Then he kissed him on the nose as well. And then on the mouth.

Morgan kissed him back, a whole load of soft, lingering kisses until they were both breathing fast and Morgan was seriously considering dispensing with all the 'take it slow' crap and dragging Hunter into the bathroom for a quickie. Or maybe they could do it right here. On his desk. Next to the shiny new Mac.

But Hunter pulled back, his cheeks flushed and his eyes glazed over. "Tomorrow, Morgan," he said, his voice croaky.

"Bright and early," Morgan said.

Hunter left the office. Morgan listened to his footsteps fading as he went downstairs, heard the bang of the front door. He leaned back in his chair and loosened his tie a little. He was hard as a rock and considered rubbing one out, just to get the use of his brain back. But he wasn't an exhibitionist, in the usual run of things, and although he was technically alone, Hunter had installed at least one camera that he was aware of. Besides. There were a few remnants of professional conduct he'd quite like to cling to.

He arrived at Dr Rosero's at five to six. The waiting room was as tidy as ever. Well, casually tidy. There was a blanket tossed over the back of a couch, artfully off-centre. The magazines were in piles that weren't entirely straight. Over in the kids' corner toys were strewn on the carpet, no longer contained by the big green toy box.

There was a bookcase full of books of motivational quotations and sayings. Morgan had read most of them, over the years. There were no actual windows, just mirrors. Morgan sat opposite one and checked himself out, as he was alone. He looked just like he always did. Appealingly untidy. Marginally scruffy hair. Smartly dressed, although he'd taken off his tie and rolled up his sleeves on account of the heat. Professional. Yes.

The door at the far end of the waiting room opened.

"Good evening, Morgan," said Ms Rosero. "Do come in."

Morgan submitted himself to the squeeze of the blood pressure cuff, the scratch of the sampling syringe and the coldness of the stethoscope while he went through his monthly physical. Ms (technically Dr these days) Rosero swept through the usual questions about his magic (Had it flared up? Had he used it since their last meeting?), his control (Rated on a scale of one to ten.) and whether he was getting enough sleep and eating properly. She encouraged him to call her Michaela now he was all grown up, but he frequently forgot to do so.

Should he tell her about Hunter? No. Hunter was nothing to do with magic.

He settled into the technically comfortable,

ergonomic seat opposite Ms Roser... Michaela. He smiled at her.

"So, Morgan," she said. "How have you been?"

He took her through the catalogue of his life for the past month, right up to the Move-U incident. Right. That, he should talk about.

"I didn't know people could look me up on a register," Morgan said.

"There's no official register. I understand there's a company that hoovers up information on majos from the Internet, so it's only if you declare it on social media, or as your occupation, or if you've appeared in any news reports."

Morgan sighed heavily. "The bloody warehouse."

"It doesn't define you, Morgan. You've done so well since then."

"But it does define me, doesn't it? Every time I think I'm past it, it just comes right back up and bites me on the arse. Sorry."

"If they knew you were majos before they hired you, they can't have minded. It's likely they thought it was an asset."

Well. Okay. He hadn't thought of it that way.

"What assets do you think your magic brings to the workplace, Morgan?"

He wanted to shrug sulkily and mutter something about being able to light the boiler. One of the problems of having the same therapist he'd had as a kid: his inner teenager tended to pop up for a bit of a strop sometimes. But he'd always liked Michaela and he trusted her completely. When he'd left school he'd been transferred to a guy in a majos centre who was heavily into circuit training on the grounds that a strong body equalled a strong mind. That hadn't really worked out. He'd been limping along with a painfully well-meaning woman, who squinted at him worriedly no matter what he said to her, when Ms Rosero turned up to give a talk at a Coven meeting. While Morgan had been struggling through college trying not to explode anything, she'd got herself a PhD from the Majos Psychology Department in Barcelona and had come back to head up Majos Support for the North East. She had been based in Durham, but she'd taken one look at Morgan and arranged to move her clinical work to Leeds.

So, he owed her more than the sulky teenager he'd been back in the old days.

"What I don't get is how they thought magic could clean the windows. It's not like I could just vanish all the shit off them."

"I don't think the people who searched for you on the database were thinking you'd clean the windows, do you?"

"I don't know."

"You don't think they might have hoped you'd charm clients for them?"

"That would be dishonest."

"Indeed it would."

She had a wry smile on her face. He wasn't sure why. "I don't do that."

Then he wondered about Alice. She'd opened up

to him so quickly. Had he inadvertently turned the *encanté* up to ten? And what about Hunter? What if he didn't really like him, but Morgan had turned the mojo on because he wanted him to so much?

"Where are your thoughts taking you?" Michaela asked.

"Nowhere good. I suppose."

She waited.

And waited.

"What if I do it without meaning to?" Morgan blurted.

"How would that work?"

"What if I'm just being nice to someone, just ordinary nice, or polite, and the encanté accelerates it and they fall in love with me?"

"Have you met someone?"

"I was exaggerating."

Another agonising pause, but this time Michaela was the one to break it. "When you lose control and your other powers flare; say your fuego, for example, do you know it's happened?"

"Of course I do."

"Even in a minor way?"

"Even a spark. I still get the tickling feeling in my fingers and toes. My lips, sometimes."

She nodded. This was old ground. When Morgan was first training with her he'd learned that tingle as a warning sign. He'd conditioned himself to use it as a trigger to clamp his control down tight.

"But I've never had that with the encanté, not

unless I'm consciously using it. Which I never do."

That was a lie. He wouldn't deliberately charm someone into his bed, or to persuade them to spend money they didn't want to spend. But there were times it seemed harmless and saved time, or made people happy. Like the time he charmed the doorman of a fancy club Caleb was dying to get into. Or when the guy at the train station tried to fine him for not having a ticket when he'd left his train pass at home.

But, conscious charms aside, he always connected quickly with people, when he wanted to. People seemed to trust him instinctively. Like Alice. And Sahil. And he knew Michaela was the same.

"Getting along with people isn't necessarily a magical skill," Ms Rosero said. "A lot of history's leaders have charisma, without being majos. Martin Luther King. Winston Churchill."

"Hitler?"

"The jury's still out on Hitler."

"But that's what scares people, isn't it? That majos can influence peoples' minds?"

"One of the things, yes."

He wanted her to tell him it was okay, that he wasn't really scary. That his power, if people knew how strong it could be, wouldn't push everyone away and get him rejected and feared and locked up. But the only person who knew he could do more than stir up a gentle breeze on a still day was Ms Rosero. And she'd been working with him since he was a child to make sure he didn't give himself away to anyone else.

He realised he was holding his breath. He let it out in an abrupt whooshing sound. "I just want people to like me for myself. But how can I know they do? What if it's all just encanté?"

"Your majos is part of who you are, and research suggests that for some of us that power gives us a certain advantage; it can make us appear more attractive to many susceptible individuals. But I'm not so sure I see that in you, Morgan. I think you're just a very likeable young man. Nonetheless, if you chose to use your power, you could be even more likeable, for the period you could sustain the encanté. But even you couldn't achieve that for long enough to maintain a friendship in the long term."

"Long enough to get laid?"

Ms Rosero was unshockable, but Morgan was cross with himself for letting it slip out.

"Not without knowing it. Morgan, you are one of the most self-aware majos I've ever worked with. Even if you didn't feel it at the time, surely you would feel the drain afterwards?"

She was right. And he hadn't, not once since he'd met Hunter. If he had, he wouldn't have flared up back at Move-U. Or in Hebden. Certainly not to the point of scaring himself as much as he had recently.

He took a deep, calming breath. "Thank you."

"Think of it like evaporation. If you leave a glass of water out but don't drink from it, you don't see it evaporate. But you can see when the water level goes down. If it makes you feel better, do the measurement exercises for a little while. I can give you some indicator strips if you'd like?"

Morgan liked when Ms Rosero brought science into things. It was very reassuring. He agreed and left her office a few minutes later with a pack of paper strips in his wallet and a fresh thought in his head.

If it was okay to use encanté to get Caleb into a club, it had to be okay to use it to, say, solve a murder.

So long as Hunter never found out.

Chapter Thirteen

It was nice to come to work and have a desk that was actually his, even if it was only for three months. Not borrowed or allocated or scheduled. Just his. Morgan shyly took out a little pen pot and put it on his desk. It wasn't anything special, just a plain grey metal one he'd picked up from the discount stationer's on the way to work. But he liked it. He put a couple of pens and a pencil in it and smiled to himself.

Hunter was hard at work already, reading through a filled fit-to-burst folder of stuff with a frown on his face, so Morgan made the coffee.

"Anything I can help with?" Morgan asked as he placed Hunter's mug on his coaster.

"Have you done those addresses?"

Morgan pointed at the pile of papers in the top of Hunter's in-tray. "Finished them last night. I emailed you the ones that are real. There's only eight of them."

Hunter let out a low whistle.

"What were they for, anyway?" Morgan asked. "It wasn't some weird initiation ritual, was it? Like sending an apprentice to buy stripy paint?"

Hunter snort-laughed. "No, Morgan." He leaned back in his chair. "It's a fraud enquiry. Those are a bunch of addresses they think were given by the same eight people applying for various kinds of credit."

"Including their real ones?"

"Looks like it. Good work, Morgan."

Morgan sat on the edge of Hunter's desk, keeping very tight control on his encanté. He'd tested himself already that morning and scored a zero point four. As the maximum was a hundred, he was happy with that. "So. Do I get a reward?"

"That depends. What do you think you deserve?" Hunter's eyes sparkled at him.

"You're the boss." Morgan leaned back on one hand and hoped he looked alluring. Whatever happened, his attraction to Hunter was one hundred per cent natural, which was a bit nerve-wracking, because what if Hunter didn't like him back anymore? What if it had all been a magic-fuelled mirage?

What actually happened was that Hunter got up, came around the desk and kissed him. And while Morgan was busy being kissed, Hunter slipped his hand on his belly, one finger slipping between the buttons of his shirt. It tickled in a really good way. Hunter didn't move much, just kept the weight of his hand there, reassuringly heavy. His tongue filled Morgan's mouth, and Morgan's magic was about the only thing he did have under control. He found himself imagining all the very wonderful and indecent things he wanted to do with Hunter, most of which involved being very, very naked. He was such a good kisser. Morgan wondered what that sinful mouth would feel like around his-

There was a buzzing noise.

What?

Bzzzt. Buzzing. A buzzer. Shit.

"Wait," Morgan pushed Hunter back, breathlessly. "Door."

"Why?"

"What d'you mean, why? Someone's at the door."

"Nobody ever comes to the door."

"Well, they are now. What if they're a potential client?"

"We could close for the day."

"Is it a good idea to turn business away?"

Hunter made a growling noise, stomped over to the entry panel by the door and pressed 'talk'. "Hunter PI, can I help you?"

"It's Jess. Open up."

Hunter swore under his breath and unlocked the door.

Morgan slid off the desk and took a steadying sip of his tea. Two sets of footsteps approached, both even, measured steps. No heels.

The door opened, and Hunter's sister stood there, with Sahil in tow. She looked around and seemed surprised by what she saw.

"Good morning," said Morgan, trying to remember

how to be professional. "Can I get you a drink or anything?"

"You have a kettle?" said Detective Shaw. Or Jess. What was he supposed to call her?

"Yes, I have a kettle," said Hunter. "I had a new kitchen put in and everything. You'd be amazed at what a functional adult can achieve when liberated from the restrictions of institutional bureaucracy."

"Tea?" said Morgan. "Coffee? I think there's some hot chocolate."

"No, thanks."

"I'll have a tea if you're making one," said Sahil. Either he didn't see the disapproving look Jess gave him or he'd learned to ignore it. Morgan went into the little kitchen, keeping an ear out for what was going on in the office. Sahil followed him. Hunter was complaining that she hadn't given him any warning, and then she asked if he had anything to hide, to which Hunter retorted that no, he didn't have anything to hide but he didn't have enough chairs for them either.

"She seems a bit put out," said Morgan. He topped up the kettle and turned it on.

Sahil visibly relaxed and leaned back against the kitchen counter. "It's been a rough morning."

"Herbal or regular tea? I've got salted caramel green tea, blackcurrant, chamomile, ginseng and vanilla, Yorkshire or Taylors breakfast."

"That's... Extensive," Sahil observed.

"I'm a big fan of tea."

"Yeah. Uh, Yorkshire, please. Milk, no sugar. My

wife's got a thing about sugar at the moment. She watches too many documentaries, you know?"

Voices in the office were getting raised. Words like 'repressed bitch' and 'pretentious twat' were being thrown about in a most unprofessional manner.

"She's under a lot of pressure. Our boss is a bit of a wanker. And then there's the whole sibling rivalry thing they have going on," said Sahil, with a little nod. "To be honest, I had enough of that when I was a kid."

"Do you come from a big family?"

"Five of us. Three boys, two girls. I was in the middle. Learned to keep my mouth shut and my eyes open." His eyes sparkled when he smiled. Morgan liked him.

The kettle boiled and he made Sahil's tea. Back in the office, Jess and Hunter stopped talking as soon as they came in, glaring at each other instead.

"Are you sure I can't get you anything?" Morgan said to Jess.

"No. Thank you. I think we'd better get on with it."

"I wish you would," said Hunter.

Sahil and Morgan exchanged a look.

"You can probably guess why I'm here," Jess said.

"To make my life a misery?"

"For fuck's sake, Hunter, will you grow up and act like a professional for once in your life?"

"If you—"

"It's about Reginald, right?" said Morgan. "Have you found out what happened?"

"I need information about drugs."

Hunter folded his arms across his chest. "And you think I can give you that information why, exactly?"

"What sort of drugs?" Morgan asked. He was aware of Hunter's eyes boring into him, no doubt less than pleased with him for getting in the way of his pathetic fraternal put downs. But Morgan didn't much care. He'd found out enough about Reginald Klyne that he genuinely wanted to know what had happened to the poor guy.

"Recreational. Is there anything new on the market that you've come across lately?"

"I don't do drugs," said Hunter, smugly. "That was your speciality."

There was a long, uncomfortable silence, broken only when Sahil slurped his tea.

Jess pulled herself up to her full height. She was wearing a tailored suit with flat pumps, practical but stylish, but she was still tall, easily passing Hunter's five foot ten-or-so and nearly up to Morgan's six foot one. Her colouring was different from Hunter's: dark hair, hazel eyes, skin very pale where Hunter's was golden. But they both had killer cheekbones, broad shoulders and a glare that could kill at twenty paces.

"Very well," Jess said, her eyes narrowed. "I'll inform the department that I won't be requiring your services on this case any further. Clearly you're more suited to fraud."

She turned on her heel and stormed out of the office while the rest of them watched. A moment later came a yell of, "Goswami! Now!"

Sahil pressed his mug into Morgan's hand with a regretful look. Morgan followed him to the door to see him out. Sahil hesitated on the threshold, then turned to Morgan and whispered, "Don't mind Jess. She's not usually like this, it's just they bring out the worst in each other, I think. I'll text you later. We'll talk."

Morgan nodded and closed the door behind him. He went and put Sahil's mug in the kitchen.

"What?" said Hunter, following him.

"What do you mean, 'what?'"

"Honestly, Morgan, I can feel your disapproval from here. We don't need her. We have plenty of clients."

"It's your business," said Morgan, holding up his hands. "If you want to give up on poor old Reginald, that's up to you."

"I do. And it is. Thank you for noticing."

Morgan poured his cold tea down the sink, rinsed out his mug and put the kettle on to make another one. "D'you want more coffee?"

Hunter fetched his own mug and set it down next to Morgan's. "Maybe I do care a bit about poor old Reginald," he admitted.

"Mmm?"

"It's just I always see red when Jess is around." He scrubbed a hand across his eyes. "Christ, that was awful. I was horribly unprofessional, wasn't I?"

"Li'l bit."

"Shit."

"It's okay. Let me talk to Sahil."

"Thanks. It's just…"

Morgan let the quiet hang there. He wasn't about to force Hunter to say anything he didn't want to. However curious he was.

"I don't want you to think I'm normally like that." Hunter picked at a bit of blu tac that had been abandoned on the wall. Probably by the previous owner; Morgan couldn't imagine Hunter sticking anything on the walls. He looked kind of lost, his intense gaze fixed on the wall and the blu tac, which dropped off along with a little chunk of paint. Morgan touched his hand. Hunter made a sort of grunting noise and meshed his fingers between Morgan's.

"I hope we're still on for tonight," said Morgan.

"Really?" There was a sulky edge to Hunter's voice, like he was a little kid who'd just got told off. "You'd go on a date with a moron who puts his own family issues above finding out why a gambling addict killed himself?"

"Just this once," said Morgan.

Hunter gave him a pouty little smile, and seriously, Morgan was in way too deep if he found it this cute.

He did find it cute, though.

Sahil rang later that morning and Morgan arranged to meet him in the park at lunchtime. They found a secluded bench by a rose bed to sit and eat. They'd bought sandwiches from the café near the entrance; it wasn't exactly up to Hunter's standards of venue for entertaining clients, but it was secluded enough that they could talk freely without being overheard.

"Are they always like that?" Morgan asked. "Hunter and Jess, I mean."

"Well, I'd never met Mr Hunter before the other day," Sahil said. "But I get the impression they had a big falling out a while ago. Families, eh?"

"Hm," said Morgan. He got along very well with his mother, providing he wasn't burning down warehouses, and he barely remembered his absent father. His uncle and cousins were okay. They didn't go in for big dramas. "So, what did you want our help with?"

"We got the lab reports back on Reggie Klyne, and it wasn't what we thought. The initial assessment was death by suicide."

Morgan nodded. The hairs on the back of his neck went up at the thought of what Sahil might be about to say.

"He had a lot of alcohol and drugs in his system. Overdose, we thought, or possibly misadventure. But then the full analysis came back, and the drugs in his system weren't normal drugs. They were infused with some kind of magic."

Morgan's mind went straight to Caleb. Shit. He swallowed down panic and said, "You think that's what killed him?"

"Not directly, no. What we wanted to know was whether there was any history of him interacting with majos. Maybe he was dealing, to pay off debts? Or could he have taken the drugs to improve his success at gambling?"

People were so woefully ignorant of majos it hurt sometimes. Even good guys like Sahil. They believed whatever the media told them and didn't think to ask questions. He had an opportunity to sort that out right here and now, of course. He could say, 'well, Sahil, speaking as a very powerful majos myself, that's bullshit.'

What he actually said was, "I'm pretty sure they can't do that. Otherwise the bookies would be up in arms. And broke. Or refusing to let people gamble if they think they're under the influence. Majos isn't the same as precognition, or mind reading, or anything like that."

"Right. So this was just Reggie taking drugs for shits and giggles, then."

"Or to feel better. He can't have been happy with the debts and the gambling addiction. I've heard that drugs like that can alter mood quite dramatically."

"He certainly seemed to be having a good time just before he died. As well as the drink and magic drugs there was evidence of sexual activity. He had a hell of a last night."

Sex, drugs and rock'n'roll? It didn't sound like Reginald-Klyne-the-loner as Morgan had come to know him. Maybe that aubergine emoji had meant something after all. "Where was he found?"

"Horsforth. His body was found in Old Mill Beck. First guess was accidental death, thought he'd got drunk, fallen in and drowned. But he didn't die at the scene, so we've started to look at murder."

"What did he actually die of?"

Sahil hesitated, and Morgan wondered whether he'd taken a step too far. But then Sahil said, "Cardiac arrest. But with no known cause. He was surprisingly healthy for a man of his age. Liver was a bit under the weather, but nothing serious. Low cholesterol, healthy heart and lungs. Which is what led us to the drug angle; we were expecting evidence of coke, maybe meth or MDMA. But all he had in his blood was the magic pixie dust."

Why did everything keep coming back to fucking Essence? Morgan was going to use every bit of Reginald's terrible fate to scare Caleb off them, that's for sure.

"He had good reason to kill himself, either directly or by taking unnecessary risks," Morgan said. "Truly horrible debts, and he didn't seem capable of not gambling. Just kept on and on, even when he'd lost pretty much everything."

"Addictions tend to cluster up in some people. Poor guy."

"Yeah."

"I could really use a close up with the drugs, though."

"They're very hard to find. So I'd heard, anyway."

"Yeah, I know. It's frustrating."

Morgan chewed on the last of his sandwich, thinking hard. He wanted to help. He really did. But it was hard to think of a way to do so without incriminating himself in a way that could easily get back to Hunter. "So, what are you going to tell Jess? About sneaking out to see me, I mean."

Sahil shrugged. "The truth, maybe? She won't be pissed off if I bring back evidence. I think she's pretty ashamed about the way she behaved, truth be told. She's usually painfully professional."

"That sounds familiar."

"Well, everyone know the sidekicks gets the real work done, right?"

Sahil put his hand up for a high five and Morgan amiably smacked palms with him.

Is that what he was now? Hunter's sidekick?

Sahil's phone buzzed. He glanced at the screen. "I have to go," he said. "Call me if you think of anything, okay? Glad to be working with you, Morgan."

"Me too," said Morgan.

Chapter Fourteen

Morgan waited until he and Hunter were actually on the train before he messaged Caleb. He'd packed a toothbrush and a few other things (including his magic book, just in case). He'd nearly packed condoms and lube, put them in and taken them out of his bag a dozen times, before finally convincing himself that Hunter would have some at his place, and if he didn't, well, maybe that meant he wanted to take it slow and of course Morgan would respect that. He didn't want to tempt fate, not when things were so new and anyway, Hunter could be called off on a case at a moment's notice.

Once they'd pulled out of Leeds station for York, though, at around the time he'd usually be getting home, Morgan decided to bite the bullet. He took out his phone and dialled, aware that Hunter was watching him out of the corner of his eye.

Caleb picked up straight away with a 'yo', and

Morgan realised he'd been hoping it would go to voicemail.

"Hi," he said.

"'Sup?" asked Caleb, popping the 'p'.

"I'm, um, going to York for the night. I might be, um…" He dropped his voice. "…back late." And then added, wishing he'd taken this call to a different part of the train, or maybe just sent a bloody text, "Or not. Tonight. Home. Um."

"Well, well. My boy's all grown up."

"I mean, I might be."

Hunter shook his head. Possibly at whatever he was reading on his phone. Possibly not.

"Have a lovely time, sweet boy," said Caleb. "Be safe and remember to say thank you for having you."

"I will not be saying anything of the sort, Caleb, just… No. Are you okay?"

"Never better."

"Are you going out?"

"I have a boxed set of something outrageously sinister on Netflix to watch. Sorry you'll miss it."

"I'm not. Well, okay then. I'll see you, um, later."

"If you're not back in a week I'll start watering your plants."

"That won't be necessary."

"Ciao, darling. Give Hunter a big sloppy blow job from—"

Morgan hung up and stared out of the train window, biting his lip. Bloody Caleb.

"Look at this," Hunter said, shoving his phone

under Morgan's nose. "Isn't that the cutest thing you saw?"

Morgan looked. On the screen a puppy climbed into a cardboard box, ran about until the box fell over, then ran about some more and rammed it into a skinny pair of guy-legs.

It was pretty cute.

"Reminds me of someone," said Morgan.

York was always beautiful, but on that evening the city surpassed itself. The sunshine made the old stone glow. The streets were alive with cafes and pubs, music and laughter spilling out. The restaurant was busy, but once again Hunter clearly got on well with the staff, and they ended up at a table in a quiet alcove, where the chatter and clatter of plates was a soft background noise rather than an intrusion. There was a whole column of vegetarian choices for each course on the menu. Hunter was going to order wine, but when Morgan said he didn't drink, he ordered them both non-alcoholic cocktails, which had strawberries in and just a hint of pepper. He didn't ask Morgan why he didn't drink.

A busker outside started playing Spanish guitar as their food arrived. It was all so perfect Morgan got really anxious that it would crash around his ears any minute.

"I wanted to say thank you for today," Hunter said.

"For cleaning the coffee grounds out of the machine?"

"For making sure my infantile behaviour didn't

affect the business."

"Jess hasn't cancelled your contract, you know."

"I suspected she wouldn't. How would she explain it to her superiors? 'I can't possibly work with my brother because he's a dick?'"

Morgan swallowed a delicious mouthful of melted cheese and flaky pastry and said, "What happened with Jess? Or has it always been like that?"

Hunter frowned, and for a moment Morgan thought he wouldn't answer. But then he said, "No. We haven't always been like that. To be honest, I don't think I'd have got through school without her. I'm the older one, sure, the big brother - but you'd never have guessed it. I used to get so homesick, so pissed off with all the circle time and the co-operative games and the ridiculous student-led assignments."

"It seems funny that a kid wouldn't like all that freedom."

"Not at all. Kids thrive on boundaries. Jess and I had been brought up by our Dad for as long as we could remember, and he never really knew what to do with us. We were both crying out for a bit of, not discipline, more… Guidance. Just a good solid example of what we were supposed to do. And then, to top it off, I hit puberty and realised I was gay."

"Was it a surprise?" Morgan couldn't remember a time when he didn't know. There were so many things that were different about him as a kid that it barely registered on the weirdness scale.

"Not really. I think I was in denial, maybe? And

then one day when we were building a free-climbing course in the gym I found myself staring at Nigel Branwell-Harding's arse."

"And what did Nigel Branwell-Harding think about that?"

"Funnily enough, he quite appreciated it," said Hunter with a little grin.

"Did he, now?"

"We ended up sucking each other off in the toilets a couple of hours later. Which was lovely, except his brother saw us leave hand in hand, no doubt dishevelled and dreamy-eyed."

"Oh God! Did he say anything?"

Hunter's eyes narrowed. "Not to us, but he told his best friend, who told someone else, who told someone… And then at circle time the next day our prefect-of-the-week saw fit to announce it. To everyone. I got three cheers and the biggest piece of cake at break time."

"Really? That's so cool."

"Not when you're a pimply fourteen year old who doesn't want anyone to look at you, never mind publicly celebrate your sexuality."

"I can't imagine you with pimples."

"Good."

"Seriously, though, at least you didn't get bullied about it."

"Worse. My sister was disappointed."

"That you were gay?"

"That I didn't tell her first. To be honest, I was, too.

I would have rather. She understood, though, when I'd explained. She was amazing that way."

"So, how did it go wrong?"

"Little things, at first. Joining the police was great. I could finally be my structured, methodical, logical self. Just… normal. Painfully normal, even. But it was tough when Jess came along and got promotion over me just because of her degree, when I'd been slogging at it for three years as a lowly community constable. It was as if all that competitive spirit we'd been squashing all those years at school just burst out. We were both desperate to be the best at everything. It probably made us better coppers, in the end. But I hated it. And then she had Liam."

"But you like being an uncle, right?"

"I love Liam to bits. But after she got married and had him things weren't the same. And then there was the divorce, and…" Hunter put down his fork and took a gulp of peppery strawberry. Morgan got the impression he'd rather it had been vodka. "Look, let's not. Not tonight. Let's leave my torrid family history to one side. Is that okay?"

"Of course," said Morgan.

"So what about you? Any brothers or sisters?"

"None. It was just me and mum."

"Sounds peaceful."

"It was, sort of."

"And where does Caleb fit in?"

"He's family, yes. I mean, not literally. But we've known each other for a long time. He's like a brother.

Or, how I'd imagine a brother to be, at any rate."

"That's good."

"Yeah. Yeah it is."

He wondered how many people Caleb had told he was out on a date with Hunter. A lot, he'd guess - Morgan going on a date was a very rare event. Hopefully he wouldn't put it on Facebook.

Oh shit, what if he did? What if Pearl found out?

He pulled out his phone and tapped wildly at the screen.

>Calb dinf tell any1 about Huntr shouldn't fragernise

"Everything all right?" said Hunter.

Morgan's phone dinged.

>Course I won't. And turn your ducking autocorrect back on.

Morgan closed his eyes for a moment as relief washed over him. Then he looked at Hunter - gorgeous, golden Hunter, who was regarding him with a sort of benign amusement - and smiled.

"Everything's brilliant," he said.

Hunter's home was a three-story town house right in the city centre. As they stood on the doorstep while Hunter got his keys out, he told Morgan he'd bought it a few years back. It had been student flats for decades, run down and neglected. He'd been lovingly restoring it ever since. The ground floor was done, and the master bedroom upstairs, but the first floor bathroom still needed work and the second floor was a mess…

Three floors. Right.

The door opened onto a hallway, with a tiled floor, carpeted stairs and three stripped-pine doors.

"C'mon in, I'll show you around," said Hunter.

On the ground floor at the front of the house there was a living room that looked out onto the street. It was decorated in theatrical red and black, with three sofas arranged in a u-shape facing a big fireplace, which had a huge TV above it. There was a wooden floor and a sturdy black coffee table. It was very dramatic and bold, but Morgan could imagine it would look cosy with the candles lit and the shutters closed.

The next room was a study, lined with books - psychology, thrillers, classics, philosophy, poetry. There was an upright piano against one wall, a desk against another. An acoustic guitar on a stand. There was a big old pub-style mirror on the chimney breast with *Rose and Crown* on it in swirly print. Very retro.

"Do you play?" Morgan asked, indicating the piano.

"Yeah, a bit. It was the one thing I liked about school."

"Were you in a band?"

"I got roped into a self-expression inclusive performance group for a term. Does that count?"

Morgan patted him on the arm.

An open plan kitchen/dining room ran the whole width of the house at the back. Large, triple-glazed windows looked out onto the back yard, illuminated by the lights from the alleyway beyond. On the dining side of the room there was a long grey-topped table with six chairs. The other side was a modern fitted kitchen, with a centre island and a long counter separating it from the dining area. It looked like something out of a showroom. Morgan leaned awkwardly on the counter, while Hunter turned on lights - just the ones under the cupboards that lit the counters, nothing too harsh - and put the kettle on. It was red, the same colour as the splash-back tiles. Most of the kitchen and dining area was glossy grey and white, with tasteful red accents. Unlike the other rooms he'd seen so far, which looked lived-in levels of untidy, the kitchen was immaculate. Morgan wondered if Hunter ever used it.

None of what he'd seen so far was what he'd expected of Hunter's home. He'd imagined a smart executive flat, maybe. Compact but comfortable. But this... Morgan felt out of place and a bit naive. Hunter and Jess had been privately educated, after all, and Hunter had his own successful business. Morgan might have expected he'd have a big house.

"So what d'you think of the place?" Hunter asked, setting a mug of tea down on the counter by Morgan's elbow.

"It's very nice," Morgan said. "What I've seen so far, anyway."

Hunter stepped in close and rested his hands on Morgan's hips. "Don't worry. You'll see the bedroom soon enough."

Morgan's cheeks went hot. "No, I didn't, I mean–"

"Shhh." Hunter's mouth was about as close to

Morgan's as he could get without touching. "We're taking it slow, remember?"

"How, um, slow, exactly?"

"Well, that depends. Do you usually put out on the first date?"

Morgan cleared his throat. His cheeks were still burning, but his cock never really cared about little things like dying of embarrassment and was getting very interested in proceedings. "Maybe."

"Well, Morgan Kerry. You little go-er, you."

"I'm not, that is I... I'm not easy."

"Hmm... You were the one who gave me a blow job about ten seconds after our second kiss."

"Ah." Hunter had him there. "I did, didn't I?"

"You did." Hunter's thumbs rubbed at Morgan's hipbones. "And I've wanted to pay you back ever since."

"You have?" squeaked Morgan.

"Very much."

Then Hunter kissed him. A quick brush of his lips at first, then a press, and then his tongue was in Morgan's mouth and they were going at it like teenagers. Morgan wasn't shy anymore, and he didn't care about the big, posh house, or the showroom kitchen, or any of it. He just wanted to strip Hunter out of his clothes and do naughty, naughty things to him. A lot of things. Quite urgently.

Hunter dropped gracefully to his knees. His slender fingers made short work of Morgan's belt and fly. Morgan's trousers were a loose fit; they dropped of their own accord as soon as Hunter had released them.

Hunter mouthed over the bulge in Morgan's underwear, his breath hot, his lips firm. Morgan cried out, knees weak, and he gripped the edge of the counter behind him. Hunter hooked his fingers into the waistband of Morgan's boxer briefs and peeled them carefully down. They joined his trousers in a tangle at his ankles, and his cock sprang up happily. Suddenly his balls were cupped in Hunter's palm and Hunter was kissing the soft, sensitive skin across his pelvis, from hipbone to belly. Morgan slid his fingers into Hunter's hair, whispering over his scalp. "Yes," he said.

Hunter took the head of Morgan's cock in his mouth, swirling his tongue around, warm and wet and Morgan hadn't don't this for a long time, what with one thing and another, and Hunter was really, really good at it, working his way down inch by inch until Morgan could feel the tight constriction of Hunter's throat around his cock, and fuck, he'd never been properly deep-throated before and it was so intense, so incredibly hot.

"You're good at that," he murmured, a masterful piece of understatement. Hunter squeezed Morgan's thigh by way of an answer. Morgan wondered if one day Hunter might let him just fuck his mouth, and thought maybe he would, but he didn't dare even ask because he had zero control and for Morgan sex was never about anybody dominating anybody. Well, apart from the thing that he maybe had fantasised once or twice about Hunter smacking his arse.

His hips twitched at that thought, and Hunter slid

off a bit, making a low groan that thrilled right though Morgan's cock.

Then Hunter took the root of Morgan's cock in his fist and got serious with his tongue, licking the spot that tethered Morgan's foreskin, just under the head, and God, fuck, right *there*. The ridge of the counter bit into Morgan's back and Hunter's fingers dug into his thigh and things were tingling in an urgent sort of way.

"Hunter, I'm gonna, I, you can—"

Hunter sucked harder in reply; everything went tight and hot and just on the edge of too much, and then Morgan's orgasm broke and his body spasmed, spilling come into Hunter's hot, sucking mouth. There was nothing in the world but the pleasure rocking through his body, the smell of sex and man and the soothing press of Hunter's tongue against his sensitive prick.

Hunter's hands moved around to stroke Morgan's arse, soothing, gentle. Inquisitive.

Oh God. Morgan had only just come and he could totally just turn around and offer himself up for fucking. But his legs seemed to be all quivery and trembling and not entirely capable of holding him up unaided.

Hunter let go of his cock with a slurping sound and stood up, pulling Morgan in, wrapping his arms around him. "You're gorgeous," Hunter whispered into Morgan's ear. "Have I told you that yet?"

"N-No," stammered Morgan, his brain still fuddled.

"That's very remiss of me. I do apologise."

Morgan chuckled into Hunter's shoulder and

hugged him tight.

Once Morgan was capable of standing without help, Hunter made fresh tea - jasmine, fragrant and delicious - and led him out of the kitchen. But not up to the bedroom, as Morgan expected. Hunter seemed determined to hold out on the bedroom. Instead he took him to the living room. He shut the shutters and switched on a few lamps. They sat on the couch opposite the fireplace. There was a wood-burning stove there. Morgan could imagine it being very cosy in wintertime, sitting here, watching the flames. Hunter tapped his phone and music came on. Morgan didn't recognise the band but it was soft and acoustic and perfect for a seduction. Not that Hunter needed to worry about that: Morgan had never felt so seduced in his entire life. He was quite thoroughly seduced, thank you very much.

Hunter slid an arm around Morgan's shoulders and cuddled him in close. He kissed him, slow, gentle, like he was savouring him. Morgan sank into a warm bubble of post-coital pillowy goodness. Hunter played with Morgan's hair, teasing at the curls that bothered his ear.

"I haven't been with anyone for a while," Hunter said. His voice was a bit overly-casual, like he'd been planning how to say it.

"Me neither," said Morgan.

"I don't really like the clubbing scene anymore and I'm not the best catch in the world."

Same here, thought Morgan, but this time he kept quiet about himself and said, "I like you. Most of the time." He nuzzled at Hunter's shoulder. "When you're not being an insufferable arse."

"That's immensely flattering, Morgan."

Morgan stroked Hunter's belly through his shirt. It was tight, a bit tense. Possibly because he was trying to say something difficult, or maybe he was still really horny. Morgan suddenly realised he'd been totally selfish, he hadn't even offered payback for the amazing blow job.

"I've never met anyone like you before," Hunter told him and boy, that was true in ways he didn't know. Yet. Morgan snuggled into him, imagining a day when he could actually look Hunter in the eye over breakfast and say, 'by the way, I'm majos' and Hunter would say, 'oh, darling, I always knew you were special' and it would all be perfect. Hunter had a good heart, under all the sarcasm and arseitude. Morgan just needed to put in a bit of work in advance. Gently introducing him to the facts of magic. He was intelligent. He'd understand, if it was presented in the right way.

"Are you falling asleep?" Hunter asked.

"No. I'm listening." Morgan kissed his neck and noticed the way Hunter leaned into it. Heh.

"I suppose I'm saying… Shit, I have no idea what I'm saying."

"You like me," Morgan said. "And I like you."

"You do?"

Morgan kissed him at the dip at the top of his jaw,

just behind his ear. A little sound escaped Hunter's throat. Excellent. "Very much. Can't you tell?"

"Blow jobs aren't the same as a meaningful relationship, Morgan."

Morgan smiled to himself. "So, you're saying you want a meaningful relationship?"

Hunter frowned, all cross-face. He'd given away more than he wanted to.

"I'd like that," Morgan continued. "But sex and cuddles are great too."

"Cuddles, Morgan?"

"What do you think we're doing now?"

Hunter looked down the length of their bodies, all nestled up together on the sofa. Morgan's socked feet were all tangled up with Hunter's. His fingers were stroking circles across Hunter's belly.

Hunter kissed him, and this same thing that happened every time they kissed happened: fire (thankfully metaphorical) shot up Morgan's spine and he stopped thinking. Everything was tingles and fireworks. He yearned for skin to skin contact - a lot of skin to skin contact - touching and rubbing and tasting. Judging by the change in Hunter's breathing, the intensity in his ridiculously gorgeous eyes when he pulled back, the feeling was mutual.

"I want you," Hunter said, helplessly. "In all kinds of ways."

"And you can have me." Morgan grinned. "In all kinds of ways."

"Oh God." Hunter kissed him again, pulling

Morgan on top of him. Morgan's necklace swung down and bumped Hunter on the nose; Hunter huff-laughed.

"Do you have lube in this bedroom of yours?" Morgan plucked at the buttons of Hunter's shirt.

"Lube and condoms, yeah."

He actually made it sound really hot.

"I don't need condoms. You tested?"

"A couple of months ago. After the last time I was with anyone. A bad decision on race day. Formal wear is my kryptonite."

Morgan stashed that little nugget away for future reference. "No condoms, then. I like a lot of lube, though." He brushed his lips against the shell of Hunter's ear. "I'm very tight."

Hunter groaned and gripped Morgan's arse. Morgan led the kiss this time, exploring the inside of Hunter's mouth with his tongue, drawing out all of these needy little moans from Hunter's throat.

"Now," Hunter gasped, when Morgan pulled back for breath. "Upstairs."

"Are you going to carry me up and throw me on the bed?"

"No, I'm not. Health and safety, Morgan." Hunter smacked his arse. "Come on."

They ran up the stairs, Hunter leading Morgan by the hand. There was a landing and doors and stairs going up again but Morgan got no more than a glimpse before Hunter flung open the door right in front of them and pulled him inside. He flipped a switch and lights came on in a warm glow. There was a huge, low bed, neatly made up with white-and-grey linen.

Hunter cupped Morgan's face in his hands and pressed their foreheads together. Morgan was aware of lust flowing through his veins, twining with his magic, his pulse a steady throb, throb, throb, drinking Hunter in. The smell and feel and sound of him.

"I want to fuck you," Hunter said. "Really. A lot."

Morgan pulled back enough that Hunter's face was in focus, grinned his cheekiest grin and said, "So what're you waiting for?"

Hunter growled and then they were on the bed, grappling with clothes and kissing hard. The grappling wasn't terribly effective, so Morgan pushed Hunter off to take the lead and pull his own shirt over his head. Hunter watched him in awe, as if this was a revolutionary notion and then followed suit. Morgan didn't take his eyes off Hunter for a second while they undressed, relishing every inch of golden skin that emerged. Hunter's body showed evidence of gym membership: muscles well-toned but not overly ripped. A dusting of fair hair over his chest led down to his belly button and a somewhat darker treasure trail beyond. He wore a chain around his neck with a tiny disc hanging from it. The long muscles in his thighs shifted as he kicked off his trousers and struggled with his socks.

Hunter won the 'who can get their clothes off first' race, and gave Morgan's boxer briefs the final shove over his hips that rendered him naked. Then he pushed him back on the bed and straddled him, kissed him, his hands running over Morgan's chest and shoulders and arms, their dicks rubbing together hard and urgent.

"I want it like this," Hunter hissed into Morgan's ear. "The first time. I want to be able to look into your eyes. Watch you come. Can you? Come, I mean, while–"

"God, shut up. Yes. Yes. Just…" Morgan slid a hand between their bodies and grabbed both of their cocks, more than one handful but a quick squeeze was enough to make his point. Hunter sucked in a breath and his eyes glazed over. "Want me to take the edge off?"

Hunter shook his head.

Morgan squeezed their dicks together again. Hunter grabbed his wrist. "No. Not yet. I've got to fuck you. Right now."

Morgan took his hand away, enjoying the heavy bounce of Hunter's cock on his and gave Hunter's thigh a reassuring pat. "Okay. Yes."

Hunter swung himself off Morgan and grabbed the lube from the bedside table. Morgan parted his legs, horniness making him brazen. Hunter settled on his knees between Morgan's thighs and tipped him up a bit, so he could get his mouth on Morgan's balls, licking and nibbling his way down. Following the line of Morgan's taint down to his hole. Suddenly everything was warm and wet and nerve endings were zinging to life that hadn't had any attention for a long time. Hunter circled with his tongue and pressed in with one long, wet finger. Morgan held his breath at the intrusion, strange and uniquely intimate.

Hunter made soothing noises, leaning his head against Morgan's thigh. Watching himself opening Morgan up with his fingers. Morgan tipped his hips up, making it clear he was one hundred percent on board with the whole being opened up thing.

Once everything was really wet and squelchy, and Morgan was considering begging because he needed Hunter's dick inside him right this minute, Hunter dropped the lube and lined himself up. Morgan steadied himself, his hands on Hunter's shoulders - he hadn't been kidding, he really was tight, so used to controlling his body it could take him a while sometimes to loosen up. He took a breath, let it out as he felt the first blunt push of Hunter's cock on his hole. Hunter didn't try to get it inside, though. He slipped his finger back in instead, worked it around his cock and Morgan's hole, spreading the slick around. Then he pushed again. This time he got a little way inside. He paused and looked Morgan in the eye as he shoved another inch or so in, and this was it, now Morgan felt the stretch and the promise of pleasure. He sighed out another breath and let Hunter in.

Hunter pushed in bit by bit by bit, until his pelvis was flush against Morgan's buttocks, and Morgan could squeeze the base of Hunter's dick with his arse. He cried out. He felt full, hot. His cock twitched itself back to full hardness, and Hunter's whole body shivered. For a second Morgan wondered whether he'd come straight away. But, no. Hunter raised his head and watched Morgan as he pulled out half way. Pushed back in. Oh

God. Right there. "Right there." Out. In. Fuck, fuck, fuck.

Morgan bucked up into it, fighting the instinct to close his eyes because, God, Hunter had never looked so beautiful. There was a flush of red over his gorgeous cheekbones. His lips were wet and plump from kissing. And every bit of his attention was on Morgan as he fucked into him again, and again, and again.

Hunter licked his hand and reached between them to wrap his hand around Morgan's cock, a hot, wet tunnel to fuck into. Morgan barely needed it; Hunter had found a sweet angle and Morgan would probably have come untouched. But Hunter was obviously on a short fuse, and he was a gentleman. He wanted Morgan to come first, just like he'd said. He wanted to *watch Morgan come*. Oh God.

"Yeah?" said Hunter, but Morgan couldn't answer. Everything was pleasure and fire and thunder rumbling deep in his balls, building and building until he gripped the sheets in his fist and Hunter thrust in hard, that final, plugging thrust that tipped him over the edge. Come splattered wetly over his chest; he imagined it coating Hunter's fingers and shuddered out another stream. And another.

"C-can I, inside you, can I–" Hunter stammered. Morgan, still in an orgasm-haze, crossed his ankles over Hunter's back, pulling him in. His arse was still pulsing, throbbing; Hunter probably couldn't have pulled out again just then even if he'd wanted to. But he obviously didn't; he squeezed Morgan's shoulders and kept his eyes open as pleasure shuddered through him. Morgan felt the throb of it inside him, everything hot and wet and, "f-f-fuuck," said Hunter.

Then he collapsed on top of Morgan and buried his face in his hair. Morgan relaxed, closed his eyes and gently stroked Hunter's back. It was so warm, damp with a sheen of sweat. He could smell salt and come and, distantly, fresh laundry detergent and an unlit scented candle. Vanilla. Nice. Like custard. Morgan giggled.

Hunter giggled back. His cock slipped out of Morgan's arse in a slick rush; some of Morgan's boyfriends had found that part icky, but Morgan didn't. It felt rude and naughty and incredibly satisfying. He sighed happily.

Hunter rolled off him, leaving space for a breeze from the window to cool Morgan's heated skin. Morgan folded his arms behind his head and watched Hunter go through a door at the other end of the room to what was evidently an en suite bathroom. Nice. The shower went on. Hunter stuck his head around the door and said, "Join me?"

Morgan didn't know how Hunter could jump about so much when he'd just come that hard, but the idea of a coolish spray of water was very appealing. And nobody liked sticky sheets.

Well, Caleb claimed he did. But he was probably lying.

Hunter's shower had three shower heads, was beautifully tiled and had plenty of room for two within its frosted glass walls. It smelled of fresh grout and foresty-scented shower gel. Morgan felt a twinge of the -I don't belong here- anxiety returning, but Hunter was still Hunter, cursing when he got soap in his eyes and wanting to touch Morgan whenever and wherever he could.

When they were back in the bedroom, clean and dry, Hunter pulled the quilt back and they slipped between white cotton sheets. Egyptian cotton, probably, with a ridiculous thread count. The heat of the day hadn't quite died off and the room was warm, so sheets were plenty; the quilt stayed crumpled up at the foot of the bed. They kissed for a while, and maybe things might have gone further, but Morgan's limbs were heavy and his breathing deep, and at some point his head dropped on to the pillow, Hunter's fingers stroking through his hair, and he slept.

Chapter Fifteen

The next morning Morgan woke curled up on his side with Hunter draped over his back, one arm holding Morgan firmly around the belly. It felt very nice, and might have developed into something else, but Hunter's phone went off. While he answered it with a grumpy, "Hunter," Morgan's bladder complained. So he went to the bathroom to pee.

By the time he returned, Hunter was pulling on his clothes.

"What time is it?" Morgan asked.

"Nearly seven. That was the client with the husband who's into furry sex in car parks. Someone put a brick through her window."

"The guy who made the videos?"

"Bates? Probably. I need to go and see her."

Morgan cast about for his own clothes. Shit. His clean underwear was downstairs, in his rucksack. "I'll come with you."

"No. This is nasty stuff. I won't risk you getting hurt."

Morgan scowled at him. "I'm tougher than I look, you know."

"It's not that." Hunter caught his arms, pulled him in close. "It's just that you're not insured."

He laughed, and Morgan laughed too, although he had a sneaking suspicion it was just an excuse. And while it was lovely to be protected, it was completely unnecessary. Still. It wasn't the first time someone had made that mistake, and it's not like Hunter knew what he was capable of.

That gave him a sharper pang than it had yesterday.

"Besides," said Hunter. "There's still the work for the fraud case. All that cross-referencing won't do itself. C'mon. I was going to take you somewhere nice for breakfast but I guess it'll be Costa and a bagel at the station. Sorry."

Actually a bagel sounded really good. Morgan quickly washed and dressed, and they set out for Leeds.

Morgan's phone started ringing on the train. First Caleb, then Sahil, then Caleb again. He switched it to silent and ignored it, enjoying the press of Hunter's thigh against his. Every now and then he'd catch Hunter looking at him, and Hunter would catch him catching him, and they'd bump shoulders. There was a tiny mole just under Hunter's left eye, so faint he'd only noticed it up close. But now he knew it was there he was fascinated by it. He wanted to kiss it. He actually wanted to kiss Hunter's eyelashes. He could imagine it, a soft whispery feeling across his lips.

The half hour journey was gone in a flash. At the station Hunter headed to the taxi rank to get a cab to the client's house. As they parted Hunter kissed him. Just a small, quick kiss, and a "see you later, darling," but it left Morgan weak-kneed and a bit head-spinny. It was in public, in broad daylight, for one thing. And for another that 'darling' kept echoing. It sounded so natural. So right.

He sat down on a cold metal bench and fumbled through his rucksack for his encanté measurement kit. Pricked his finger quickly with the lance and dripped blood onto the test papers.

0.4. Same as always.

He pulled out his phone and called Caleb.

Caleb answered in three rings and yawned pointedly down the phone at him.

"You called me first," Morgan said. "Less than half an hour ago."

"And you didn't answer. So I went back to bed."

"What did you want?"

"Well, obviously I was nosing around to see how your date went. I presumed that as you didn't make it home, Mr Big Shot PI rocked your world."

Morgan tried to think up a grown up and slightly huffy response to that, but what he actually said was, "He's amazing." No doubt his eyes were dewy and fluttery as well. It was probably a good thing Caleb couldn't see him.

"Are you grinning your head off? You sound like you're grinning your head off."

Yeah. He totally was. He could tell by the way his jaw was aching. "Don't be ridiculous." And then, as an afterthought he couldn't stop from popping out, "He kissed me goodbye. At the station. He called me darling."

Caleb made gagging noises at the other end of the phone.

"You're just jealous," said Morgan, happily.

"Hm. Why'd he leave you at the station?"

"He's gone to see a client. I'm just about to go to the office. D'you have work today?"

"No, I took the rest of the week off."

"Sex party drained you dry, did it?"

"Oh, very funny. Actually I got a note from Mr Appleford himself. I've got free tickets for a show at the club on Friday."

"You're going back?"

"Yes, Morgan," Caleb said, slowly and distinctly. "I thought it would be polite to take Dave and Jennifer, seeing as they introduced me to the scene and everything."

"Oh, it's a scene now, is it?"

"You can take your moralising attitude and shove it up your arse, Mr Shag-the-boss."

"I worry about you."

"And I worry about you. Strange, isn't it? Anyone

would think we're friends."

"I'm serious. Just be safe. Can you drop by the office later?"

"Why, so you can harangue me further?"

"There's something I want to ask you. For work. But… Not now. Not on the phone."

"Ooh, skullduggery! Is there skullduggery?"

"Can you? Come to the office?"

Caleb sighed dramatically. "If you insist, Mr Manly Morgan. God, you're always so bossy when you just got laid."

With that he hung up. Morgan took a moment to appreciate that, yes, he really had got laid, and then he headed for the office.

Caleb turned up at lunch with a two wraps and some wild honey flapjack from Sophie's, and a couple of large Iced Shaken Hibiscus lemonades from Starbucks. He pulled an upended storage box over to Morgan's desk to sit on and they had a picnic.

"I should cost out some visitor's chairs," Morgan pondered.

"Never mind that. Tell me about this skullduggery. And if you want to give a thrust by thrust account of your night with your golden Adonis of a detective along the way, feel free."

"He's not a detective. He's an investigator. Although he was a detective, once. In the police force."

Caleb frowned. "An actual proper copper?"

"Yes."

"Isn't that a bit… I dunno. We live at the fringes of society, man."

Morgan snorted. "Speak for yourself. We don't all take time off work for orgies. Anyway, he's not with the police anymore."

"Once a copper–"

"Stop it."

Caleb took a bite of his avocado and cream cheese wrap and chewed. "What did you want me for, then?"

"We're working on this case." Morgan looked down at his wrap to avoid Caleb's 'oooh, you're working on a *case'* face. "This guy died, and they found traces of Essence in his system."

Morgan glanced up to find Caleb rolling his eyes.

"I need you to promise me to be really careful," Morgan said.

"Essence doesn't kill you. What was the actual cause of death?"

"Cardiac arrest."

"There you go. Being a bit happy or horny or excited can't give you a heart attack."

"A cardiac arrest isn't the same as a heart attack."

Caleb shrugged.

"I'm serious," said Morgan. "Until we know what happened, no Essence. Promise me."

"Do you have any evidence to say it was the Essence that killed this guy? Not a regular drug? There's plenty of those that mess with your ticker."

Morgan was rapidly losing patience in the face of sheer panic at the thought of Caleb being fished out of a muddy pond. "They don't know yet. But the fact remains that magic is volatile and unpredictable, and you could do yourself some serious harm. Paranoia, depression, majos-related anxiety disorder. I'm not kidding around here."

"I can tell."

Caleb pointed to what had been Morgan's cup of iced tea with extra ice. The plastic cup looked saggy and melted and the drink inside was steaming gently.

"Shit!" Morgan sprang up to get a cloth. He scarcely managed to get the melting cup in the bin before it oozed warm, pink fluid all over his desk. Caleb passed him paper towels.

"Sorry," Morgan said, once the initial panic had abated.

"It's okay," said Caleb gently. He knew how rare it was for Morgan's magic to manifest spontaneously these days. But Morgan hadn't had time to meditate that morning. And he was so scared for Caleb. And it felt horrible, doing magic here, in Hunter's office, even accidentally. As if Hunter would inevitably pick up on the fact that Morgan had desecrated his space with magic.

But all Morgan said out loud was, "Yeah. Yeah, I know."

They sat down again. Caleb tipped half of his lemonade into Morgan's empty tea mug, broke a corner off his flapjack and popped it into his mouth.

"You said Jennifer has a dealer," Morgan said.

"An old friend, apparently. Look, I don't think she

uses regularly. And I won't do it anymore. Not if it bothers you this much."

"Thank you." Morgan hoped he could trust him to be good as his word about that. "Do you have a name for this dealer?"

"Why? You're not going to get them dragged off to majos jail, are you?"

"No, of course not. It's just the police want a sample. To see what it actually does."

"You said yourself, no two majos make the same Essence. What Jennifer gets from a posh bloke in Horsforth would be totally different from your average street Essence.

"Wait."

Caleb put another bit of flapjack in his mouth and raised an eyebrow.

"Horsforth. Is that where it was? That party you went to?"

"Yeah. Off Town Street. You go up a road between Morrisons and the betting shop, past the car park, there's an old office building. We went in round the back. I suspect it might not have a license, if you know what I mean."

Morgan stared at him. "What betting shop?"

Caleb frowned. "William Hills, I think. Why?"

"I need to call Sahil."

"What?"

"I think our vic might have been to the same club."

"Okay, first, since when was the word 'vic' in your vocabulary? You sound like one of those cheesy miniseries cop shows. Secondly, who's Sahil, and thirdly, what the fuck?"

Morgan didn't answer; he was too busy rubbing the sticky flapjack mess off his fingers before he touched his phone screen.

"Morgan, really, I–"

Morgan tapped dial, and Sahil picked up on the second ring.

An hour later, Morgan and Hunter met Sahil and Jess outside Morrisons in Horsforth. Hunter looked like he'd had a rough morning; a lot of the spring had gone out of his step and he didn't even seem to have the energy to be rude to his sister. He did manage a smile for Morgan, though, and bumped the back of his hand against the back of Morgan's when he came to stand next to him. Morgan felt a bit guilty for the conversation he'd had with Sahil where they'd debated whether or not it was wise to put Jess and Hunter in the same place again. It would have been Hunter who'd missed out, as Jess was leading the investigation. But in the end they'd decided perhaps this was the ideal opportunity for everyone to get over themselves.

Jess was the last to arrive, having stopped off to talk to the staff in the bookmaker's first.

"Bubble seems to be well known in the area," she told them. "There's burlesque shows here on a regular basis."

"The building's owned by a guy called Wallace Sturgess," Sahil said. "Lottery winner. The building is part of his rapidly expanding property portfolio. There's been no official change of use registered. Could be he's let it out, or maybe he's branching out into entertainment."

"Check him out when we get back to the office. Anyway, there's a caretaker, so the locals say. Let's go and have a chat to him."

Morgan half-expected Jess to tell him and Hunter to hop it now they'd got all the information they needed and were doing the police thing. But she didn't, so they followed her and Sahil down the alley that led to the old office building that apparently turned into a den of iniquity at night. Jess rang the bell to what would once have been quite a fancy lobby, and eventually the big glass doors jerked open. A guy stood behind a completely empty reception desk. There were a bunch of silk-printed screens piled up against the wall behind him. Morgan could imagine they'd go a long way to transform the place from dilapidated office to sensual sex club, especially at night.

"What can I do you for?" The caretaker was jovial with Jess, but Morgan could see his beady little eyes were taking in everything.

Jess smiled sweetly. "Actually, it might be more what I can do you for." She flashed her ID at him.

The caretaker's joviality washed away in an instant. "What d'you want? I've got a rental agreement. I live here and I get paid for looking after the place. It's all above board."

"And this place," said Jess. "What sort of

establishment is it?"

"It's a club. And before you ask, yes, we got an entertainment license. I can get that for you as well."

"That would be splendid," said Jess. "And we'd like to have a look around, please."

The caretaker looked a bit taken aback. "Don't you need a warrant for that?"

"Only if you refuse to let us in," said Jess. Her eyes narrowed. Hunter coughed 'bullshit' behind his hand. Morgan hoped the guy did what Jess said before the Hunter and Jess started yelling at each other again.

The caretaker was wearing an ID badge that said 'Kenny Crossley, Estates'. There was a logo that matched the one etched into the glass doors; presumably Kenny had been inherited with the building. Morgan gave him an apologetic, man-to-man, receptionist-to-receptionist kind of look and said, "It's really important. D'you think...?" He left it hanging, just kept eye contact and tried to look trustworthy and non-threatening.

Kenny shrugged. "Well, it's not like there's anything to hide. Knock yourselves out. Down the corridor there, past the old boardroom, there's a double set of fire doors, then you're in the club. I'll get the paperwork for you while you're having a look."

"Thank you," said Jess.

As Kenny promised, the space beyond the fire doors had been redesigned as a club. What was once an atrium with balconies of offices was now a ground floor bar and stage area, overlooked by tiers of higher level tables, some with internal walls still intact to create private boxes to see and be seen in. Morgan wondered if that's where Caleb had been taken by Jennifer and Dave, a pretty boy to be shown off to the room.

"Okay, this is seriously weird," Hunter said. "I'm never going to look at call centres in the same way again."

"Enterprising, in its way," said Sahil.

"Where's this dungeon?" asked Jess.

"Downstairs," Morgan said. "And it's not actually a–"

"It has to be that one," said Sahil.

He pointed to a pair of faded crimson curtains which outlined a fake-wooden door. It looked like part of a stage set. Jess went to it immediately. The door opened as soon as she tried the knob, swinging as if it were lighter than the curtains that framed it. She flicked a light switch and went through the door.

They followed her inside and down a flight of stairs that opened out into a big room.

Jess sighed. There was everything Caleb had described: big four poster bed, cushions, silk sheets. Except in the harsh strip-lighting it looked tacky and sad. Everything smelled of disinfectant, which was comforting and disturbing all at once. Morgan took a step back and bumped straight into Hunter, who slipped an arm around his middle. Morgan froze. This wasn't Leeds station, or a mostly empty train carriage, or the office, or Hunter's house. Hunter's sister was standing *right there* and she'd notice any second.

"There's another door here," Jess said. "Locked. Morgan, d'you think you can charm the caretaker for the key?"

"I'm not sure," said Morgan. "He seems pretty loyal to his boss."

"No," snapped Jess. "I don't mean bat your pretty eyelashes at him. I mean charm him. Encanté."

Hunter laughed. Morgan didn't. Sahil looked very hard at the drapes on the four poster.

Morgan said, "I don't–"

Jess looked at Morgan and Hunter. Hunter's arm went very still and heavy on Morgan's belly. "Oh for fuck's sake, Damien," she said. "You don't know he's majos, do you?"

"What?" said Hunter. His arm dropped away from Morgan.

"You didn't even do a background check!" Jess said.

"But you did, Jess," murmured Morgan. He wanted very much for the earth to open up and swallow him.

"Of course I bloody did! We're trusting you with all kinds of sensitive information. I can't believe he didn't bother."

Hunter stepped away.

"You, of all people." Jess shook her head.

"Excuse me," said Morgan, turning towards the door. "I should probably–"

Hunter caught him by the arm. "Tell me this is bullshit, Morgan."

Morgan shook his head. He couldn't trust himself to form words; his stomach was churning and his legs twitching with the need to run.

"You're a fucking dwimmer?"

Magic surged through Morgan, every injustice and misunderstanding his magic had ever brought him bright and alive inside of him as happiness slipped through his fingers. It wasn't fire, though. Not this time. There was a mains water pipe beneath them, under the cheap laminate and the floorboards and the hard packed earth. Morgan clenched his fists, clinging to every last shred of control. He had to get out of here. Now.

He heard Jess say, "What the fuck," as he wrenched his arm from Hunter and ran. Ran out of the dungeon, up the corridor, through the club, out of the reception-that-wasn't, across the car park, kept running down Town Street, feet pounding on the pavement, following his magic to Hall Park. He thundered down narrow paths and finally ducked through an arch in the wall to reach the Japanese Garden. Rocks were arranged on carefully maintained gravel like miniature standing stones. Next to the gravel was a pond, serviced by a little stream with a bridge, the whole area bordered with carefully placed trees and rocks and grass. This was the closest patch of open water his magic could find. He didn't have time to check if he was alone. He held out one hand, gripping his necklace with the other, and his magic burst from him. The shallow water in the pond surged up like a geyser, splashing the whole garden on its way down. Morgan fell to his knees and threw up water, three long, sobbing retches.

Everything went quiet and he knelt there, gulping in harsh, painful breaths. But the magic was building again. He couldn't stop it. It hurt too much, everything hurt too much. He couldn't think straight.

A gentle voice behind him said, "Okay, mate. I'm going to ground you now. All right? Just take a deep breath for me."

Morgan looked over his shoulder through the chaos of tears and panic. He made out familiar features on the face of the man behind him. Thick, worried eyebrows, black hair cut into a short police-cut.

Sahil put his hand on Morgan's shoulder, and everything went black.

Chapter Sixteen

Morgan came round wrapped in an emergency blanket and surrounded by paramedics. Sahil was keeping the public, who were, as always, interested in a spectacle involving someone else's misfortune, at bay. The paramedics took Morgan's pulse and blood pressure, checked out his registration card, measured his esper rating, and let him ring Caleb. Caleb came in a taxi and took him home as soon as the paramedics declared him fit and well. They gave Caleb a load of numbers to call if he blacked out again.

Caleb didn't ask him what had happened, or what was wrong, although Morgan knew he was desperate to find out. When they got back to the flat Morgan shut himself in his room, crawled under the covers (despite the suffocating heat) and fell asleep.

He awoke sticky with sweat and threw off the duvet in

disgust. Then everything came back to him in a rush, the whole clusterfuck that ended in that single, horrible word that ended everything.

He rolled over and reached out to his bookshelf. There was a gap between *Great Expectations* and the *B&Q guide to DIY*. He went cold all over. Shit. His book was still in his rucksack. In Hunter's office. Locked in what used to be his desk. Fuck, fuck, fuck.

He picked up the nearest book he could reach, which happened to be *Forbidden Blood*, and threw it across the room. It hit the wall and sank in a sad flutter of pages to land on the floor.

The door opened and Caleb stood there. "Are you okay? What happened?"

"My book," Morgan said. Tears stung his face.

Caleb went and picked up *Forbidden Blood* and carefully laid it on the bed next to Morgan. Morgan gave a bitter kind of laugh and said, "Not that one. My book. I took it to work. To Hun... to York, I left it at work. In the office."

"Oh. All right. Um. Look, don't worry, okay? Why don't you lie down? Get more rest. I'll bring you some tea."

Caleb brought him the tea, and Morgan drank the tea, and then he felt really, really sleepy. He lay down and drifted off.

When he woke up it was dark, the only light coming from a small spotlight on his desk. The desk chair had been pulled up by his bed and Caleb was asleep in it, his feet up on the bed. He'd slung a blanket over his legs,

Forbidden Blood open, upside down, in his lap. Morgan pulled himself up to sitting, his head still thick from sleep. Then he spotted his magic book resting next to him on the bed. He looked around: there was a cardboard box on the bedside table. In it was his rucksack, a Kit-Kat, a packet of paracetamol, a clothes repair kit, his own personal stapler with his name on it and a spare phone charger. And a mug with *Keep Calm and Investigate* on it.

Pain surged in his heart and with it his magic. He quickly ran his fingers around the edges of his book, flicked it open and thumbed to page seventy three. With a huge sense of relief his magic surged into the book, and Aiyeda appeared. She checked herself over, poking at her blue-black scales with her nose. "Sheesh," she said. "Someone's had a bad day."

Caleb stirred under his blanket, and his eyes flickered open. Aiyeda settled into Morgan's lap and crooned to him.

"Okay?" said Caleb and yawned.

Morgan nodded.

"You can see he's not okay, Carinyo," said Aiyeda. "I mean, look at the state of me. I'm the colour of the midnight sky. This is not a good colour for me. It makes me look like the inside of a cave."

"I'm sorry," said Morgan.

Aiyeda nosed at him and murmured, "Be quiet, Guapo. You sound pathetic. You want to be pathetic? Of course not. Nobody wants to be pathetic."

"D'you want tea?" asked Caleb.

Morgan nodded. Caleb padded off to the kitchen.

Morgan took his iPad out of his bedside chest of drawers and fired up YouTube. He flicked through his bookmarks to a kids' cartoon series and put the iPad on the bed in front of him with the volume low. Aiyeda perked up straight away, trotted off Morgan's lap and sat in front of the iPad, immediately entranced.

Caleb returned a few minutes later with two mugs of tea, which he put on the bedside table. He sat back in the chair.

"What did they tell you?" Morgan asked Caleb.

"The paramedics said there had been an 'incident'. Sahil filled in the rest."

"Oh."

"He said Hunter found out you had magic. And reacted badly."

"He called me a dwimmer."

"Fucking bastard."

"Yeah. Only… I've only got myself to blame, right? I hid it from him."

"If he's so uptight about it, he should have run a background check."

"That's what his sister said. Pretty much. Well, for other reasons. Like, for all he knows I could have a criminal record long as your arm."

"Well, no. Pearl makes sure we come all fresh and squeaky-clean legal, with a money-back guarantee. All it means is he didn't ask any specific questions."

"Oh. I suppose. I hadn't thought of that."

Aiyeda chuckled at her cartoons. Her tail wafted

happily.

"It's still no excuse to treat you that way," Caleb said. "Majophobia is never acceptable."

"He has his reasons. And I knew what they were. His mother abandoned him, for fuck's sake."

Caleb flinched. "And I say again - majophobia is never acceptable."

Morgan sighed.

He watched a giant robot form on the iPad screen, a reflection of a blue dragon on the glass.

"Sahil said you'd been to Bubble. It was a bust, just so as you know. After you ran out leaving puddles of water behind you they refused to let anyone do anything else without a warrant."

"Shit."

"What the hell were you doing there, anyway?"

"I told you. Investigating a murder."

"Actually, you didn't mention the word 'murder'. You were mostly lecturing me about the perils of illicit magical substances the last time we spoke."

"It doesn't matter anymore. Hunter hates me. I think I can safely say I'm off the case."

"Hmm."

Morgan buried his face in his hands. "How did I manage to fuck things up so badly? Last night I was so happy. I thought it was the start of something, I thought..." Tears came. Normal, non-magical tears; Aiyeda was channelling his excess magic into a whole bundle of cartoon-excitement. But Morgan couldn't stop thinking about lying in Hunter's arms and how right it felt. How totally, fucking right.

Caleb put a hand on his knee, which was the easiest bit of him to reach, and let him cry.

"I lost everything over one stupid lie," he said, when he could speak again.

"One stupid lie which was supposed to protect you," Caleb said. "And a lie of omission at that. You weren't the one throwing abusive language around and being a git."

Morgan sniffed.

"Okay," said Caleb. "So tell me. What happened to the murdered guy?"

"He had a lot of gambling debts. Left work one night, went out and got a bit pissed, a bit high on Essence, had a lot of sex and ended up dead in a river."

"So, why's it murder? I mean, I'm sorry for the guy, but these things happen, right? People have heart attacks all the time, and if stress and bad habits were his lifestyle and he had a death wish…" Caleb shrugged.

"He didn't actually die in the river. They think he'd been dead for several hours before he went in the water."

"Okay. So, what's the theory?"

"There isn't one. At least, not that anyone shared with me. I'm pretty sure Jess knows more than she's letting on."

"Jess?"

"Hunter's sister. Detective Sergeant Shaw. Sahil's boss."

"Oh, she was the one who let the cat out of the bag

to Hunter, right?"

"The very same."

"Hunter's sister?"

"Oh, it's this whole thing. I don't know."

Morgan took a sip of tea. It was hot, fragrant and soothing. He took a deep breath of its fumes and felt his shoulders relax a little.

On the iPad the giant robots were fighting. Aiyeda swept her tail from side to side, the feathery tip creating a nice little breeze.

"So," Caleb said. He was leaning forwards, his forearms on his knees. "Maybe I know something."

"About what?"

"About a great many things, young Morgan," Caleb said in a Gandalf voice. "But, seriously. Your gambling friend might not the only person who's had a little bit too much fun and ended up dead in a ditch."

Morgan frowned. "What?"

"Well, not an actual ditch. More a warehouse. Other side of town. But rumour has it he'd been at Bubble. And he was epileptic or something. And really wasted. I thought it was an urban legend."

"Where did you hear it?"

"A couple of people there mentioned it. Everyone at Bubble seemed to know. No foul play mentioned though, just a tall tale of an old dude who had too much of a good time. But it seems like a bit of a coincidence, right?"

"Did he have Essence in his system?"

"I don't know. Probably? Most people who go there

do. It's safer than Viagra and gives you a really mellow buzz."

"Always?"

"Yeah, pretty much. Everyone I saw downstairs seemed to be having a great time, relaxing, kicking back, having amazing sex."

"Doesn't that strike you as a bit weird? Why would everyone have the same experience? Essence is notoriously inconsistent. It's really difficult to channel exactly the same mix of magic at the same dose."

"Maybe there's a really good majos out there who's saving up to send their kids to Uni, or buy a flash car or something?"

Morgan took another sip of tea. A plan was forming in his mind. He couldn't turn back the clock, and he wanted to punch Hunter in the face as much as he wanted to beg him to take him back. That side of things was a horrible, painful mess he was better off leaving alone. But the reason he was in that miserable club in the first place was still one hundred per cent valid. He could still find out what happened to Reginald Klyne.

"When are you going back?" Morgan asked.

"Back where?"

"To Bubble. You said you had a personal invite."

"Well, yeah, but after all this–"

"No, no, you must go. And take me with you."

"What? Morgan, you shouldn't decide anything too hastily."

"I need to get hold of one of those Essence tabs. Then maybe I can find out where they come from."

Caleb sighed heavily. "I don't suppose I could just bring you one?"

"I'd rather get it myself. I might recognise whoever's selling them from the Coven."

"Well, all right then. You'll have to decide how to get out of going to the play room and joining the orgy. Just so you know, you're one hundred per cent Mr Appleford's type, all dark and willowy. He's bound to ask us. I get the feeling Dave would never have got in without me, you know."

"Of course he wouldn't. Why do you think he asked you?"

It was out as soon as he'd thought it, and Morgan regretted it instantly. But Caleb just sighed and said, "Doesn't mean it wasn't a great night. We all had fun."

"I know. I just–"

Caleb squeezed his knee again.

There was a lot to sort out. He'd have to tell Pearl he'd blown the contract. He'd have to see Dr Rosero in the next forty eight hours, because he'd very definitely lost control. And then there was the Coven meeting on Thursday. There was a chance that Jess might want to see him, too. It made Morgan's head hurt to think about it all, even without the ache in his heart that was Hunter.

"You should rest," said Caleb. "I'll keep an eye on the dragon, make sure she doesn't get square eyes."

"I heard that, Carinyo," said Aiyeda, but she didn't take her gaze from the screen.

The next morning Morgan took the coward's way out and sent Pearl an email telling her he'd left Hunter PI and was taking a couple of weeks off. Then he went to see Dr Rosero.

She kept morning appointments free for emergencies like this, and fitted him in for ten o'clock. He arrived at nine thirty and wandered around the block several times before finally going to sit in the waiting room at quarter to. Not long after he'd begun to stare at the familiar bookshelves, half hoping to come across something titled 'so your boyfriend called you a dwimmer' the door to Dr Rosero's office opened and someone Morgan recognised came out. A woman called Galatia who went to his coven. They acknowledged each other with the standard and slightly embarrassed 'hi, you okay?' that was reserved for majos meeting each other in therapeutic situations, and Galatia went to the appointment desk. Dr Rosero came to the door and ushered Morgan inside.

"Something happened," Morgan said, plucking the lumpy cushion off the chair before he sat. There was nowhere else to put it, so he rested it carefully on the floor.

"I thought it must have, seeing as I wasn't supposed to meet you until next week." Ms Rosero was wearing a green summer dress and matching sandals. Her hair was tied up with a green scarf. He'd never seen her showing so much skin before; usually she wore trousers and long-sleeved blouses. Her skin was freckled and there were definite signs of wrinkles, but she played a lot of tennis and it showed: her body was lean and fit, with strong arms and impressive calf muscles. She sat opposite Morgan and folded her hands in her lap.

"I lost control," Morgan said.

"Uhuh. And how did that happen?"

Morgan told her the bare minimum of what happened in Bubble. Just that there had been an argument and he'd got upset.

"Well, you channelled water. I want you to remember that. It's easier to manage than fire, isn't it?"

Morgan wasn't so sure about that. He supposed it had done less damage than fire would. But it hadn't felt safe, either. Far from it.

"Have you seen the papers?" Dr Rosero asked.

Morgan shook his head. Oh god. What if someone had filmed the whole thing and put it on YouTube?

"They're saying that there was a giant airlock in a water pipe in a park in Horsforth. It caused a geyser worthy of Yellowstone park."

"Did you fix that?"

"Goodness, no. There was a policeman at the scene. He was on the news. You owe him a big thank you."

Morgan relaxed a bit. "No mention of a rampaging majos spewing water everywhere?"

Ms Rosero shook her head. "Not a peep. You've been very lucky, Morgan."

He didn't feel lucky.

"I'd advise you to stay away from places like Bubble in the future. They attract bother."

Because he'd met her when he was still a child, Michaela still fitted the role of teacher in some part of Morgan's mind. That part felt told off and ashamed, especially as he had no intention of taking her advice. He murmured noncommittally.

"What was it about the argument that drove you to lose control, Morgan?"

"It was this man I've been working for. He's a Private Investigator. He had a bad experience as a child and now he loathes all majos with a deadly loathing. And I gravely underestimated the deadliness of his loathing."

Ms Rosero said nothing.

"He found out," Morgan continued. "And now he loathes me."

Again, she waited.

"I liked him a lot," said Morgan.

And then the tears came.

Having bawled in Michaela's office for half an hour and come away with an extra hour's worth of meditation exercises to do every morning for the next two weeks, Morgan found himself at a loss. Then he got a text rom Sahil, who was very kind and sympathetic and came over to make him lunch. Morgan thanked him for the cover story and explained he was feeling a bit wrung out after therapy. He couldn't bring himself to say what kind of therapy, even now when he knew Sahil knew he was majos. But Sahil said he'd had therapy himself after attending a particularly bloody crime scene as a novice copper, so he understood.

And then, as he put a plate of sandwiches on the coffee table in front of Morgan, Sahil said, "You don't have to worry about Jess, by the way."

"What d'you mean?"

"Well, she understands more than your average copper might. She's majos."

"She's…" Morgan stared at the sandwich in his hand as if he'd never seen one before. That was impossible. If Jess was majos, how come Hunter had never mentioned it?

"She doesn't like people to know unless they need to. There's always a level of suspicion about majos in the police force, and she wants to succeed on the strength of her policing skills, without exploiting any advantages. She knows what it can be like. So you won't get any trouble from her."

Morgan took a bite of bread, cheese and chutney and chewed without really tasting it. Well. No wonder Hunter didn't get on with his sister.

"We didn't find anything at the club," Sahil said. "The investigation's focusing on the drugs now. Thing is it's hard to prove, without any substances for forensics to get their paws on."

"You still think it's connected to Bubble?"

"Mr Klyne placed a bet using his phone at ten forty two on the night he died. He was at Bubble at the time. That was the last time he used his phone, despite the fact that his greyhound actually came in the winner fifteen minutes later. Now, Mr Klyne doesn't sound like the type to miss a win, but according to his phone records he never read that message."

"So you think that's when he died?"

"Looks like a possibility. The only question is, if he did, why didn't anyone at Bubble notice?"

"If he was in the orgy room, maybe people were too involved with their own, um, activities. Or too high."

Sahil shrugged. "It's possible."

After Sahil had gone, Morgan did some online research on cardiac arrest, sex party etiquette and Essence. It was a popular drug among the orgy crowd, apparently. The encanté varieties of Essence could strip away your inhibitions and give you a hit of happy like ecstasy, along with a libido rush that turned you into a sex machine. The problems though, went further than any questionable choices you might make under the influence. Like any drug, it could be cut with just about anything. The majos making the drug could bleed in other effects without even knowing, especially if they were unskilled. Sometimes Essence was cut with other drugs to encourage crossover trade. Cocaine, speed, even heroin. A cocktail like that could definitely stop someone's heart. By accident or design.

After an hour of research, Morgan put his iPad away, made a cup of ginger tea and numbed his brain with TV. Caleb came back at dinnertime with armfuls of takeout, and Harlequin and Darius in tow.

"She/her pronouns," announced Harlequin, as she marched through to the kitchen. She was wearing a vest top and a little flippy skirt. Her hair was held back by a sparkly purple band. "Have you got any soy? They never put enough on."

Darius kissed Morgan on each cheek, 'muah, muah'. "Caleb said some ignorant twat of a man let you down. We've come to cheer you up."

Morgan's heart sank. Being cheered up was hard work, in his experience. People tended to get upset if it didn't work, and really, he'd rather it was just Caleb, who never expected very much of anything from him. Except trouble, possibly, which Morgan could reliably supply. But Darius and Harlequin were quick to prove him wrong. They didn't expect him to talk; nobody suggested DVDs or board games. They just gave him really nice Thai food and hung out and tried to talk Caleb into going with them to this new karaoke bar. Well, Darius did. He seemed to have got a bit carried away with the whole Spice Girls act and was demanding a reunion.

"So, what's the plan with you?" said Harley.

"Plan?" said Morgan. "I'm not going to be Posh Spice. I already told you."

"Not that plan, your plan. We want to help. Seems the most positive thing to do, given that your boss is a jerk and doesn't deserve you."

"So Caleb said," Darius added. "And he usually picks the right team."

"I really can't ask you—"

"You don't have to. Caleb did. And we said yes."

Morgan glanced at Caleb, not sure whether to be angry with him or pleased.

"Harley's right," Darius said. "We need a plan."

"Lucky for you," Caleb said, "I have it all worked out. Gather round people."

Morgan presumed that to be rhetorical, as they were all gathered anyway.

"We go to Bubble tomorrow," Caleb said.

"Who's we?" said Harley.

"Us four."

"I don't think that'll be happening," said Harley. "Honestly, I'd be one big panic attack from beginning to end."

"Oh. Oh, well, okay. You can be nearby, in case we need you to get help."

"I'll wait in the cafe in Morrisons," she said. "I'll be fine so long as there aren't people having sex everywhere."

"Should be safe from that in Morrisons," Darius said. "So long as you don't go in the gents after eight on a Saturday."

Harlequin rolled her eyes.

"Okay," said Caleb. "So the three of us go into Bubble on my free ticket. We'll get a table, have a few drinks - it's okay, Morgan, they have fruit juice - and I'll look out for Jennifer's dealer, score some Essence for you to experiment on. We'll keep very low key, lurk in the shadows so we don't get noticed, then toddle off home as soon as we've been there long enough to not cause suspicion. I don't want to piss them off, it was a sweet night I had there. I wouldn't mind going back one day under less cloak and dagger circumstances."

Morgan thought it through, prodding for potential problems. Surprisingly, he couldn't find any, so long as they didn't get spotted by anyone who knew who he was, and what his connection with Hunter was. "If the police or Hunter turn up, we leave," he said.

"Naturally," said Caleb. "We could use a lookout for that, just in case."

"I can hack into Bubble's security camera on my phone," said Harley, her voice as level and matter of fact as if she'd just said she'd order a cinnamon latte in Morrisons.

"Can you?" Morgan asked, wide-eyed.

She shrugged. "Easy. I wrote this app."

"We've got your back, Morgan," said Darius. "No problem."

Chapter Seventeen

Morgan changed his clothes about eight times before he finally checked with Caleb and was informed he looked fine for a prelude-to-a-sex-party event. He wore skinny black jeans, a button-down grey shirt and a black waistcoat. He considered a bow tie, but Caleb gave him a searing look, as if he'd disown him the minute he put it on, so he put it back in the drawer.

Caleb put some kind of product in Morgan's hair so it lay flat, with a side-swept fringe and a lot of shine. Darius liked it. Harlequin opened and shut his mouth a few times and finally settled on, "You look very un-you."

Which was the point, after all.

Harlequin drove them to Horsforth in his car - a fairly old Ford Kia, which Darius was a bit too tall for - and parked in Morrison's car park.

Morgan's nerves mounted as they reached the door

of Bubble. What if the caretaker doubled up as a doorman and recognised him? But to his relief the bouncer on the door was a complete stranger. He checked Caleb's ticket and let them in. As they walked away Morgan thought he heard him say something into the headset he was wearing, but he couldn't pick up the words. They weren't out of the woods yet, that's for certain.

To say the place looked different at night was an understatement. They were shown to a table on the first floor, up a set of spiral stairs which Morgan presumed were not original to the office building. The tables were laid with white linens and the lighting brought warmth and sparkle to the surroundings. Their table had a good view of the ground floor below, in the centre of which was the stage, with dancing poles to each side which Morgan hadn't noticed before.

A waiter came to take their drinks order. Caleb and Morgan stuck to soft drinks, while Darius ordered wine. When they arrived the waiter told them they were on the house, compliments of Mr Appleford.

"Was he that quick to notice you before?" asked Morgan.

"No," said Caleb.

"Well, we are extra specially gorgeous," said Darius. "I'd certainly notice me if I was looking for pretty people. Cheers, boys."

Morgan clinked glasses with them both and gulped a mouthful. It was pleasant, sharp lemonade with mint and a hint of peach juice.

"Okay," Caleb whispered in Morgan's ear. "I see Jennifer's contact. I'll go score."

Morgan nodded.

As Caleb left the lights went low, highlighting a spotlight in the middle of the stage. Curious, Morgan leaned forward to take a proper look. He'd never seen burlesque in real life before.

Two women came onto the stage, each holding a leash with a man on the other end. The men prowled onto the stage on all fours. They wore skin-tight black catsuits, with ears and tails and collars studied with sparkling stones. The women tied their panthers to the poles and the music started. The women were dressed in corsets that matched cut-away skirts, revealing fishnet stockings beneath. The skirts had bustles bristling with feathers, and more feathers erupted from their elaborate up-dos. Silky gloves stretched up their arms, past the elbow.

"Very classy," Darius murmured. Morgan wasn't sure whether he was being sarcastic or not. It did seem classy to him, or at least, not tacky. There was very little skin on show. The women danced sensuously with each other, flirting with the audience. The room was hot. Morgan downed the last of his lime and soda, and a waiter immediately appeared with a refill. Just as the song finished Caleb appeared. "Done," he said, sliding into his seat next to Morgan. "Shall we go?"

"May as well finish our drinks," said Morgan. He really wanted to see the men dance too. "Keep up appearances and everything."

They had another couple of drinks and watched the show. The panther-men really lived up to his expectations with slow, sensual body rolls and acrobatics around the poles.

Morgan felt hot, and horny, and annoyed with Hunter for not being around to have sex with.

"It was so good," he told Caleb. "Did I tell you how good it was?"

"What was good?"

"Hunter. He fucks like… God. So hot and he has a great dick, but he was… Sensitive, you know? Caring." He took another swig of fizzy lime. "Bastard."

"That sucks, mate," said Caleb.

Darius said, "You need to move on, honey. Rebound shags have a lot going for them. Seriously, so cathartic."

"Catharti-licious," said Caleb with a giggle. "Hey, are you offering, Dar?"

Darius looked Morgan up and down like he was something delicious. "Are you serious? Who wouldn't want to tap that?"

"Thanks," said Morgan, squirming a bit; he wasn't used to compliments. But it felt really good. "You too."

Caleb leaned in conspiratorially towards Darius and said, "Between you and me? You won't believe it, but we never fell into bed, him and me. All these years, not so much as a drunken snog."

"There were reasons," Morgan said. He frowned. He couldn't exactly remember what those reasons were. "I think."

The waiter popped up at Morgan's elbow, so unexpectedly that Morgan jumped and giggled.

"Mr Appleford sent this over for you boys," the waiter said. He presented Caleb with a silver tray, upon which was a key and three feathery masks.

"Well, shit," said Darius. "Y'know, it seems a shame to turn a guy down."

"Yeah," said Caleb. "Man, it was fun last time."

They both looked at Morgan.

He knew there was a reason this was a bad idea, just like there was a reason he'd never had sex with Caleb. He did. But it was a foggy sort of thought that kept slipping away. His dick was really hard, and maybe if whatever it was that had denied him Caleb had led him to Hunter and disappointment, he'd got it wrong. Maybe Darius was right, he needed a rebound… something. He really wanted to get off. No, not just that. He wanted to touch, God, just to feel another person's skin. To let down all his walls and protections, to let go of his precious control just for once in his fucking life and have fun. *Fun.*

"This won't wreck our friendship, right?" he said to Caleb.

Caleb's face lit up like a summer sunrise. "You mean it? You want to do it?"

Morgan grabbed the key from the tray and stood up, a little unsteadily. "Lead the way."

Just like the rest of the club, the basement room looked totally different at night. The lighting was flattering and the room filled with soft moans and cries of pleasure. There was a sense of continual movement, one touch flowing seamlessly into the next. There were other people there, a lot of them, but Morgan was sandwiched safely between Caleb and Darius on the bed; naked except for their masks. Darius kissed him, his tongue and lips insistent, masterful, while Caleb pressed up against Morgan's back, rubbing his cock lazily into the dip at the base of his spine. He reached around to stroke Morgan's belly, slid down to touch his dick. Morgan was so hard, so pleasantly achy. Caleb pulled him onto his back and slid down the bed; Morgan kept his fingers in Caleb's hair, enjoying the sense of intimacy, of connection. Caleb slurped Morgan's cock into his mouth and started to suck. Morgan arched into him with a moan.

Time floated along. Morgan licked and nuzzled at Darius' cock, his hand around Caleb's. Caleb gasped between sucks of Morgan's dick, "I need to get fucked, fuck me, Morgan, tell me you'll fuck me," and Morgan replied, "yes, yes, of course, shh, baby, shhh…" And then Morgan came, an exquisite pulse that started deep inside and flooded over Caleb's tongue and lips and cheeks and-

The lights went on.

There was no sense of panic, maybe because he was still kind of coming, but Caleb squeaked and sat up, wiping spunk off his face with the back of his hand, and Darius growled, and Morgan blinked into the harsh, white light that had shattered their pleasure.

And then there was Hunter.

"Shit," said Caleb.

Morgan was so pleased to see Hunter. He reached out a hand across the bed to him and said, "Join us?"

Hunter said, "What the fuck?"

And then all hell broke loose.

It wasn't like when his magic came from anger or despair. There was no flood, although Morgan felt the tug of the water surging through the pipes below the basement more strongly than ever. There were no flames, no wind, no tempest. But Morgan sparked and fizzed, and he laughed because, wow, there were little bolts of lightning crackling between his fingers; he shook his hands and there were more and bigger and it felt so good, freedom and energy and it was so damn pretty he—

"Morgan, I'm going to ground you."

Morgan looked up to find Harlequin standing in front of him. There were other people who hadn't been there before, too. One of them was in a police uniform. Sahil? No. A flash went off.

Harlequin put his hand on Morgan's shoulder, and Morgan fell back into Hunter's arms. The last thing he noticed was a strange, treacly burning smell and the distant sound of a motor humming. Then the humming filled his head like a swarm of bees, his magic faded, and he was out.

Caleb was holding Morgan's hand when he woke up.

He was covered in a blanket and it felt really soft. It smelled nice. Wait, not a blanket. A shirt. Morgan nuzzled into the collar. Hunter. It was Hunter's shirt. And although Caleb was holding his hand, it was Hunter who had his arms wrapped around his middle; Hunter whom he was leaning against.

Hunter looked down at him, eyes glowering but his body cradling him.

"What happened?" Morgan asked. He was wearing trousers again. How strange.

"You took drugs, had sex with a bunch of strangers and let your fucking magic loose," said Hunter. His voice was really harsh.

"You don't know what you're talking about," said Caleb. "He was trying to do your bloody job for you."

"How? By fucking the truth out of people?"

"God, you are one hundred percent arse, you know that?"

"It has been mentioned once or twice, yes. Fortunately I don't much care for your opinion."

"Could we not?" Harlequin's voice cut through the rising boil of anger. "He's only just stable. We need to get him somewhere quiet and safe."

Morgan looked around. He wasn't in the basement anymore; he was in the main part of the club, on the ground floor, by the stage. He wondered if Hunter could pole dance.

"Stay with us, Morgan," said Harlequin. He put his hand on Morgan's arm. "For some reason your magic spiked really hard and fast. You need to keep calm until we can get you home."

Oh. That explained things. Morgan didn't really care about his magic, but everyone seemed worried. His book was at home. Perhaps he needed Aiyeda. But he felt okay. Better than okay.

He tipped his head up and saw Hunter glaring down at him. "Can you pole dance?"

Hunter swallowed down a laugh; Morgan felt him do it, the rumble of mirth in his belly rushing up in him, only to be firmly stopped by his harsh, unforgiving mouth. It reached his eyes, though.

Caleb laughed out loud.

"Where's Darius?" Morgan asked. "I bet he'd pole dance."

"He's with the paramedics," Harlequin said.

"Why?"

Hunter looked more closely at him. "Don't you remember?"

Morgan shrugged. How could he remember if he'd forgotten? That made no sense.

"You ran a bolt of lightning through most of the room," Hunter said.

What?

Everything went still while Morgan's mind raced and panic rose. He wanted to brush it away, to enjoy the buzz, the warmth of Hunter's body, the soothing rub of Caleb's thumb over his wrist. But something was shifting, pushing through the fuzzy blanket of lust and magic, screaming to make itself heard. A memory.

You hurt people. Your magic hurt people.

Morgan couldn't frame a question, couldn't think, couldn't remember. He burst into tears: messy, confused tears.

"We really need to get him out of here," said Harlequin. "Damian, can you carry him?"

"Yes." Hunter hugged him. It felt good. Made him feel safe. "C'mon Morgan. It'll be all right."

"What about Darius?" said Caleb, and Morgan had another sudden shot of memory: Darius, twitching and shuddering, power surging through him.

"It went through the floor," Morgan murmured. "Oh God."

"It was a good thing it did," Hunter said. "It meant no-one died."

"They must have a grounding mechanism, I guess," said Caleb. "Makes sense."

Harlequin tossed his car keys to Caleb. "You bring the car around the front. I'll go find Darius."

Morgan phased in and out as Hunter carried him to the car and settled him in the back seat. He ached with magic, and it took all he had to keep it inside. He didn't dare think about what had happened back there, how he'd lost control, how much trouble he was in or how strong and warm Hunter's arms were. He didn't understand any of it. But he did breathe a sigh of relief when he saw Harlequin and Darius walking towards the car. Darius was walking slowly, but he was walking. Morgan had a flash of a memory. Darius surrounded in a deep, blue glow. A shield. Darius was majos too; he must have protected himself.

Harlequin held the passenger door open and Darius got in.

"D-Darius, I-I'm s-sorry." Morgan strained forwards, but the seatbelt kept him firmly tied to the back seat.

"No sweat, honey," Darius said. "I'm fine. I just lost most of an eyebrow and a few pubes. I mean, you could call that a treatment and people would pay for it, right?"

Morgan wondered if he was telling the truth.

Hunter checked Morgan was properly strapped in, then ducked out of the car.

"Aren't you coming home with us?" Morgan said.

"I've got things to deal with here," said Hunter, and then, to Caleb, who was sitting next to Morgan, "Call me, tell me how he gets on, okay?"

"Will you look at that," Caleb said, nastily. "He cares."

"Don't," said Morgan. Caleb made a disgusted sort of noise and stared out of the window. Harlequin started the car and they pulled away.

Morgan watched Hunter until they turned a corner and he was lost to view.

"I don't get it," Morgan said, frowning. "He hates me. Doesn't he?"

Caleb patted his leg. "Just take it easy, mate. Okay?"

Aiyeda appeared with mottled scales, a blend of sickly green and yellowy blue with patches of white.

She proceeded to have a dramatic coughing fit that

ended in a long, painful-sounding wheeze.

"So that's Morgan's magic?" Harlequin asked.

"An outward expression of his magic, yes," said Caleb.

"What's wrong?" wailed Morgan. "I don't understand. There was the club and we were having a nice time and then Hunter was there and everything went weird and now Aiyeda's doing … That."

Aiyeda gave another pathetic cough.

"It looks like your magic is sick, Morgan," said Harlequin.

"Yes, but I don't–"

"Shut it, *cabrón*," said Aiyeda. "Don't you think you've done enough? Now, someone run me a hot bath. And I would like a smoothie made of, ah, let me see…" The little dragon counted off items on her claws, popping each one out as she went. "Jalapeños, the hot kind, not that rubbish you get at the supermarket. Also some peach juice, a lot of ice, a spoonful of sherbet, a banana and a generous measure of vodka. In fact, make that two measures of vodka."

"Will a mashed up peach do?" asked Darius, from the kitchen.

"In a pinch," said Aiyeda, shaking her head sadly. "We must work with what we have, I suppose."

"Morgan doesn't drink," Caleb pointed out.

"Carinyo, Morgan doesn't do the kissy kissy with lots of people at once, or take the stupid drug. We are paddling in uncharted waters. Please, let me work."

"I didn't take drugs," said Morgan, but nobody

seemed to be listening. They just patted him or smiled sweetly at him. They were humouring him. Shit.

Darius came back with a tall glass full of pale pink liquid with flecks of red through it. Morgan stared at it in horror. There was no way he was going to drink that. Darius popped a straw in the glass and set it down on the coffee table.

The little dragon hopped over to the drink and sniffed at it. She took the straw delicately between her rubbery little lips and drank it all down.

Everyone in the room held their breath, including Morgan.

Then Morgan hiccupped, at the exact same time that Aiyeda burped out a little plume of greenish smoke.

"Great jalapeños," said Aiyeda. "You went to the market?"

Darius shrugged. "I found some chilli powder in the cupboard."

Aiyeda's eyes narrowed. "You are dead to me."

"Hey," said Caleb. "You're changing colour."

The greenish cast to Aiyeda's scales was getting worse. Morgan was suddenly worried. What if she threw up fire? What if what she'd drunk made him throw up? What if-

Aiyeda burped a lick of flame. "I beg your pardon," she said. "It must be the inferior ingredients."

Then her scales fluttered and changed colour once again, this time to a pretty aquamarine.

"Better," she said, and waddled over to the remote.

Morgan pulled himself together as best he could,

and helped her to pick a CBBC channel. He put subtitles on and turned the sound down. She made a big show of peering at the screen to read them, although her eyesight was way better than any of theirs and she could read in six languages.

Morgan felt a little drunk, or at least he supposed he did. What the fuck was wrong with him? He tried to get up but the other three moved in to stop him. Darius fetched him a glass of water. It was the best thing he'd ever tasted in his life, so he asked for more. Darius brought him a jug full, with ice cubes in it.

He felt guilty that Darius was running around after him: after all it was Morgan's fault he had a very unusual style of eyebrow and apparently less body hair than he'd used to. He'd been unconscious for ten minutes. But he seemed unfazed by the whole experience.

"I didn't take any drugs, did I?" Morgan said, because he was desperate for certainties and that seemed like a safe one. But the others looked at him with an assortment of worried frowns.

So much for that idea.

"Our drinks were spiked," Caleb said.

"I would have noticed," said Morgan.

"Hunter found our waiter. The guy said someone paid him to put Essence in our drinks, but he claims not to have known who it was; he just got an envelope with the money, Essence and instructions in it. The way he saw it, he was doing us a favour. Free drugs."

"Moron," muttered Harlequin.

"It was the same as the stuff I had the other night," Caleb said. "Or at least it felt the same. It's pretty amazing."

"Completely fucks with your inhibitions," said Darius.

"Remember that, Mor," said Caleb, with a little pat to Morgan's arm. "Whatever you did, don't blame yourself. "

And that was when Morgan realised exactly what he had done. The water and Caleb's gentle reassurance sloughed off the last of the Essence high and it all crashed in. He'd gone down to the dungeon. Joined a sex party. He'd had sex with his friends in front of a bunch of strangers. He and Caleb had broken their promise. He remembered coming down Caleb's throat.

"Oh God." Morgan tried to get up again, but the others gently stopped him. Aiyeda shot him a glare over her shoulder.

"It's okay." Caleb rubbed his arm again, soothing.

"I couldn't help it. The relámpago, I mean. I'm so sorry."

Harlequin gripped the other arm, none too gently. "The lightning wasn't your fault. It's the idiot who gave Essence to a majos."

Darius murmured, "And your ex, for going off on one at you when you were high. That was a dick move."

Morgan vaguely recalled Hunter yelling at him. He probably deserved it: he'd behaved like an idiot.

"Are you okay?" Morgan asked Darius. "You didn't seem to… You didn't lose control."

Darius chuckled. "Oh, believe me, honey, I did. I just don't have the firepower you do. I can fling a shield up and charm the pants off a monk, but that's about it. So, no harm done, okay?"

"I'm so sorry," Morgan said.

"You have nothing to be sorry for," Caleb insisted.

"I should never have trusted anything about that place. I shouldn't have gone off snooping on my own. I'm such a fucking idiot."

"Hey, stop that," said Caleb. "We all fell for it. If you're an idiot you're in good company."

"I didn't," Harlequin pointed out.

Aiyeda chuckled at something on the TV, and Caleb said, "We all came out of it intact. Nobody got seriously hurt. And we got what we went for."

It didn't make Morgan feel any better, but it was something to cling to, he supposed. "Did you give it to Hunter?"

"Don't be ridiculous."

"The police?"

"I still have it. It's all yours, to analyse to your heart's content. You can still impress the constabulary and show you're twice the detective Hunter is. You might even find who made the shit that fucked up your sad, dead bookie."

Is that what all this was about? Morgan was so disorientated he couldn't really remember. He'd just wanted to help. Hadn't he?"

"For what it's worth," said Harlequin, "Hunter was nice to you, when he realised you weren't deliberately trying to hurt anyone. He was worried. I think he really likes you."

"Shame he's a majophobic arsehole," murmured Caleb.

"It doesn't seem to have changed his opinions very much," Harlequin acknowledged. "But it says something that he blamed the magic for what happened. Not Morgan."

Aiyeda ruffled her scales and got to her feet. Credits rolled on the cartoons she'd been watching. "I am ready for my bath now. With fragrant oils, please. Yes?"

Chapter Eighteen

Morgan woke at noon the next day, after a series of repeating dreams in which he ended up blasting lightning at Hunter again and again. Aiyeda was still curled up next to him on the pillow, but her scales were a healthy, gleaming silver-blue.

"Morgan?"

The door was ajar, and Caleb stood on the other side of it. Morgan flushed pink at the memory of the warmth of his mouth, that moment of shared pleasure. If it was shared. Fuck. He scrubbed at his face with his hands and sat up. Aiyeda grumbled a little, but didn't properly wake.

"Come in."

Caleb sidled into the room and put a cup of tea down on Morgan's bedside table. "I'm sorry."

"Why?"

He shook his head.

"Caleb, you can't have known they'd spike our drinks."

"No, but I knew it was risky, I mean, that's why I like that kind of place, for fuck's sake. But it's not your thing. I should have gone on my own."

Aiyeda raised her head and yawned a long, steamy yawn. Morgan petted her scales gently, and she curled up again.

"It's not your fault. You know that normally, I would never… Christ, Caleb, I just, what happened between us…"

Caleb waited, but Morgan just didn't have the words. He tried out a few phrases in his head; 'I had a nice time but…', 'I'm sorry I came in your mouth without asking…' None of it sounded right. Eventually he came up with, "I would never hurt you."

"I take it this is about the sex." Caleb rubbed at a bit of lumpy paint on the door frame.

"Yes."

Caleb sighed.

Aiyeda pointedly shoved her head beneath her tail, covering her ears.

"I'm so sorry," Morgan said, helplessly.

Caleb came and flopped himself down on the bed. "Me too."

"We always said–"

"I know. Can you forgive me?"

"Of course, there's nothing to forgive. I just wish…"

"Wish what? That it had never happened?"

Morgan frowned. "No. No, just that I wish I knew

whether it was what you really wanted. If you hadn't been high."

Caleb looked up at him. "Are you serious?"

"Very."

"Sweetheart, who wouldn't want to have sex with you? Look at you."

Morgan squirmed awkwardly, but he did feel flattered. Even if Caleb said things like that all the time, just because he was Caleb, he got the sense that maybe this time he meant it.

"It's not that, at all," Caleb continued. "It was great. But we always said it could ruin our friendship."

Great, huh? Morgan sat up a little straighter. "So…"

"So, has it?"

A chink of hope dawned. "Well. Look at it this way. We've seen each other naked before."

"Often."

"It's probably safe to say that we've seen each other at our worst way before this."

"Definitely. God, that New Year's Eve party, with the strippers and I drank a whole bottle of Baileys, and you—"

Morgan put up a hand. "We swore we'd never mention that again."

Caleb nodded, pale just from the memory.

They fell silent for a few moments, and then Morgan said, "So. Maybe our friendship can survive one drug-lubricated one night stand, yeah?"

Caleb's face was all wobbly like he was about to cry,

but his eyes were bright and shining in all their ice-blue magnificence. "Yeah."

"And I'm really sorry I didn't get you off. I'm not usually a selfish lover, I promise."

"Who says you didn't get me off?" Caleb said, with a very naughty smile. And then they both burst out laughing. Aiyeda muttered into her tail.

"Anyway, here it is. What we went for." Caleb held out his hand and uncurled his fingers. A very small plastic bag lay there and, inside it, a purple and green capsule. There was a decoration around the join, a linked chain.

"Essence," said Morgan.

"It looks exactly like the one I took the first time, and I've never seen this design or colouring before, so it's got to be from the same manufacturer. According to Hunter, it's what the waiter said our drinks were spiked with. So I'll leave you to do whatever you need to do, okay?"

"Thanks."

"Unless you want me to stay? In case anything happens?"

"It won't. If it worked just by touching or breathing it they wouldn't have had to spike our drinks."

"I know. I know. Just…"

Morgan shook his head, no. This required magic, and he'd done enough of that in public lately to last him a lifetime.

Caleb squeezed his shoulder. "Don't forget your tea, twink."

Morgan cleared everything off his desk and laid out some equipment from the old wooden chest in his wardrobe. First he covered the desk in a clean, white cloth. If you looked closely, it had threads that shimmered gold running through it, but otherwise it just looked like an ordinary table cloth. On top of this he placed a pewter dish on a tripod and assembled the channelling apparatus: a glass tube, flared at one end and narrowing to a tiny hole at the other, supported on two wooden stands. He sprinkled a trail of dried dandelion petals around the edge of the cloth and picked up his book. Aiyeda perched on the back of the chair next to the table, watching closely.

Morgan flicked to Chapter Six, *Divination*, part 12.4, *Composition and source of magical materials*. There was an ornate, ornamented diagram of a table laid out exactly as his was. First, he popped the Essence tablet in the centre of the dish. He placed his right hand on the centre of the image in the book and held Aiyeda's paw with his left.

"*Definis*," said Morgan.

Aiyeda repeated the word, and then breathed softly into the channelling apparatus. Morgan watched the shimmering, gold-flecked breath flow through the glass tube to surround the Essence. It lingered there for a moment, wrapping itself around the tablet, seeping inside the break between the two halves of the capsule. Then it flowed back into a small cloud above the dish. Aiyeda leaned forwards and breathed it all back in.

Morgan's fingers tingled where he touched the dragon's paw. She closed her eyes, took in a couple more deep breaths, and then settled back on her haunches.

"All done," she pronounced. "Are you ready?"

Morgan fetched a notepad and pen from the bed and wrote as she spoke.

"Composite materials include: magnesium stearate sorbitol, distilled essence of majos in form encanté: focus inhibition and wellbeing."

"Is that it? No coercion?"

"None, or I would have said so, would I not?"

Well, at least that meant nobody forced him to have sex with anyone. They just forced him not to care.

"And origin? Who made it?"

Aiyeda blinked, her long, whiskery eyelashes brushing her cheek, and said, "It is a flavour familiar to us."

"Great! Do you recognise the signature?"

He stood, pen poised and ready, but she turned her back on him and said, "I am not sure."

"What do you mean?"

"It is not clear."

"Then we can do it agai–"

"No."

Morgan reached out and touched one iridescent wing tip. "Aiyeda. Please."

Her scales flushed a deeper shade of blue, her tail almost black. She looked over her shoulder at him and said, "Dr Rosero, Guapo. You can taste it yourself, I think? If you try?"

Morgan held his hand over the dish and took a long breath in. It had to be a mistake. Michaela would never do something like this. Everything she had taught him, all her advice and encouragement, had been about control. As he breathed in he caught a hint of lavender and the rubbery smell of new tennis balls. It stuck at the back of his throat. Tears welled in his eyes. Not her. Not this.

"You know it is true," Aiyeda said, bumping his arm with her nose. "It is sad, but it is true, no?"

Morgan nodded. A tear plopped from his nose to hit the pad he'd been writing on, making a big, rugged blot on the paper.

"Enough of this. We can watch cartoons now, yes?"

Morgan set up the iPad and propped it on the bed for Aiyeda to watch while he set about clearing up his things.

The door to Dr Rosero's waiting area was open, as usual. Clients were welcome to let themselves in, make a drink in the kitchenette and peruse the bookshelves while they waited. For the first time, Morgan didn't have an appointment. Michaela hadn't answered her phone - she wouldn't, if she had a client - so he hadn't been able to make one. But technically it was an emergency, as he'd lost control, never mind that it was for the second time in less than a week. The waiting room was empty. When the next client arrived he could beg for a quick five minute chat. People had done that with him before, when they were desperate, and he'd let them cut in. Karma had to be good for something.

He sat on the sofa opposite the door and prepared to wait. He rehearsed his opening line in his head: 'This isn't easy'… No, that was crap. 'I have a question…' Better. 'There's something I need to know'. Yes. And then-

Morgan's gaze sharpened on the door to Dr Rosero's room.

It wasn't shut. It was ajar. He listened carefully. No sound. Yet the door to the building had been open; that only happened when she was with a client, or was expecting one. Maybe the person before hadn't turned up. That must be it.

Okay. Morgan should have been pleased, but his hand shook as he knocked on the door. There was no answer. He opened it.

The first thing he saw was the office chair, which belonged at the back of the room, by her desk. But there it was, right in front of the door, lying forlornly on its side. So out of place, so *wrong*. Then the rest of the scene crashed in on him all at once: cushions pulled off sofas; a smashed vase; the filing cabinet with the bottom drawer open, spilling its contents across the floor.

Morgan pulled out his phone. He scrolled through his contacts frantically, but the names were a blur. He sat down suddenly on the floor, his phone shaking so much he could barely keep hold of it. He was shaking. He was…

He closed his eyes and breathed. Not now. No. No,

no, no.

He let the phone fall to the carpet in front of him and let his breath out slowly, focusing on the screen. He saw 'Sahil', and jabbed dial.

The police were kind to him. He guessed they assumed any client at their therapist's office was likely to be vulnerable and treated them accordingly. It wasn't Sahil who'd come, of course. He'd patiently listened to Morgan stammering at him down the phone, and he'd told Morgan to try and relax, and he'd take care of things. So Morgan had breathed, and waited, until eventually the local constabulary arrived to find him shaking in the waiting room. Once he'd given a statement they let him leave. He kept the statement simple: he turned up to see her, she wasn't there, the room was in a state. They presumed he'd come by for an appointment and he let them.

He didn't know where to go after that, so he stood on the doorstep and called Michaela one more time, just in case. She didn't answer.

But from the bins in the alley by her office, a phone rang.

For a split second Morgan considered grabbing it himself and taking it to Hunter or Sahil and getting them to use it to find her. He didn't like the idea of this one, clear piece of evidence being in someone else's hands. But he'd made enough mistakes lately to last him a lifetime, so he did the right thing. He trailed back into her office and told the constable who was grappling with a roll of incident tape about the phone.

He was standing in the alley, watching the police swarming around the bin like wasps round a cider bottle, when his own phone went off, the alert so loud it made him jump. Not a call, though, and not Michaela. A text.

>My office. 6pm. Pearl

Chapter Nineteen

Morgan went home, showered, put on clean clothes, drank a lot of water and forced down a banana. He sorted out the post that had come that morning and added another envelope to the pile of unopened ones for Caleb on the hall table. He hadn't asked yet, but he guessed they were from Caleb's mother.

Caleb wasn't the only person avoiding things. Morgan hadn't told anyone except the police about Michaela. Nobody else knew her personally, not even Caleb. Morgan had known her nearly all his life, and he couldn't believe she'd do something like that without a good reason. Until he'd asked her about it, face to face, and God, he hoped he'd get that chance, he'd keep it to himself. She'd kept his secrets for nearly two decades. This was the least he could do in return. She was out there, somewhere, he was certain of it. He'd find her, talk to her, and she'd give him a perfectly rational explanation.

When Caleb got home from work, Morgan was staring out of the window at the pigeons squabbling on their tiny rooftop patio. He couldn't have said how long he'd been there. Time had gone a bit weird. Everything had gone a bit weird.

"Hey," said Caleb. "Have we got any of those energy bar things? I'm starving and I have to go straight out."

Morgan checked the time on his phone. "Me too."

"Pearl's called me in for 6."

"Oh. Me too."

They looked at each other.

"Shit," said Caleb.

Pearl wasn't angry. She was disappointed. Or so she claimed.

"You're my boys," she told them, pacing back and forth behind her desk. "I didn't just sign you up to my agency. I took you under my wing. I trained you. I bent over backwards to find the right positions for you. I protect you, I nurture you, I rely on you. And how do you repay me?"

She smacked the newspaper down on her desk with such a thwap that Morgan and Caleb both flinched. Morgan didn't want to look at the picture on the cover of the paper, but he forced himself to. Then he couldn't stop looking, even though the longer his looked, the more sick he felt. It was a photo of him, Caleb and Darius. Naked, their key body parts blacked out with thick black lines. Darius and Caleb had their masks on, but Morgan had lost his completely; he was totally naked apart from his necklace.

He was grateful it was only local. If his mother saw it she would never forgive him.

"I know what you're thinking," Pearl said. "'Ignore it, Pearl. It was just a bit of fun.' Never mind that pesky clause in your contracts about not bringing *Oyster* into disrepute. 'Boys will be boys. It'll blow over in a day or two.' Well, you better hope none of them online sites picks it up. Or the tabloids. Always out for a bit of scandal, aren't they? Did you think of that, when you were taking your clothes off in a public place?"

Morgan hoped that was a rhetorical question, because he couldn't think of anything to say that wouldn't just make things worse.

"It wasn't a public place," Caleb said. "We weren't working."

Pearl leaned across the desk, her eyes narrowed. Caleb squirmed under her attention. "Did you read what it says here, child?"

Caleb snatched up the paper - Morgan had to say, he was being extremely brave - and read. 'Local nightclub Bubble was raided by police last night after they received reports of wealthy executives indulging in decadent, drug-fuelled orgies in what is normally a quiet residential area-' Honestly, that's bullshit, it's right next to Morrisons, there's maybe one bungalow. '-a quiet residential area. Exotic dancers Morgan and Caleb, moonlighting from the...' Oh. 'The Oyster temp agency.' Shit."

"Yes, Caleb. That is exactly what you are in right now. Deep." Her devastating gaze darted to Morgan. "Up to your pretty little necks."

"How the hell did they find that out? All it says is 'a source'. Who was it? Anyway, we weren't working there," Caleb said. "We went to have fun, and our drinks were spiked."

"Denise from the front office said you'd been there before," Pearl said. "You were bragging about it by the photocopier. And on that occasion you went with Jennifer Cotterall."

Caleb swallowed and said, "So what? Are there restrictions now on what we can do in our own time?"

Morgan groaned. "Caleb, stop."

But Caleb seemed determined to keep the train wreck going. "C'mon, Pearl, you can see they lied. I've never danced for money in my life and you know Morgan can't."

"Wouldn't," Morgan murmured. He wasn't that bad at dancing. Just chose not to. "That's not the point, Caleb. It's us. There. At a known sex club. With no clothes on."

"Jennifer Cotterall," Pearl repeated. "From Slytho and Fitch, Solicitors. Where you have worked on several occasions."

All the fight went out of Caleb. All he could muster was a helpless stare.

"And you." Pearl turned her sights on Morgan. "I found you a long term contract with a very well-paying local business, who asked for you by name. But you not only walked out with no notice, without bothering to talk it through with me first - and not for the first time, either - you didn't even pay me the courtesy of a visit to explain. You saw fit to tell me in a text. So I rang Mr Hunter. Do you know what he said?"

Morgan shook his head, hoping it wasn't what he was imagining.

"He told me if you hadn't resigned, he would have fired you for being unable to control your temper."

Okay. That could have been a lot worse, in the circumstances. Hunter could easily have said 'majos' instead of 'temper' and then Morgan would probably never have worked again.

"And now this." Pearl snatched the paper back from Caleb and slammed it on the desk. "Nobody plays me for a fool, and nobody taints my reputation with this filth," said Pearl. "Get out of my sight. And don't expect a phone call any time soon, either of you. You're off my books."

They went to Starbucks, where Caleb got a caramel latte and Morgan got a peppermint tea. They didn't say much, just sat together at a table and sipped at their drinks in shared misery. Morgan felt kind of numb. Things had piled up so fast he didn't know where to start. And Caleb always went quiet when he was truly angry, until the edge wore off and he started throwing things.

Morgan hoped he wasn't around when that

happened. His magic was already pushing at his skin. He needed to keep calm.

His phone pinged. Sahil's personal number.

>DrMR left the country. Safe and well. Sxx

"Oh," Morgan murmured. He had a hundred questions: why had Michaela gone? Where? Why hadn't she said anything? But he knew the police wouldn't say. With a dull sick, feeling, he realised he might never know. Michaela was his mentor, his therapist. A professional. He had no right to know anything.

"What?" Caleb said.

"Nothing. Nothing, just… nothing."

Caleb grunted.

Morgan noticed the day on his phone as he was putting it away. Thursday. Right.

Coven night.

Just as well, really.

The Leeds District Coven meetings took place in the local medical centre, in an area which was a waiting room during the day. Three nights a week the chairs were switched from rows to a big circle, the medical doctors went home and the majos 'mentors' took over. Morgan was a few minutes late but there were still a couple of seats left. He tucked himself into the one nearest the door and exchanged a polite smile with Galatia. She had been coming to this group nearly as long as Morgan. Her power wasn't huge, but she was every bit as terrified of letting it loose as Morgan was.

He wondered if she'd heard about Michaela yet.

The group was led by Rick, an earnest, middle aged man with lightly spiked hair. A runic tattoo ran down the side of his neck, which looked exotic and out of place next to his smart shirt and financial-advisor suit. He wasn't a financial advisor, though, he just dressed like one. Brooke, the mentor who ran the Monday sessions, was in the staff kitchen, clinking around the cups for after-meeting refreshments. Like most mentors, she and Rick always worked in a pair, unlike Michaela, who used to run Sunday groups all on her own, until she gave them up to free up more time for her university research. Morgan liked Rick and Brooke well enough: Rick was almost painfully understanding, and Brooke had a dry sense of humour that was a good foil to Rick's earnest approach.

"Good evening, everyone," Rick said. "Quick intros as usual, please: name and in one sentence anything you'd like to bring to the meeting tonight, along with your estimated risk factor on the one to five-star scale, and then we'll have a chat. Okay?"

Everyone murmured assent, and they started to go around the circle.

Eddie, nothing special, risk one.

Debra, apologetic smile, still having trouble sustaining control of light manipulation - risk three.

(She was never really a three. She just saw shadows and panicked.)

A murmur that was a roughly equal blend of 'God, not again' and 'poor Debra' went around the room.

Cliff, nothing special, risk one.

Jamil, got into a fight at school, risk two.

"Morgan. I had a major episode, no, wait, two major episodes this week. So. Um, risk five. I guess."

There were a few swift intakes of breath, a lot of eyes on him, and Rick leaned forward. "Are you okay, Morgan? Is your primary advisor aware of these episodes?"

"It's Dr Rosero. She's, um, left. Suddenly."

Galatia gasped.

Brooke appeared in the doorway, tea towel draped over one shoulder and gave Rick a questioning look.

"Oh yes. I had a call," said Rick. "We can talk after the session and make sure you're properly supported, Morgan. You too, Galatia. Any other clients of Dr Rosero here this evening?"

A buzz of interest went around the room, but nobody else came forward. The fact that Rick and Brooke seemed to have it all under control was a lick of comfort which Morgan welcomed so much he could have sobbed. He knew, theoretically, that someone would be assigned to him. But he also knew it could take time. It felt weird, like he was somehow keen to cheat on Michaela. Who may or may not be a manufacturer of illegal drugs. No. Who *was* a manufacturer of illegal drugs.

"I only saw her last week," said Galatia. She was as white as a sheet. "What happened?"

Brooke appeared at Galatia's side and whispered something to her. Galatia nodded and got up. She followed Brooke out of the room.

Rick smiled at Morgan, and said, "Okay?"

Morgan nodded, and the rounds of the room continued. People spoke quickly now, more interested in Morgan's 'episodes' than their own concerns - all apart from Tim, who tended to be oblivious to any problems other than his own. He'd fought in the Falklands and some of the things he'd seen (and done) had really fucked with his sense of empathy and compassion. He wasn't a bad sort, and Morgan was happy enough to shrink back and listen to the small speech Tim gave in place of the sentence he'd been asked for. It kept Morgan's brain busy, and stopped him from thinking too hard about Pearl or Hunter or Michaela.

"Let's come to Morgan first," Rick said. "If you could tell us what—"

The door clicked open behind Morgan. Someone rushed to the empty seat next to Tim and sat down, apologising for her lateness. Morgan was preoccupied planning out what he could and couldn't share of recent events with the group, so it was only when he was about to get to his feet to speak that he looked the late arrival in the eye.

His legs felt like noodles and magic churned in his gut.

It was Jess Shaw.

"Hi, I'm Jess, majophobia incident, risk one. Again, really sorry I'm late, everyone. I'm not from this Coven, just visiting. So. Hi."

Everyone chorused 'Hi, Jess', including Morgan. She darted him a few glances, shoving her hair behind her ear. It was as if all her police attitude had been peeled off with her uniform and revealed a flustered, somewhat shy young woman in her place. She looked so vulnerable.

"I'm sorry to hear that," Rick said. "As always, we will invite everyone who wishes to share in order of stated risk. Today Morgan had the highest risk, at five. So, Morgan?"

Morgan got to his feet. He kept his eyes on Rick, because otherwise he'd just have stared at Jess and not been able to say a thing. "I've encountered some very emotional situations this week, and someone had to ground me both times. I got through it, but I'm really scared and then Michaela..." His throat closed up; he was trying very hard not to cry, not to look at Jess, not to think about Hunter, and he was failing. He sat down. "Sorry."

"You have nothing to be sorry for," said Rick, gently.

Rick asked him a few general questions - they never talked about circumstances in the group unless the speaker wanted to, and Morgan very much did not want to tell everyone he'd taken Essence (even unwittingly) and got involved in an orgy. Neither did he want to tell them he'd broken up with his boyfriend who couldn't stand magic and, oh yeah, was Jess's brother. But he did talk about how scary it was to be that out of control, and how he felt stupid for not being able to deal with it on his own. He snuck a glance at Jess to gauge her reaction, but she was staring at the floor, head down.

"You've done all the right things, especially coming here," said Rick. We'll get you some ongoing one to one help sorted out after the session, yeah?"

Most of the group chipped in with sympathy for Morgan and shared a few things Morgan already knew about meditating and control exercises. It felt good to be heard, and nobody seemed afraid of him, which was reassuring. Caleb and his friends were great, but nobody could really know what it felt like to be consumed by your own magic unless they'd experienced it. Nearly flooding a building wasn't quite the same as Debra's tendency to leave non-existent lights on when she left the room, but fear was fear and all majos had felt it at one time or another. Morgan thanked everyone and leaned back to listen to the others. Galatia returned, just after Debra had shared her latest accidental illumination of a dark spot in the stacks of the library where she worked. Galatia and Morgan shared a little smile. She looked like she'd been crying.

As Jess was only a risk one and she'd arrived late, she went last.

"I have quite a responsible job dealing with the general public," she told the group. "Frankly, I'm used to getting all sorts of abuse. But this time it was personal."

"Would you like to share with us what was said or

done to you?" Rick asked. "If it's not too painful?"

Morgan braced himself to hear more bad things about Hunter that would make him question his own judgement all over again. But instead Jess clasped her hands together nervously and said, "It was a colleague. Someone I'm really close with."

Not Sahil. He'd been so good with Morgan, and he'd sounded protective towards Jess. He'd even covered for him. So, who?

"We joined the organisation at the same time and I always thought he understood. He played tennis with my husband, and his little boy and mine have playdates. We often ask each other for advice. He works in a different department, it's good to get perspective."

Definitely not Sahil. Thank fuck. Morgan didn't think he could stand anymore betrayals.

"I'm working on a tricky project right now." She glanced at Morgan, probably without meaning to, and she snapped her gaze away again immediately. "I went to this particular colleague for advice, and the topic of magic came up. He was extremely dismissive."

"Is that it?" said Tim. "No disrespect, but people are dismissive of magic all the time. In fact, if my family would stop at being dismissive I'd be hunky dory and wouldn't need to come here anymore."

"We are a little more than a support group, Tim," Rick said, his big brown eyes delivering a sad sort of admonishment to Tim.

"You know what I mean," said Tim, and crossed his arms in front of his chest.

"It didn't stop there," said Jess. "The next day, he told me his little boy wouldn't be coming to my house for sleepovers anymore."

"Oh no," said Debra.

"It's hard enough being a woman in my line of work," Jess said. "And I'm younger than most in my position. Having to deal with this as well feels like too much sometimes."

Morgan really felt for her and, judging by the buzz of sympathy that went round the room, he wasn't the only one. Knowing exactly what Jess's job was, and that she had to deal with her own brother's prejudice as well - and her mother's desertion - made it all the worse.

"I'm sure we can all relate to Jess's position," said Rick. "Can anyone share ways in which they've coped in situations where they've been discriminated against for their gifts?"

"I suck it up and get on with it," said Tim, gruffly.

"I try not to get into fights," said Jamil. "Violence doesn't help. Even when it feels like it might. Like this week."

"Talk to someone," suggested Debra. "You did well coming here tonight. Didn't she, everyone?" She started, tentatively, to clap. Nobody seemed quite sure whether or not to join in, so Morgan did, to encourage them. For Debra's sake more than anything. It was all a bit awkward.

When the applause died away, Rick stood up. "Remember, Jess, as hard as it can be with the world the way it is, discrimination in the workplace is illegal.

If he shows any signs of prejudice there I suggest you visit your HR department. Or any coven can provide you with advocacy."

"Thank you. I will."

Rick led them in a closing meditation, and then Brooke came out with a tray of tea and biscuits. Morgan gratefully helped himself to a peppermint tea and a piece of shortbread, and was going to talk to Galatia, or maybe Jess - he wasn't sure if she'd welcome that or not. Brooke took the decision out of his hands when she passed the tray to Rick to finish taking round and said to Morgan, "See me in the office, mate?"

Morgan obediently followed her into a consulting room just beyond the kitchen. She turned on the lights and indicated for him to sit in the patient's seat.

"Am I in trouble?" asked Morgan.

"Not at all. Like Rick said, we need to sort you out with some support, right?"

Brooke was from London, or so Morgan assumed from the accent. She was quite short, with hair braided back from her face to fall down her back. She wore cut-off denims and a t-shirt with 'Luton Girls' on it, along with purple Converse with rainbow laces. She logged into the computer and pulled up his file.

"I'm sure Dr Rosero will come back," Morgan said. "It's probably just a misunderstanding or something."

"Hm. Okay, says here you used to see her every other week, is that right?"

"When things were going well, yes."

'That's a bit more than most of us."

"Is it? I never really thought about it."

"You've been seeing her a long time."

"We get on really well."

"It must be tough on you that she disappeared." Brooke's sympathy was as matter-of-fact as Rick's was syrupy. Morgan liked that.

"It's horrible. I went to her office and found it in a mess and…" To his horror, tears welled up.

Brooked popped a box of tissues in front of him and leaned towards him, touching his arm. "Would you like to talk about it?"

Morgan shook his head. "It's just…" He blew his nose. "I'm worried about her."

"Of course you are, mate."

"And I'm scared. My control is shattered right now and it's selfish but without her…"

"Without her, what, mate? Tell me what you're frightened of."

"I'm frightened I'll hurt people."

"Right. Listen to me, Morgan. Look at me."

He looked up. Brooke's eyes were pretty, hazel-green, but most of all, kind. Her gaze was steady.

She said, "You've got this."

"I do?"

"You've had two major incidents in the last week, and you came through both times. You have inside you more power than all the majos in tonight's meeting put together, and you manage it day after day after day. What do you do when you start to lose control?"

"Get out of the situation. Breathe. Discharge the

magic safely, if I can."

"And that's all you can do. You're not alone. You have your totem?"

Morgan's hand went to his necklace, traced the outline of the tree with his forefinger. "Yes."

"You do all your exercises? Channel to your familiar on a regular basis?"

Morgan nodded.

"Then you're more dedicated than most of the majos I see. Take it easy, and try to keep out of stressful situations until you're feeling better, okay? This isn't your fault, Morgan. You're doing your best. Now, shall we get you sorted out with a new mentor to look after you until Dr Rosero gets back?"

Morgan drew in a long, shuddering breath. "Yes. God, yes, please."

"Good. Well done, Morgan. You'll be okay."

Brooke tapped a few things on the computer, and then she grinned at him. "Would you look at that?"

"What?"

"I just put you through the mentor matcher, and look who it popped out." She turned the screen so he could see the name.

Brooke Anderson.

She stuck her hand out for him to shake. "Welcome aboard, Mr Kerry. When would you like our first meeting to be?"

Morgan hadn't expected to leave the meeting with a new mentor, not even a temporary one. When he'd got up that morning he hadn't even expected to need one. It was all a bit daunting and confusing, although he didn't have a problem with Brooke. He did have a problem with his life being turned upside down on a regular basis. By the time he'd got back to the main room everyone else had gone, and Rick was moving the chairs back into formation for the next day's GP surgery. He said his goodbyes. Rick gave him a hug.

Out on the street he spotted Jess striding off towards the car park. She must have left only a little before him. She'd recaptured her usual confidence, by the looks of things: she held her head high, her stride was even and confident, and her dark hair swung jauntily in its ponytail. She looked like a different person. Maybe that's how she coped with things. Putting on a brave face in a hostile world. Morgan had never got the hang of that.

He thought about running after her, maybe talking to her about Hunter and whatever bullshit she was putting up with at work. But he figured if she'd wanted to talk to him she'd have waited. Besides, she'd probably had quite enough of Morgan and his misadventures for a lifetime. So Morgan headed to the bus stop and went home.

Chapter Twenty

Morgan was surprised to find Caleb, Darius and Harlequin sitting around the dining table when he got back to the flat. It had been cleared of the DVDs and books and odds and ends that usually covered it. Morgan had forgotten it had a rather swish marbled blue top. It looked quite posh.

"I hope this isn't an intervention," he said. "I've already been to Coven tonight."

"Not an intervention." Caleb got up and ushered Morgan to one of two spare seats at the table. "D'you want a drink?"

Darius, Harlequin and Caleb had bottles of beer in front of them. "Water, please," Morgan said. "So what are we doing? Monopoly tournament? Dungeons and Dragons?"

"Darling, please," said Darius.

"Hi, Morgan. Female pronouns," said Harley. "We're here to form Plan B."

Caleb set a glass of iced water in front of Morgan, just as the doorbell rang. Morgan looked at the empty chair. "Who else are we expecting?"

Nobody would quite meet his eye. Caleb rushed off to answer the door.

He heard a voice from the hallway outside, swapping pleasantries with Caleb's. He knew that voice. He pushed his chair back from the table.

"Morgan," Darius said, gently.

"I can't believe this."

"He wants to help," said Darius.

"You can tell him to go away if you want," said Harley. "You have a choice."

Morgan gave Harley a grateful smile. At least she grasped how out of order it was to ask his ex here to his home, even if no-one else did. Darius picked at the label on his beer bottle and avoided eye contact.

Morgan braced himself and looked calmly at Hunter as he came in, determined to appear aloof and composed. All that happened was that Morgan's heart skipped a beat at how beautiful Hunter was. He was wearing a soft-looking t-shirt which clung to his shoulders and hung loose over his stomach. It wasn't tucked in. Morgan could have his hand up there in a matter of seconds. He remembered what Hunter's belly felt like: the scattering of soft blond hairs, the smooth, flat skin.

"Let me get you a beer," Caleb said.

"Thanks." Hunter's voice was warm and rich and didn't have an ounce of arrogance about it, for once.

This wasn't Damian Hunter, PI, it was the Damian Hunter who'd had dinner with Morgan, taken him home and made love to him until his heart sang.

Morgan kicked out the chair for him. Hunter sat.

"How are you?" Hunter asked him. He sounded genuinely concerned.

"Fine."

"And your magic…?"

"All back to normal. Don't worry, I'm not going to make a water feature out of the table. Or electrocute anybody."

"Good."

"Honestly, I'm fine," said Darius. "It was just a tingle."

An awkward silence settled over the table. Morgan was relieved when Caleb came back, even if he did want to kill him for letting this happen.

"So, thanks for coming, everyone," said Caleb. "I asked you here because I have an opportunity to get back into Bubble. And I think I should take it."

"No," said Morgan.

"Hear me out."

"Christ, Caleb, you've already lost your job and had your naked arse plastered all over the local press. That's enough."

"On the contrary. Those things give me all the more reason to go back and solve the mystery," Caleb said. "Revenge."

"And because the danger gets you off."

Morgan and Caleb glared at each other.

"If they thought the place was dangerous they'd have closed it," said Caleb.

"Only if they had proof," Morgan shot back. "They can't close down a business without evidence."

"You should have pressed charges about them slipping you Essence." Hunter looked annoyingly smug.

"Hunter has a point," Harley said. "Why didn't you?"

Morgan said, "Because it's irrelevant. And I don't want my arse all over the national press. The local papers is quite enough." And now he knew who'd made the Essence, Morgan didn't want the police sniffing around it. "I just want to forget the whole thing."

"I'm not asking you to be a part of this," Caleb said.

"Great. I won't be, then. It's a terrible idea."

"I mean, I thought you cared that people are getting killed, but if you really just want to forget it all…"

"What do you hope to gain from going back, hm? Loyalty points? Or are you going to hide under a blanket somewhere and wait until the murderer turns up and starts talking to himself about what he did?"

"Ah, that's the exiting part. This isn't just an ordinary invitation. Dave and Jennifer and I have a personal invitation directly from the mysterious Mr Appleford," Caleb said. "I'm going to find out exactly who he is."

"We know who he is. He's the owner of the club."

"Actually, he's not," said Hunter. "The owner is Wallace Sturgess, the lottery winner, remember? Sahil interviewed him. He lives in London and all he's interested in is acquiring buildings, mostly recommended by his business manager. He's never met Appleford in person, the lease was arranged by an agency, which, it turns out, doesn't actually exist. The events are managed by a woman called Candice, who runs the burlesque show. She said no-one's ever seen Appleford. Supposedly he remotely watches the security cameras at the entrance and messages the security staff to tell them who's picked for the playroom."

"What?" said Caleb.

"That makes sense," said Harley. "Most sex parties are quite exclusive, you know. Only the prettiest are allowed."

Darius said, "Maybe they film it and sell it as porn. Hey, has anyone checked PornHub?"

"On it," said Harley, tapping at her phone.

"That would finish Pearl off good and proper," Caleb said.

"Or maybe Wally Sturgess watches it on livestream from his office in London," said Darius.

"There's CCTV in there?" Morgan was just wondering if his day could get any worse and hey presto, there it was.

"You're quite safe," Hunter, with a totally unnecessary smirk. "There's no CCTV in the play room, and they record over the previous night's footage from the entrance every night."

Harley said, "To be honest, most of these orgy

videos could be shot anywhere, you don't really see the surroundings. None of them look like you, though."

"That was fast," Hunter said.

"I wrote an app," said Harley. Morgan could tell that Hunter was dying to ask more about that, but there was something about the decisive way Harley turned off her phone and put it back in the pocket of her shorts that said no questions would be answered.

"We should be leaving this to the professionals," said Morgan.

"The thing is, we professionals are stumped," Hunter said. "Both victims died of cardiac arrest, with Essence in their systems and evidence of recent sexual activity. The police have eliminated all their suspects, and they've found no other connection between the victims except for one. They were both invited to Bubble personally. By Appleford."

"You've got to be kidding me." Morgan turned to Caleb. "You hear that? And you want to go right back in there?"

"It's the ideal opportunity," said Caleb. "I'll go along with the invitation, and find out all I can about him."

"That could work," said Darius.

"I don't think you understand what's happening here," said Morgan. "It's obviously a trap. Both of the other victims got invitations like this. Caleb's putting himself directly in the line of danger. Are you seriously comfortable with that?"

"It's not like they can lock them in that room and

throw away the key," said Darius. "He can leave any time if things get dodgy."

"I know exactly what I'm getting into," said Caleb. "Besides, I'll be with Jennifer and Dave."

Morgan snorted. "And they've always been so good to you, right? You're fooling yourself, Caleb."

"Morgan has a point," Hunter said. "I don't like any of this. Remember, people have died, and we have no idea why. If anyone's doing this it should be an undercover police officer."

Caleb said, "How long would it take them to get as close as I am now? And how many people might die in the meanwhile?"

"So, let's look at things a different way," said Harley. "Did you find out anything about the Essence, Morgan?"

"It's an advanced formula. Encanté, with a focus on reducing inhibition, and a high thrown in. Very clean." Morgan kept his voice steady. It was tempting to charm them all to make the lie easier when it inevitably came. But he resisted. Magic had done nobody any favours recently, after all.

"And the maker?" asked Hunter.

"Nothing. Didn't register the signature. It's probably imported."

The others' disappointment was tangible, and Morgan felt like shit. He hated lying, especially to his friends. But Michaela wasn't around to defend herself. What if she'd produced the stuff for perfectly acceptable clinical reasons, and it had been stolen from her? Until he could ask her, face to face, her secret stayed with him.

He said, "Whoever it was who made it, it's a clean drug. It's the people selling it who are fucking dangerous."

"All the more reason to talk to whoever this Appleford guy is," said Caleb. "For fuck's sake, people, someone spiked our drinks. Darius got hurt, Mor and I both lost our jobs. We have to do something. And I think Appleford knows what's going on."

"Oh, and he's going to just tell you," said Morgan.

Caleb glared at him. "I don't need your negativity."

"Get used to it. I'm going with you," said Morgan.

There was a chorus of 'what?' from around the table.

"I'm not letting you get hurt. And I know you; whatever we say, you're going anyway, aren't you?"

"Yes," Caleb said, stubbornly. "Yes, because it's the right thing to do."

"Right. We enter separately. I'll get there first and wait downstairs, near the entrance to the party room. You go in with Jennifer and Dave to meet Appleford, and if you haven't come back within an agreed time limit, I'll come and get you."

"I like that idea," said Harley. "Good one, Morgan."

"It's a ridiculous idea," Hunter said. "What on earth makes you think they'll let Morgan back in there after what he did?"

"I have my ways," said Morgan, with a smirk that

was probably less than pleasant.

"Magic," said Hunter, as if Morgan was something nasty he'd found in a bowl of strawberries.

"It makes sense," said Harley. "Caleb's cool because he's invited. They'd recognise Darius straight away because he got hurt."

"And because I'm hung like a donkey," said Darius.

Was he? Morgan couldn't remember. That whole night seemed more and more like a particularly unsettling dream.

"But Morgan can charm the pants off them," Harley said.

"I'm doing it," Morgan said. "I won't let him go in there without back up."

"Cool with me," said Caleb.

The others nodded, all except Hunter, who was thinking, hard. Morgan could tell by the little crease between his eyebrows.

"Can this," Hunter swallowed. "This magic, can it get more than one of us in?"

"Who were you thinking?" said Morgan. He supposed he could convince the door staff that Darius wasn't Darius, especially if he dressed differently, maybe wore glasses? And kept his dick in his pants.

"Me," said Hunter.

"You?"

"I'm a professional, Morgan. In case it's slipped your mind, this is my case. I have a responsibility."

Morgan sighed. "So long as you keep quiet and don't contradict me."

"Do you have to do anything to me?"

"No. The encanté will be aimed at the doorman, and any other security. Maybe at anyone who looks too interested in us, to make them go away." Morgan gave Hunter another of those nasty smirks. "I promise I won't get any of my filthy majos-juice all over you, babe."

Hunter looked down at his drink. A muscle in his cheek twitched.

Harley said, "So. We have Caleb going in to find out who Mr Appleford is. Morgan is going in to watch out for Caleb, and Hunter's going in to watch out for Morgan."

"To make sure I don't do anything overly magical," said Morgan.

"You can drop the attitude," said Hunter.

Morgan glared at him. "Gonna make me?"

It was meant to sound angry. But somehow the tension that fizzed between them was something quite different. Morgan got the sense that Hunter was within three breaths of slamming Morgan down on the table and fucking him within an inch of his life.

And to add insult to injury, the thought made Morgan hard.

"Fuck my life," he muttered, tearing his gaze away from Hunter. He fixed it determinedly on the ice cubes bobbing about in his glass of water instead. If they melted in double quick time, so be it.

Harley cleared her throat. "Well. I suppose we have a plan, of sorts. When's all this happening?"

"Tomorrow night," said Caleb. "Can you be our driver again?"

"Yes."

"I'll wait with you in the car, honey," said Darius.

"Great," said Caleb. "Let's drink to it."

"Wait," Hunter said, turning his sharp, blue gaze on Morgan. "Are you sure you can handle yourself? The last two times you went to that place you ended up–" He waved his hands about in an extravagant gesture that Morgan presumed was supposed to imitate some kind of spell-casting.

"Of course he can," said Caleb. "So long as you don't piss him off or slip him Essence."

Hunter still looked worried.

Morgan scraped up the remnants of his dignity, smiled sweetly at Hunter and raised his glass. "Well. Third time lucky, eh?"

They all clinked glasses.

Hunter came into the kitchen while Morgan was clearing up. Darius and Harley had gone home and Caleb was double checking porn sites to make sure the Bubble's orgies weren't out there for public consumption. At least, that's what he claimed to be doing.

"I think I owe you an apology," Hunter said.

"You think?" Morgan shook a glass to get a particularly stubborn bit of lemon rind out of it. It clung right 'til the last minute before plopping sadly into the sink. Morgan put the glass into the dishwasher.

"I was disappointed and angry," Hunter said. "But that's no excuse for calling anybody names."

"Right."

"So I'm sorry."

Morgan stacked the rest of the glasses and reached for the jar of dishwasher tablets.

"You lied to me," Hunter said. "Why?"

Morgan peeled the completely unnecessary plastic wrapper off the detergent, his mouth tightly shut. He hated the word 'disappointed'. He hated that Hunter thought an apology could put things right between them. And he hated that he'd lied.

"I should have reacted more... professionally," Hunter said. "But you see why I don't trust people who have magic."

Morgan swallowed. "Not entirely. What I see is why you don't trust liars." He risked a look at Hunter. His frown had softened somewhat: he looked more puzzled than anything. "I can understand that. But I had my reasons. Hasn't anyone ever hated you for something you couldn't change about yourself? Your sexuality, for example."

"It's not the same."

"It must have been an issue when you were a police officer. I know you see a bunch of smiley coppers at Pride these days, but I'm not convinced they're representative of a one hundred per cent out and proud force."

"No. No, not exactly."

"Must have been a shock, coming out of a happy-clappy liberal private school and running into homophobia."

"Not really. My father was pretty disgusting when I came out to him. But I never lied about it."

"So you tell everyone you meet?"

"Don't be ridiculous, Morgan. It's not the same."

"Why not? Come on, Hunter, tell me. Do you think we should wear some kind of bracelet with a danger symbol on it, like they do in Texas?"

Hunter flinched.

"Or maybe a tattoo, in case we leave the bracelet at home. Like they used to in Ireland."

"Stop it."

"I would have told you, when the time was right." Would he? He'd imagined it. That must count for something. "Besides, it's not like it changes anything. I knew you'd dump me when you found out. It's probably best it happened fast. Before anyone got too attached."

Hunter made a soft, low sort of noise and turned to the kitchen door. Morgan slammed the dishwasher shut and followed him; he was on a roll now and didn't want his quarry to escape so easily.

"I'm sorry I wasn't good enough," Morgan said. "Is that what you wanted to hear?"

Hunter span around and grabbed Morgan's arms; Morgan braced himself for violence, thinking he'd pushed too far. He didn't care. But Hunter didn't hit him. Didn't even shout at him. He just looked at him, and he wasn't angry so much as hurt, and sad. Morgan felt a pang of shame through the fury.

Hunter pulled Morgan in and kissed him, hard. Morgan surrendered to it like a switch had been flicked. His head was spinning. His body trembled.

"You might not have got attached," Hunter said. "But I fucking did."

Morgan stared at him, helpless.

"Goodnight, Morgan."

And Hunter walked away, leaving Morgan with a clump of damp, gritty soap dissolving in his hand.

Chapter Twenty-One

Morgan smiled at the man with the cash box and said, "Two, please."

It was the same smile he'd used on the bouncers outside, and it had worked on them. But the cashier - late twenties, pierced everything and a neck tattoo - frowned and said, "Don't I know you from somewhere?"

Hunter tensed at Morgan's side. Morgan smiled again, putting a little extra twinkle in his eye, and tried to relax enough for both of them.

The cashier said, "Wait, I know! Leeds Station. Starbucks."

Morgan thought he'd seen those tattoos before. "You work there."

"And you buy tea there."

The guy smiled at him, and Morgan turned the twinkle in his eyes down a tad. "Moonlighting here, then?"

"Yeah, well, Starbucks pays the bills; a guy's got to think outside the box if he wants a social life. Speaking of, here you go." He produced two tickets from his cash box, matt black with the tiniest gold lettering in the lower right hand corner, announcing the date and the name Bubble. "Fifty each."

Morgan took care not to flinch as he handed over a hundred pounds in cash. Hunter had better buy the drinks. The guy quickly counted the notes and stashed them away in his cash box.

"Have a great night, now." He winked at them.

"I'll claim it on expenses," Hunter whispered, as they followed the screen lined corridor into the club.

They reached the curtains that led to the ground floor, and Morgan could hear music and chatter beyond. An old music hall song on the speakers, packed with innuendo about a chamber maid, an earl and a feather duster. He didn't sense anything out of the ordinary. Hunter held back the curtain for him and ushered him inside. The room was about two thirds full.

"That table," Hunter murmured, indicating a spot to their right. "Good view."

It was, of course, the perfect pick: it gave them a clear view of the dungeon door and the main entrance. Their view of the stage was marginally impaired by a pillar, but that was fine. Morgan wasn't here to watch the show.

They sat down and Hunter asked, "Do you do that often?"

"Do what?"

"That magic you worked on the doorman. Getting people to like you."

"It doesn't work quite like that. But, no, I don't. And for the record, I never used my magic on you in any shape or form."

"That wasn't what—"

"Yes it was."

Hunter grunted and stared down at the table.

"I wouldn't. On anyone. Not without their permission. Not unless it was really important."

"So long as you're in control."

"I usually am."

"Usually. That's why magic is so dangerous, isn't it? You can't be a hundred per cent in control all the time. Nobody can."

"You could say the same about cars. Or guns. The only difference is I can't put it down. It's part of me. I work damn hard to stay safe. And it's not like I chose to take Essence. Someone else did that to me against my will."

Hunter bit his lip against whatever counter argument he might have come up with (and Morgan had heard a lot in his time, most of them infuriating) and called a waiter over. He ordered two posh lemonades, the sort that came in screw-top bottles with wax seals on top. Tamper proof.

"If there's trouble tonight, will you lose control?" Hunter asked.

"No." Morgan hoped that was true. His track record hadn't been exactly stellar lately, but he knew how to handle himself. He'd put in a whole morning of meditation and training. He just had to keep a hold on his emotions.

"And if you do?"

Morgan smirked at him. He couldn't help himself. "Run."

Hunter rolled his eyes and opened his lemonade. "Sahil said he did something to you to stop you going ballistic. In the park. Like Harlequin did here."

"They grounded me. That's when someone who doesn't have magic acts as a conduit to help a majos regain their control."

"Just by touching you?"

"There's a bit more to it than that. Didn't they train you in the police force?"

Hunter looked a bit uncomfortable.

"Or did you skip the majos part of the curriculum?" said Morgan. "Bloody hell, you did, didn't you?"

"It was optional."

"Like hell it was. Is that why you got turned down for promotion?"

"Wait." Hunter put a hand on Morgan's arm. "There's Caleb."

Caleb strode across the room with Jennifer - who looked stunning in a clingy red dress and matching stilettos - and a slender, dark-haired guy who must be Dave. He looked older than Morgan had imagined, but undeniably handsome. Caleb was wearing a sparkly silver top. He spoke animatedly to the bouncer by the dungeon door. Morgan kept his eyes down, showing no apparent interest, but watching out of the corner of his eye.

The bouncer spoke into his walky-talky. For a moment Morgan thought he was getting Caleb chucked out. But instead a waiter arrived with a tray, bearing the now familiar masks and key. Caleb and his dates were shown into the playroom. Just as the door opened, the house lights dimmed, obscuring Morgan's view, and the music changed. The dancers were on their way to the stage. Morgan pulled out his phone and set a timer for twenty minutes. He felt it was way too long, but Caleb had wanted an hour, so they'd compromised.

"You okay?" Hunter asked.

"Fine."

"You seem a bit…"

"I'm fine."

Morgan took a gulp of sharp, bitter lemonade. The door to the playroom opened a few times, letting masked people through. Morgan tried to focus on the stage, like Hunter was, but his eyes were continually drawn to that big fake-wood door and he itched to rush in and find out what was happening behind it.

The minutes ticked down: Fifteen to go, ten to go. One of the fan dancers threw her bra and it landed on Hunter's head. Morgan forced himself to laugh, just like he would have if he hadn't been increasingly terrified for Caleb and residually mad at Hunter.

The door to the basement opened again, this time from the inside. Morgan hadn't seen that before; it seemed that once they'd got in, people stayed down there 'til the place shut. The guy who guarded it from all except the lucky key holders gave the opening door a startled look, then held it open as the person came through from the other side.

It was Jennifer. She was crying.

Morgan nudged Hunter's elbow, but he was busy disentangling himself from the bra. Jennifer returned her mask to the doorman. He tried to console her, even offered her his handkerchief, but she shoved him away and went straight to the bar.

Hunter and Morgan exchanged a glance. Hunter flicked his eyes at the bar. Morgan nodded and headed in that direction, trying not to look conspicuous.

Jennifer had a queue of different-coloured jelly shots lined up by the time he got there, and she was making short work of them. Morgan asked for another lemonade and said to Jennifer, "You okay?"

"No." Jennifer downed another shot and let out a long hiss of a sigh. "It's Morgan, right? Did Caleb tell you about this place?"

"Yes. Hi. Can I ask what's wrong?"

Her eyes flashed with fury. Morgan fought the urge to flinch. "Men. Bloody men. Specifically, my husband. It was his idea to invite another guy into our bed. It was supposed to be a threesome. To think, I was worried he'd get jealous. Ha! How wrong can you be?" She picked up her last shot and raised it in the air. "Thank you Caleb Davies, for ruining my marriage."

"Oh dear."

"Apparently my husband prefers the company of

men. Well, one man. Do you?"

"Do I what?"

"Prefer the company of men?"

"I, uh, well…"

"Of course you do. The ones with the prettiest eyelashes are always gay. Excuse me!" She waved at the bartender. "Another rainbow. And a vodka tonic."

"I'll be with you in a moment." The bar tender put down Morgan's lemonade. "Shall I put this on your boyfriend's tab?"

"Oh. He's not, I mean, yes."

"You're blushing," Jennifer observed.

"It's hot," murmured Morgan. "Are they still in there, then, your husband and Caleb?"

"Oh, no. No, no, no, no. Dave - that's my husband, the slimy piece of shit - took him off to a private room, no less. To meet the great Mr Appleford himself." She burped, none too delicately, then added, "Without me."

"Perhaps they're just going to talk," Morgan suggested.

Jennifer laughed, bitterly, and finished her last shot.

"So." Morgan kept his voice as casual as possible, although the state she was in he didn't suppose she'd notice. "Where are these private rooms? I haven't heard of them before."

"Me neither," said Jennifer, darkly. "It's all very hush hush."

A cold chill ran down Morgan's spine.

"Sorry, got to go." Morgan jerked his head towards Hunter. "Um. I'm sorry." He was about to flee, but turned back at the last moment and said, "You know, Caleb's a good guy. He would never knowingly hurt you. You should know that. Right. Bye."

Then he hurried back to Hunter, who got to his feet the minute he saw Morgan's expression.

"We have to get in the playroom. Caleb's in trouble."

"What? How do you–"

Morgan gave Hunter a stern 'trust me' look, and took his hand to drag him over to the door. The doorman blocked their way, ready to turn them back. But then Morgan's encanté hit him and he said, "You'll need these." He produced a couple of masks and a key, opened the door and ushered them inside.

"I'm not taking my clothes off," Hunter said, as they approached the changing area.

"Me neither. We're not here to socialise. We're looking for another exit from the playroom. Follow me."

"There is no other exit. We checked every square inch. Twice, now."

"There must be somewhere down there. What about the pipes?"

"What pipes?"

"There's a water pipe goes under the playroom. I could feel it."

"Must be the mains."

"No, that runs up the street and under the reception area. This was different. Part of the heating, or the cooling system, maybe?"

"There's nothing there, Morgan."

"Not that you can see."

"What do you mean?"

"There's ways to hide things, Hunter. Even from you."

A secret room, then. The perfect place to murder someone. Morgan felt sick. Not Caleb. Please, not Caleb. "There's a door in there and we need to find it. Where would you look first?"

Hunter frowned in concentration. "Probably not the walls. Two are exterior and the others are behind furniture. The floor, though. There could be a basement, I suppose. There's an alcove, in the southwest corner. Behind the curtain, where there's those shelves with the fancy flavoured lubricants on it. It's the only logical space. Everywhere else is in full view of people or buried under furniture."

Morgan could have kissed Hunter just for the power of his logic. "Right. That's where we're headed."

"I don't see how we'll get there fully dressed without being challenged."

"Well, there is a way."

"How? Can you do your little Jedi mind trick with the whole room?"

"I could. But it would take a while. So... okay, you're not going to like this."

"Like what?" said Hunter, suspiciously.

"I could use majos on us."

Hunter took a step back.

"It won't hurt. It really won't."

"No." He actually looked quite pale.

"Okay, okay. You stay here. I'll go in alone. If I'm not out in ten minutes call Sahil."

"Oh. Right."

Morgan took a breath, pulling magic around him like a cloak.

"Wait." Hunter touched his arm. "I'm coming with you."

"Better get your kit off, then."

"No. Your way. I'll do it. Or let you do it." He lifted his chin bravely, every bit of him tense, bracing himself. "Invisible me."

"I'm not going to make you invisible."

"But you said–"

"That's not how it works. Here." He folded one hand around Hunter's arm and touched his tree necklace with his other. He took a few deep breaths and let the magic flow around them both. "People will see us, if they look straight at us. But they won't care. We'll be as unremarkable as a cloud on a rainy day. Unless they know us. It won't work on Caleb, but it might on whoever's in there with him. So stay quiet and don't do anything unexpected."

"All right, then." Hunter squinched his eyes shut. "Do it."

Morgan leaned in and whispered in his ear. "I already did."

Then he led Hunter down the corridor to the play room. It was taking all he had to keep things tight, to stop him from tearing through the room with magic and fury until he knew Caleb was safe. They made their way around the edge of the room, stepping carefully over a couple sixty-nining on a pile of cushions.

"Here," said Hunter, voice so low Morgan barely made it out over the chorus of moans and slapping flesh around them. Hunter edged the curtain back with one elbow. Morgan held his necklace and whispered, "*Veritat.*"

The illusion that had been laid over the floor peeled away, leaving the seam of an old-fashioned wooden trap door.

"Shit," said Hunter, wide-eyed.

"What was here before?" Morgan asked. "Before the offices, I mean?"

"An old merchant's house, according to the records."

That explained the old brick walls and the thick floorboards under the rugs. And the trapdoor. "Down there has to be the basement of the original building, then."

"Looks like. A cellar, maybe?"

Morgan reached out a hand to the trap door. His fingers tingled. He closed his eyes and listened. There was the roar of water, rushing through the pipes. Except, now his mind was clear of drugs and devastating emotion he could sense more deeply. It wasn't ordinary water. No wonder he'd manifested aigua that day. Those pipes were full of it. "Open the door," Morgan said. "I'm going down."

"Let me go first. You're–"

"Puny, yes I know. And I'm also majos. I know what I'm dealing with down there. You don't."

Hunter blanched, but he opened up the trapdoor and peered inside. Morgan peered with him. There was a step ladder leading down to a corridor - more of a tunnel, really - dimly lit by a rope of LED lights, like some kind of seedy disco.

"Here goes," said Morgan, lowering himself onto the first rung of the ladder.

He went down slowly, careful not to make any noise. When he was at the bottom he indicated for Hunter to join him, and padded as softly as he could to a door at the end of the passageway. He paused to listen again, his ear pressed tight against the rough surface of the wood. The rush of water and magic purred along with the whirring of some kind of machinery.

He felt Hunter's presence behind him.

"There's something very wrong here," he whispered.

And then Caleb screamed.

Chapter Twenty-Two

Morgan kept his magic coiled up tight and pushed the door open. He took in as much as he could of the scene beyond in the first few seconds. Caleb was naked and strapped down in a metal chair, his mouth taped over. The room was lit with harsh strip lights and a couple of naked bulbs, but the pipe against the back wall glowed, aigua writhing around its surface. Dave, dressed in a greyish-white bathrobe, was leaning over Caleb, fiddling with something on Caleb's arm. He was muttering unconvincing reassurances: "It's only a bit, he won't take it all, you don't mind, do you? Help a mate out, Caleb, there's a good boy."

Caleb wasn't moving.

"What the fuck?" Hunter murmured.

Morgan's mind ran fast. Dave hadn't noticed them yet, and it gave Morgan time to take in the whole room. The pipe full of aigua was connected to an engine at one end and a tarnished brass tube at the other which was in turn connected via a spigot to a long rubber hose. Shit, he knew what this was. He'd seen it in books.

"Hunter, that's a life-taker," he whispered.

Hunter flashed him a look of total incomprehension.

"The machine. It drains people of their esper."

"Majos."

"Sorry to break it to you, but everyone has esper to some degree. Even you."

Hunter looked suitably horrified. "But–"

"Shh." Morgan took a step closer. The hose seemed to be connected to the chair. Wait - no. Not the chair.

It was connected to Caleb, by a crude approximation of a cannula and plastic line stuck into the crook of his elbow. Dave was taping it in place with duct tape, while a trickle of Caleb's blood fell down his arm and onto his bare thigh.

Morgan's magic surged; his mind filled with thoughts of water, a wave surging, soaking, drowning. *No.* Not now. He evened out his breathing, replacing the panicked flow of images with logical, calming thoughts. They were going to free Caleb and get him out of here. Dave didn't look to be in the best physical shape: he was pale and thin; sweat beaded at his temples and his hands shook as he wound the tape around Caleb's arm. To Morgan's relief he saw Caleb's chest rise and fall. He was alive, at least.

"You be ready to distract him if necessary," Hunter

whispered. "I'll restrain him from behind, quick as I can."

Morgan made his way slowly towards Caleb, while Hunter moved behind Dave. Dave's head was down, tearing off a strip of tape with his teeth. He didn't stand a chance. Hunter grabbed him and in one smooth, economical movement pulled his arms back behind him, tugging enough to elicit a yelp of pain. He caught the tape before it hit the floor and wrapped Dave's wrists up tight.

Dave yelled, "What the fuck?!" as Hunter shoved him down to his knees.

Morgan froze half way to Caleb. The door he and Hunter had come through was still open, and Morgan sensed something, someone, in the corridor. Morgan spun around to see a man step into the room. Not very tall, but wide and solid, with a neck like a bulldog. He was dressed in a beer-stained Man U vest and tatty jeans. The door closed behind him.

Dave struggled in Hunter's grasp like a fish on a line.

"Well, well," the man said. "What have we here?"

"N-nothing," Dave said. "An in-inconvenience. We can still do it, he's still–"

"Paul Bates," said Hunter.

The blackmailer who'd filmed the furry in a car park. Who'd put Hunter in hospital. Shit.

"Damien Hunter," said Bates. "Private dick." He drew out the word 'dick' and clicked his tongue against his teeth at the end, sending a string of spittle flying across the room.

"You're Appleford?" said Morgan.

Bates took a deep mock-bow. "At your service."

"We're taking these men out of here," said Hunter. "And you're not going to stop us."

"Am I not?"

Morgan felt the surge of magic a split second before it manifested. A ball of ice appeared in the air just ahead of Bates' outstretched palm. He sent it with a savage shove and the ice shot towards Hunter's chest.

Morgan deflected it with a flick of his wrist.

Paul Bates wasn't majos. The magic in that ice wasn't his. It was a confusing mess of a thing, like common street Essence. The product of more than one majos.

"Will you look at that," Bates said, his gaze settling on Morgan with a greedy leer. "He's oozing fucking fairy juice like piss from a drunk."

Hunter glanced nervously at Morgan. "If we keep calm and think sensibly, we can all leave here alive," Hunter said. He took a few careful steps away from Dave, towards Bates.

"Where's the fun in that?" Bates said. "I mean, it's not like I need any of you to be breathing."

Dave sobbed.

"Not even your mate here?" said Hunter. "I know how keen you are on taking care of your mates."

Bates laughed. His laugh was even nastier than his leering. "Oh, but Dave isn't a mate, are you, Dave? Dave is a pathetic middle aged weasel who can't get it up for his wife anymore. He promised me a nice juicy battery and in return I promised him a little something to slip into his tea when he wants to get frisky. Have you ever taken Viagra? No? Well, big strapping boy like you, probably never needed to. It fucks up your heart, they say. Keeps you hard for hours. Whether you want it or not. My little bottle of fun? Entirely different. No side effects, no unwanted post-coital stiffie. Just the libido of a healthy teenager and a high like nothing else. Ain't that right, weasel?"

Dave wailed. It distracted Morgan just enough that Bates' magic almost slipped past him. A block of ice materialised above Morgan's head, threatening to crash down on him. Crude. Fast. Powerful. Morgan dashed it away at the last moment, but his magic was seething and the struggle to keep it under control made him slow.

Next time the magic came faster and it was aimed not at Hunter, Morgan or Caleb, but at Dave. The tape around his wrists dissolved in a flash of fire. He screamed; Hunter lunged for him, but Bates was too fast. No magic this time; Bates got his head down and charged like a bull, thudding into Hunter's stomach and forcing the air out of his lungs. The man looked freakishly strong; his muscles rippled as he pinned Hunter down, sitting on his thighs and holding down both wrists. He yelled at Dave. "Forget the twink, get the majos, you moron!"

"I don't know," whined Dave, cradling his scorched hands to his chest. "This isn't what I signed on for, Paul.

I didn't want anyone to get hurt."

"Jesus fuck, do I have to do everything my fucking self?"

Hunter thrashed around wildly, but Paul's grip stayed firm. With a sick feeling in the pit of his stomach, Morgan realised there was something very unnatural about that strength. Then he noticed Bates was wearing a silver bracer on one arm, a gleaming serpent twisting around his right bicep. It took a fuck of a lot of life to make a tiny bit of esper, especially from people who weren't majos. How many people had died for that bracelet?

Morgan took a few steps backwards, towards Caleb, with his hands up. "Let Hunter and Caleb go, and you can have my magic instead. No need for violence. I'll give it up voluntarily."

"No!" Hunter gasped out, breathless under the pressure Bates was applying to his chest.

"I mean, what have you got to bargain with, really?" Bates said. "Seems to me I'm the one with all the cards here." He looked at Hunter with a nasty grin on his face. "Shall I dislocate the other shoulder this time? Or break that wrist I pulled out of whack? I wouldn't want to make a mess of that pretty face of yours… Or would I?"

"I get it," said Morgan, keen to keep him talking. "You're the one who blackmailed your mate."

"One of my best customers. Until his wife found out. Nasty business." He tightened his grip on Hunter's wrists.

"Same business, different venue," Hunter spat. "Did you get chilly finding punters in the car park and decide to take the party indoors?"

Morgan took another step backwards, while Bates was busy scowling at Hunter.

Bates said, "A good businessman never puts all his eggs in one basket, Mr Hunter. Now then, what to do with you? Maybe I'll just kill you. But I'm going to make sure your dwimmer boyfriend gets sucked dry first. Dave. Get that scrawny waste of space out of that chair."

Hunter roared and made a monumental effort to throw Bates off, but all Bates did was laugh.

Morgan rolled up his sleeve.

Dave scuttled to the chair while Hunter writhed and scrabbled. Morgan couldn't look, couldn't listen. He was too close to the edge as it was. He had to keep control.

Come on, Guapo. Take out the bad guys. You know what you can do. This is what you were born for. Not all that nonsense in the office. You're a spirit of fuego and aigua and hielo. I think the time for caution is passed, no?

Morgan smiled.

Yes.

God, yes.

He held out one hand, and in his palm coiled a ball of energy, flickering gold and silver, crackling with blue-black sparks. "Let them go," he said. "And this is yours."

Bates laughed at him. "That all you can do?"

Morgan tossed the ball of relámpago to his other

hand. "Oh, no. This is just the beginning. Do you want it, or not? Or, should I say, how do you want it? In that machine or between your nasty little eyes?"

"If you let that off you'll kill yourself too." Bates' voice had lost some of its certainty. "And your friends."

"If it was in the hands of a charlatan like you, maybe. Not me. See, I know exactly what I'm doing with this. I control it. I say where it goes, who it hurts."

"Like you did with your friend the other night? Is that what you call control?"

Morgan felt so strange. So calm. Caleb and Hunter needed him. That was all that mattered. He couldn't have cared less about anything this pathetic little man had to say.

"Nice bit of bling you've got there on your arm," Morgan said. "Silver, is it?"

"Silver and a little bit extra," he smirked.

"Perfect," said Morgan. He pulled a thread of energy from the globe still spinning in his palm, drawing it out like soft caramel. He let it settle into its own ball, no bigger than a pea.

"Any lightning you throw my direction, it's going straight to your boyfriend here."

Morgan flexed his fingers; lightning danced around him.

"I'm not afraid of you," Bates said.

"But you should be," said Morgan, and flicked the extracted energy at Bates' arm.

It popped and crackled into the metal of his bracer; Bates' face contorted into a grimace of pain. Footsteps scuffled in the direction of the door; Morgan didn't turn, just said in a calm, clear voice, "Stay where you are, Dave. You're far more conductive than your friend here."

Dave made a sobbing, retching sound, but he stopped running.

"Good boy," said Morgan, and then, to Bates, "Let Hunter go, and lay face down on the floor."

Bates snatched up Hunter's arm, holding his forearm with one hand and his fingers with the other. "You try that again and he better learn to wank left handed."

"Get off him, or you'll have to learn to wank with a fried dick," Morgan replied, surging power through the ball of relámpago in his hand.

Bates' bracer responded, the silver shimmering with contained magic. Morgan smiled. He fixed on the smooth, shiny surface of the metal, and let his magic seep into it, a steady flow of liquid energy, until there was screaming and Bates was staring at him with bulging eyes; he let go of Hunter, who scrambled to his feet and ran towards Caleb. Morgan kept pushing power into the silver bracer, charging and charging, until the pain got too much for Bates and he clawed at the lethal cuff, trying to get it off.

Morgan broke the flow just as the circuit closed and the bracer discharged itself, forks of lightning sparking over Bates' arms in pulses, running through his body to arc into the pipes behind him. Magic called by magic.

Bates sobbed, wrenching at the bracer. Finally it

fell, empty and useless, thudding to the floor, leaving Bates' arm a blackened mess. The power left him all at once and he fell down.

"Is he dead?" whimpered Dave.

"No," said Morgan. His skin prickled, his blood fizzed. He squeezed his eyes tight shut and fell to his knees. "But you'd better run, you'd all better run, or you will be."

Morgan heard Hunter's yell of "Morgan!", and there were scuffling sounds, and Dave was crying again. Morgan tried to shut it out, fighting to pull the power back inside of him. He grasped his necklace but it wasn't enough. His muscles went rigid; he shook his hands and sparks flew and then-

"Morgan, I'm here." Caleb's voice. Shaky and rough, but Caleb. "I'm a bit rusty at this, but I'm going to ground you, okay?"

Morgan didn't dare move enough to speak. Caleb grasped Morgan's shoulder and his power swirled and solidified, ready to strike. The world stopped; colours went bright; the roar of the machine was deafening. Morgan focused on Caleb's breathing, ragged but familiar, and let him take over.

Morgan's magic discharged harmlessly into the ground beneath their feet, through the concrete and brick and the rubble and into the sweet, clean earth beyond.

"I got you," Caleb said. He cradled Morgan's body as he fell back. "I got you."

"I think that's my line," Morgan said, and then he

passed out cold.

Chapter Twenty-Three

Morgan's magic simmered under his skin. He had a hold on it, but it was still very much there, bright and alive, making everything sharp and ultra-real. It was a relief to be in the familiar surroundings of the flat, Caleb sitting close to him on the couch. He looked really pale, but God, it was good to see him alive and awake and talking and mostly okay. Harlequin sat on the other couch, opening up the containers of take out they'd bought on their way back from Bubble, once the paramedics and the police had let them go. Jess and Sahil had done a great job of keeping the focus away from Morgan's magic and firmly on Bates and Dave. Eventually there would be statements and interviews, and for Morgan a full majos review and all the documentation and risk assessments that went with it. But for now, they were free.

Hunter and Darius joined them from the kitchen with a tray of drinks. Morgan gratefully picked up his mug of valerian tea and nestled it in his hands. The others mostly had alcohol, and he couldn't blame them, but he noticed Hunter was drinking tea, too - Yorkshire tea with milk and sugar. Morgan remembered making tea in the office for Hunter, and got a little ache in his chest.

Darius handed round plates for the food. Morgan hesitated; he wasn't really hungry, as if the magic had filled the gaps in his stomach, but he knew he should eat.

"Let me," said Hunter, taking his plate from him. "What do you like? Pakora? Bhuna? Pilau? Naan?"

"Thank you. Anything. Not too much. Oh, and no meat."

"I remember," said Hunter. Was it Morgan's imagination, or did he sound a bit wistful?

"Here." Morgan patted the space to the right of him on the couch. "I promise you won't get majos cooties."

Hunter ducked his head, and piled Morgan's plate up with food.

"Can we talk about what happened?" Harlequin asked. "I'm a bit sketchy on the details, but if you don't want to talk about it, that's fine."

"Morgan saved us all," Caleb said.

Morgan expected Hunter to protest or mutter something about magic, but instead he said, "He fucking did." Then he gave Morgan a huge plate of food, looked him in the eye and said, "It was the most amazing thing I've ever seen."

Morgan's breath stuttered, and he almost dropped Leeds' finest Indian cuisine all over the floor. Hunter steadied his plate for him.

Harlequin cleared his throat.

"I wish I'd seen it," Darius said.

"It was awesome," Caleb said. "But seriously, no, you did not want to be there."

"You were the awesome one," said Morgan. "If you hadn't grounded me the whole place would be one great fireworks show right now, with us in the middle of it."

"I'm sure Hunter would have done it if I hadn't," Caleb said. "Police training, right?"

Hunter muttered something non-committal and sat down next to Morgan. His thigh was very warm against Morgan's thigh, even through layers of denim. Morgan could smell his aftershave, woody with a hint of citrus. He shovelled a forkful of vegetable pakora into his mouth to keep his mind off it. It was delicious, as if every taste bud had sprung to life. He let the others' conversation fade into the background and focused on eating.

"It's all right," Caleb told Hunter, when Morgan paused for breath half way through his plateful. "Using magic takes energy. He needs this."

"Stop talking about me like I'm not here," Morgan grumbled.

"We weren't entirely sure you were," Caleb said.

Now he'd taken the edge off a bit, Morgan slowed down and ate the rest of his meal at a steadier pace. When he'd done, Hunter gave him seconds, and he ate that too. Finally he refused thirds, let Hunter take his empty plate and leaned back in the sofa, comfortably full, lips tingling from the spices. It was heavenly.

Caleb's voice drifted into his consciousness again. "So basically. My lover sold me for a shot of magic Viagra."

"I still don't know what you saw in him," Darius said. "You can do so much better, darling."

"Yes, you can," said Harlequin.

"He was very eager to please," Caleb said. "He didn't seem to have any trouble getting it up when I was fucking his wife."

"His wife thinks he chose you over her," Morgan said.

"Is that what they were fighting about?" Caleb said. "I couldn't hear. Dave said she was on her period."

"He's such a wanker," said Morgan.

"It's not exactly a good advert for polyamory," Hunter pointed out.

"Don't blame polyamory," said Harlequin. "Any relationship is only as good as the people in it."

"Thank you," Caleb said, with a little bow in Harlequin's direction. "Besides, Damian, I think you'll find yours and Morgan's relationship was nearly as much of a clusterfuck. Would you blame monogamy? I mean, I presume you were monogamous, Morgan's kind of old fashioned that way."

"Actually, I blame myself," Hunter said.

Morgan looked at him, startled, but Hunter didn't quite meet his eye. He was suddenly very busy stacking plates and sealing up leftovers instead.

"At least you two have a healthy relationship," Morgan said to Darius and Harlequin, at least partly to take some of the attention off Hunter.

"It's all about boundaries, darling," said Darius. "Knowing which ones you can cross, which ones are fundamental. Which ones are up for negotiation."

He looked at Caleb when he said that.

Hunter said, "I'll just go and, um," and got up to take the plates and things into the kitchen.

"I'll help," said Morgan, quickly.

He followed Hunter with a tray full of crockery, which he deposited on the draining board.

"You should rest," Hunter said.

"I'm fine. Besides. Something was going on back there and I'm not sure what it was."

"Glad it's not just me."

"It's been a very strange night."

Morgan leaned back against the kitchen counter and watched Hunter load the dishwasher. He was very efficient about it. When he'd done that he carefully stacked the leftovers in the fridge.

"So," he said, once everything was tidied away. "I should probably go."

Morgan realised he'd zoned out again, watching Hunter. He hadn't helped with the dishes at all, he's just been staring. Still, Hunter didn't seem to mind.

"Well, um, thanks. For everything."

"It's nothing. So. Right."

Morgan opened the kitchen door to let Hunter

through. He felt unaccountably sad.

They didn't get any further than the living room, though. Caleb was curled up in Harlequin's arms, but not in a romantic way, as Morgan had half-expected. He was crying. Harlequin was comforting him, while Darius knelt in front of him, a worried frown on his face.

"What happened?" Morgan asked.

"I'll get some tea," said Hunter.

Morgan sat next to Caleb and took his hand. Caleb hung on with a surprisingly strong grip, sobs stuttering to a close. "G-god, I'm s-such a mess."

"You've been through a very traumatic incident," said Harlequin. "A bit of psychological distress is to be expected."

"You're safe now," Morgan said. "You're home. Nothing's going to hurt you here."

"One minute I was going through the trapdoor, next thing I know Hunter's slapping me in the face and I was hooked up to that thing. If you hadn't–"

"We did," Morgan said, firmly. "That's all that matters."

Darius asked, "What did they do to him?"

"Bates had a machine that distils esper from peoples' blood. He must have got majos to make things out of it for him."

"Including Essence?" Harlequin asked.

"Yes."

Caleb sniffed. "So that's why you couldn't trace the Essence. If he was making it, and he's not majos, you wouldn't have recognised it."

Harlequin frowned. Morgan let Caleb's misapprehension go unchallenged, and continued the story. "He used sex parties to find punters and victims. All sorts of sex parties. He blackmailed or bribed people into that basement."

"Then there's more than two victims?" said Harlequin.

"Probably. If anyone survived the machine I suppose he shut them up one way or another."

"Oh God," Caleb whimpered.

"Come on, sweetie," said Darius. "Let's get you all tucked up in bed."

"He asked we'd stay the night," Harlequin said to Morgan. "Is that all right? He's scared of sleeping alone."

"Of course."

Hunter returned with a tray of tea, and Caleb took one with a grateful shadow of his usual smile.

Morgan stroked Caleb's hair back from his face. "You should get some rest." His cheeks were flushed from crying and there were dark smudges under his eyes, a mix of eyeliner and exhaustion. Caleb nodded.

"Do you need blankets or anything?" Morgan asked.

"Bed's plenty big enough for three," said Caleb and took a sip of tea.

"We'll be fine," said Harlequin.

The three of them went off to Caleb's room, leaving Hunter and Morgan alone with four cups of tea and a suddenly quiet living room.

"Right," said Hunter, eventually. "Definitely time to go. You need your rest, too."

Morgan saw him to the door. The pile of letters from Caleb's mother was a little taller. He'd have to ask him about that soon. When he'd recovered a bit.

Instead of opening the door, Morgan paused with his hand on the handle, looked at Hunter and said, "For what it's worth, it's not only your fault. You were right, I shouldn't have lied to you."

"It must have been difficult."

"It was. It always is."

"What you did today, it was… I had no idea what magic even was. In the right hands. What you did was so brave and selfless. I keep thinking about you standing there with that ball of fucking lightning in your hand. You were so bloody beautiful."

Morgan was a barely-balanced blend of magic, impulse and intuition, his control run ragged and thin, and thinking wasn't his strong point at that moment. Should he keep his dignity, gracefully accept the compliment and show Hunter out?

Whether he should or not, he didn't. He got up really close to Hunter, close enough to take a deep breath of his aftershave. And then, when Hunter didn't move away, Morgan hugged him. The next thing he knew, he was being pressed into the door while Hunter kissed him insensible.

"I'm sorry," Hunter gasped out, pressing his lips to Morgan's temple. "I was such an arse and I don't deserve you, but, please, could we give it another chance?

Morgan's brain wasn't working quite right. This was not how he'd expected this weirdest of all days to end. "Just to be clear. Are you offering me a job or a fuck?"

Hunter pulled back just far enough that Morgan could see his expression. He was grinning. "How about both? And, maybe, if you want, more than a fuck. I don't want to rush you. I can wait, if you're not–"

"Yes. No waiting. Please, no waiting." Hunter groaned and squeezed Morgan's arse. A shot of lust ran up Morgan's spine and his magic surged. Shit. "Wait."

"What?"

"Just a minute. Not wait-wait, just, give me a moment, okay? One moment."

He fled to his room and shut the door.

His spell book was waiting for him on the bed where he'd left it. He quickly flicked it open and put his hand on the picture of the dragon.

The air above the book shimmered and glittered into Aiyeda. She shuffled onto the bed and regarded Morgan sideways out of one golden, slitted eye. "You've been busy, Guapo."

"It's been a bit of a night. Look, I need you to be very, very good, okay?"

The golden, slitted eye narrowed.

"Please, Aiyeda. I need you to hide in the wardrobe."

"What?" The word came out with a little puff of smoke.

"There's things I need, want, I mean, well, probably both, anyway, the thing is Hunter doesn't exactly know how this whole majos thing works, especially," he flicked his finger from himself to Aiyeda and back again, "this, and I don't want to freak him out."

"I understand. It is perfectly simple, yes? Make him go away."

"I don't want him to go away. I want him to be here. As in," he pointed at the bed, "here."

Aiyeda wrinkled up her snout. "You want to do the kissy kissy thing?"

"I really, really do. But he's not ready to meet you yet. Please, Aiyeda. I need you, I've got so much magic and sometimes when I–"

"Yes, yes, I know. I remember what happened when you were watching that movie with the naked men in it. It was all very messy."

"That was a long time ago."

"And yet, here we are again. Very well. I will do as you ask. Under certain conditions. First, there will be a pillow in there. A nice fluffy one."

Morgan quickly took the fluffiest pillow off the bed and put it in the bottom of the wardrobe, shoving a pile of shoes into the corner.

Aiyeda watched him, clearly unimpressed. "I want cartoons in there."

"I can't. The iPad's out of battery."

"Ah well. No kissy kissy for Morgan."

"I know! There's an anime festival at the cinema next week. I'll take you."

Aiyeda's jaw dropped. "At the cartoon theatre?"

"Yes. If you're good. You'll have to be quiet, not like when we went to see Frozen and I had to charm the woman in front of us before she'd believe you were just a very realistic stuffed toy."

"She'd have been cool."

"Not the point. Do we have a deal?"

Hunter's voice came from the hall. "Morgan, are you okay?"

Morgan looked at Aiyeda with the most pleading expression he could muster.

"Very well," said Aiyeda, shuffling her way off to the wardrobe. "But please don't make too much noise. I shall be trying to sleep."

"That's a great idea. Good. Sleep well." Morgan shut the door the second the little dragon had hopped inside, and called out, "Okay! Ready."

The door opened and Hunter took a tentative step inside. "All right?"

"Yes. Just had to tidy up a bit. You know. Embarrassing stuff. Underwear and… Stuff."

Relief washed the uncertainty off Hunter's face. "Is that all? You shouldn't have worried. It's actually a relief to know you're not a hundred percent tidy and organised at all times."

"Well. You know. Ninety nine per cent."

Hunter chuckled. His eyes flicked to the bed and Morgan's followed. He moved quickly, scooping the magic book up and popping it back on the shelf. Fortunately Hunter didn't comment; he just put his arms around Morgan and kissed him. His mouth was warm and the enthusiastic side of gentle. Morgan kissed him back and tumbled them both onto the bed. Hunter slid his hand up the back of Morgan's tee-shirt; his hand was cool - or perhaps Morgan was just hot, it was hard to tell when he'd been using magic - and he touched all the places Morgan liked best. The base of his spine. The tips of his shoulder blades. The sensitive, mostly-ticklish, soft spot at his waist. Then he gripped Morgan's hipbone, rather possessively, and Morgan let out a happy yelp.

"I missed you so much," Hunter said, between ravishing kisses to Morgan's neck.

Morgan pressed his thigh meaningfully against Hunter's hard on, which was threatening to break free of his jeans of its own accord, it was so eager. "I can tell."

"Not just sex." Hunter kissed his mouth. "All of you."

"But, including the sex."

"Yes, okay, I also missed the sex."

"God." Morgan deftly unbuttoned Hunter's fly. "Me too."

"And I only had you once."

"Twice. I sucked you off in the office, remember?"

"I barely knew you then."

"Oh, I see. So it didn't count."

"Of course it counted, I–"

"Shh. I'm teasing."

Hunter's body relaxed into Morgan's. He sifted his

fingers through Morgan's hair. It might have felt quite innocent, if it weren't for the way their hips were grinding together in a firm, rhythmic manner. Like a heartbeat.

Hunter's eyes drifted closed, and his head tipped back. Morgan nuzzled and licked at his throat, enjoying the way it made Hunter's fingers grip tighter at his hip. He kissed Hunter's Adam's apple as he swallowed, brushed his thumbs over the dip between his collar bones. Hunter's skin tasted of salt and the alcohol-tang of aftershave, and he smelled of magic. Morgan's magic.

"I need you naked," Hunter said.

There was a sneeze from the wardrobe.

Morgan quickly got to his knees and ripped his shirt off, and Hunter gave him a long, appreciative look. But then his eyes flicked to the wardrobe. A puzzled frown pulled his brows together.

"Fuck me," said Morgan, ignoring the frown and the wardrobe as best he could. "Please?"

Hunter may have been one of the most observant people Morgan had ever met, but he was also human with keen sexual interests. He said, "God, love, yes, yes, lube, we need lube," and had Morgan out of his jeans, socks and underwear in seconds while Morgan stuttered at him.

"In the d-drawer by the bed."

Hunter retrieved the lube and Morgan snatched it from him. "Take your clothes off." He flipped the cap.

"You want to do me?" Hunter sounded surprised - but not in any way disapproving.

Morgan had intended to prepare himself while Hunter undressed, because it was a sexy thing to do and anyway, things were likely to be pretty tense down there what with one thing and another. But the idea of Hunter spread out on the bed underneath him, those muscular thighs tight over Morgan's hips as he sank into him… "You switch?" Morgan's voice came out a bit high and strangled.

"Sometimes." Hunter's smile was lopsided and very, very naughty.

"And is this one of those times?" Morgan tried to sound casual, but judging by the flare of arousal in Hunter's eyes, he wasn't very successful.

"It might well be," said Hunter, and pulled his shirt off.

Morgan licked his lips and flicked the cap off the lube.

Hunter kicked off his jeans and underwear, and Morgan shuffled between his legs. He kissed Hunter's belly, his hipbone. He ran his tongue delicately over Hunter's cock, following the big vein that ridged the shaft. He tasted the fluid beading at the tip and his tongue tingled, part from magic and part from pleasure.

Hunter's fingers nestled into his hair again, and Morgan turned his attention to Hunter's balls, licking and nuzzling at them. Hunter rocked his hips back a bit and Morgan ran his finger down to Hunter's hole, just a kiss of his fingertips that brought a gasp out of Hunter and a twitch to Morgan's cock.

The hairs stood up on the back of Morgan's arms,

a tiny crackle of magic. He squeezed a dollop of lube onto this fingers and spread it about, another dollop and pushed it in. Hunter cried out and his hands tightened in Morgan's hair. Morgan waited until Hunter released his grip, and then he started properly to explore. He found the place that made Hunter gasp and whimper and jerk his hips to get more; he emptied half the tube of lube, ignoring Hunter's protestations that he was absolutely ready and Morgan needed to fuck him right now. And finally, Morgan slicked his cock, lined himself up and, so slowly it brought beads of sweat to his temples, he slid inside.

He held himself up, just barely, hands planted either side of Hunter's head and his elbows locked to keep him there. To feel that heat, Hunter's body holding him tight and safe. There was a look in Hunter's eyes that took Morgan's breath away. Fierce with need but vulnerable. Like this was a step he was afraid to take. But wanted to. Not the sex. More than sex.

Morgan took a deep breath, and brushed the hair out of Hunter's eyes. He kissed him, just a gentle touch of lips, and said, "I love you."

Hunter pulled him down, wrapping his arms and legs around him. Morgan's cock slipped out but it didn't matter. Hunter held him so tight, so safe, and said, "This is so fucking scary."

"I know," said Morgan. "Me too."

"I want to be with you. All the time."

There might have been another noise from the wardrobe, but this time Hunter didn't seem to notice.

He was kissing Morgan's face, all over, like an excited Labrador, and said, "I'm glad you said it first, I'm such a fucking coward," and Morgan laughed and then Hunter said, "I love you, I love your magic, I am so very, very fucked."

"You soon will be," Morgan said, breathlessly. He kissed Hunter on the mouth, firmly, thoroughly, until their bodies relaxed and he could get back inside him. Because it felt so very right to be there, to be as close as it was possible to be to another person, where every movement felt important and sweat slicked their skin and everything was so bloody right. He fucked Hunter with long, slow thrusts, his hand wrapped around Hunter's cock, and when Hunter was close he pushed deep inside and stayed there, moving just enough to keep the pleasure sparking. Hunter came with a yell; his arse clenched hard around Morgan and he shot long streams of come over himself and Morgan's hand. Just the smell of it tipped Morgan over, and it only took three quick thrusts for him to get him there. He felt Hunter's body twitch around him; he felt the blessed throb of relief through his balls and his magic surged the instant he let go.

"I love you," Hunter said. "God, Morgan, you crazy wizard, I love you."

And then the wardrobe door crashed open, and Aiyeda belched fire at them.

Chapter Twenty-Four

"I s that a—"

Morgan quickly scattered the carpet with ice, before the sparks that had settled there decided to catch. Flameproofing only went so far.

"I am sorry." Aiyeda hissed to him. "Do you think your amante noticed?"

"It's a dragon," said Hunter, weakly.

"Oh, he noticed," said Morgan.

"I could not help it. You were all kissy kissy and with the passion and the declarations. Would you prefer I set fire to your cupboard?"

"Of course not."

"Well then." Aiyeda waved a claw in Hunter's direction. "Am I to be introduced?"

Well, if Hunter ran away now, at least Morgan had one more happy memory to keep him company. "Okay. Come along."

Hunter was kneeling on the bed, his lower half

wrapped in a sheet. Morgan picked Aiyeda up and cradled her in one arm. She was a bit trembly; for all her bravado he knew she had really done her best to help him. And if it wasn't for her he'd have set fire to the whole room when he'd come, never mind scorched the carpet.

He popped her onto the end of the bed and sat down next to Hunter. "This is Aiyeda," he said. "Aiyeda, this is Damian Hunter. He's a very close friend of mine."

"Phfft, you don't need to tell me that. The door to that cupboard is paper-thin." She gave Hunter a long look, then bowed her head. "A pleasure, I'm sure, Señor Hunter."

"Um," said Hunter. "Hello?"

"Aiyeda is my familiar," Morgan said. "Or, more accurately, she's my magic. A manifestation of my magic."

"Is it real?"

"Oh yes. She's a part of me, but when she comes out into the world she's a separate entity. She has her own personality, and she can think for herself. Magic is more than power, you see."

"You make it sound like possession."

"Modern researchers think it's a kind of symbiotic relationship between the energy of human life and something else. But nobody really knows. Aiyeda's a great help when my magic is a bit too full on and I need to release it safely. It's a bit like grounding, I suppose, except it doesn't make me woozy."

"Does she do what you say?"

Aiyeda snorted. "I am still here, you two who are talking about me as if I was something in a boring book. Of course I do what he says. Now, how about a bit of entertainment, hm? That cupboard was very dark and dull."

"I told you," Morgan said. "My iPad's out of charge."

"Well, this is no problem now I am out of the cupboard, is it?" She gave an evil little waggle of her not inconsiderable eyebrows. "You can plug it in."

Morgan gave Hunter a sheepish grin. "Sorry about this."

Hunter said, "Fine," with a somewhat hysterical edge to his voice. But he watched without comment while Morgan set up his iPad on the desk. He pulled the pillow out of the cupboard and plumped it up on the chair. Hunter did flinch when Aiyeda launched herself with excited little wings to fly over to Morgan, but he didn't protest. Morgan settled her with a very, very long playlist of Roadrunner videos on YouTube, and went back to bed.

"I'll understand, if you can't take all this," Morgan said. "I know it's a lot."

Hunter looked from Aiyeda to Morgan. "It's fine. I mean, no, it's not, you have a fucking *dragon*, but she seems very nice and, um. I meant it."

"Meant what?"

"I love you."

Something blossomed in Morgan's heart, the sort of

magic that wasn't about fire or ice or dragons, and he nestled himself into Hunter's arms.

They propped themselves up against the headboard with pillows, the covers pulled up comfortably to their hips. They held hands, fingers threaded together. Morgan traced Hunter's knuckles, memorising every ridge and hollow. "So, if all this detecting brought us together, any chance you can make up with Jess?"

"What d'you mean?"

Morgan said gently, "I know she's majos."

Hunter sighed. "She's not like you."

"No, but it sounded as if you were so close when you were kids."

"We were. She was different, then." Hunter sighed. "You remember I told you about Mum and the whole magic pregnancy thing? Same thing happened to Jess. Only, she didn't tell me. I found out by accident at Liam's second birthday party."

"How?"

"We were in her kitchen. She was putting candles on his cake, I was waiting to carry it into the living room, where the party was. I had a box of matches all ready in my hand. But she just–" He wiggled his fingers, "–and they lit. By magic."

"Oh."

"She looked horrified. Obviously she hadn't meant for me to find out."

Morgan could imagine that all too well. "It's not her fault, though. It's not like she chose it, anymore than

336

you chose to look at that boy's arse in the gym that day at school."

"But she could have told me."

Like you could have told her you were gay, Morgan thought. But he didn't say it. He and Hunter were at the beginning of something good, and he didn't want to risk it. Twelve hours ago the guy had been terrified of magic. Now he was sitting in Morgan's bed while Aiyeda snorted at cartoons and idly rustled her gleaming golden scales. That was excellent progress for now.

"We bluffed through the party for Liam's sake," Hunter continued. "Liam's dad collected him afterwards. Suddenly the whole divorce thing made sense. Jess and I screamed at each other for a couple of hours. Said some disgusting things, most of which we probably didn't mean, but some we did. And that was that. I left the force, set up on my own, we didn't see each other anymore, until I got that phone call out of the blue about Reginald Klyne. As you've seen, things haven't exactly improved between us."

Morgan ached for Jess. For Hunter. For every majos who found themselves burdened with a talent so few understood, and that everyone was afraid of.

But maybe, for Hunter at least, things could change.

Chapter Twenty-Five

There were no books or research experiments in Brooke's office, and nor was there so much as a hint of Essence. It was just an ordinary GP's room, except that Brooke sat on a plain, plastic chair, like Morgan, instead of the office chair at the desk. There were tissues on the table between them, and a small globe that would crackle with pretty coloured lights inside if anyone's magic got too excited.

It was very different from Michaela's office, and Morgan was pleased about that.

Brooke sat cross-legged in her chair and guided Morgan through an initial meditation. Her voice was soothing and Morgan let himself relax into it. He didn't need to worry too much about his control or focus; he'd been diligent in the week after his encounter with Paul Bates, and Aiyeda had made an appearance most days. Last night she'd fallen asleep on Morgan's lap while Hunter stroked her head, although it had taken a fair bit of firm instruction on her part to make sure he did it right. Hunter seemed to be - well, not warming to her, exactly, but he certainly wasn't so scared.

"And we're back in the room," said Brooke. "How are you feeling, Morgan?"

"Okay. No, um, good. Things are better."

"How are you feeling about Dr Rosero?"

"I haven't thought about her much."

That wasn't strictly true. At first, when Sahil told him she'd turned up in Barcelona, alive and well and not at all kidnapped, he'd been relieved. Then, as it seemed she had no intention of coming back, and there was no explanation for why her office was left how it was, and Sahil assured him the CCTV in the road outside showed her leaving in apparent good health and unaccompanied, an uneasy suspicion set in. Morgan found himself considering that she'd left because she knew, somehow, that the jig was about to be up about her making Essence. Which made him feel terribly disloyal and angry. But he couldn't tell anyone any of that. Not even Brooke. And so it tended to go round and around in his brain when he lay next to Hunter at night and couldn't sleep.

"You said last time that her leaving felt like a betrayal."

"I've known her since I was in primary school. She didn't even say goodbye."

"I'm sorry, Morgan. That sucks."

"Yeah. Well. It's up to her, isn't it? She doesn't owe me anything."

"Doesn't she?"

Well, perhaps she did. Morgan sat up a bit straighter in his seat. Yeah, perhaps after all he'd been through a civil 'Goodbye, I'm off to Spain, here's the number of your new counsellor' had been in order. And with the recognition, the anger faded away, just like that.

That out of the way, he spent most of the session talking about Caleb. He'd gone back to work at Oyster, and if Morgan had had to charm his way around Pearl to make that happen, well nobody need ever know. Everything about Bubble was at the centre of a police investigation now and, as it was a majos-related case, full press restriction was in force. It hadn't taken much to convince Pearl, anyway. Caleb had always been her golden boy. She'd offered to take Morgan back too, but, well, he had other plans.

"Oh yes?" said Brooke. "What plans?"

"Oh, nothing special," Morgan said. "An old client took me on permanently."

"It must feel really good to have more security," said Brooke.

"Yes," Morgan's heart fluttered. "It does."

Morgan put his rucksack on his desk in Hunter's office, next to the shiny computer and a small pile of papers that had accumulated. He stacked the papers neatly and put them in his in tray.

Then he opened his bag and got out his mug, a pint of milk and a small pot plant.

Hunter emerged from the kitchen. "I've got the kettle on, Mr Kerry."

"Thank you, Mr Hunter. Would you like me to make tea?"

Hunter leaned casually on his own desk. "That would be awfully kind. Could you come here a moment, please?"

There was a twinkle in his eye, and he looked ridiculously hot, with all the leaning and stretched muscles and his soft, golden hair. Morgan stalked across the room to him.

"What can I do for you, Mr Hunter?"

"Three things. Firstly, as it's your first day, I would very much like to take you to lunch."

Morgan moved a little closer, so his thigh touched Hunter's.

"Second, I'm going to need your help putting the Klyne case properly to bed."

"Of course."

Hunter's arms slipped around Morgan's waist.

"And third–" Hunter kissed him on the nose. "–I rather want to ravish you on my desk. Do you think that might be arranged?"

"On my first day? Mr Hunter, you are so forward."

"Says the man who couldn't wait to ride my cock to oblivion last night."

Morgan sighed in mock martyrdom. "All right, then. Ravish me. If you must."

Hunter quickly spun them around so that it was Morgan who felt the sturdy wooden desk behind him, and then he kissed him, bending him backwards so his hair brushed Hunter's blotter. Morgan's mind was whirling with possibilities, and he was about to hop himself properly onto the desk when he heard a knocking sound. Like someone knocking. On a door.

The door.

They sprang apart just in time; the door to the office swung open and a woman came inside. She wore bright red lipstick, an immaculate skirt-suit, high heels and the silkiest blouse Morgan had ever seen. Her hair was an ebony sweep across her forehead, a perfect chignon at the back.

"Mr Hunter?" she asked.

"That's me," Hunter said.

"Oh, thank goodness," said the woman. "I really need your help."

Morgan whispered discreetly to Hunter, "I thought you said strange women never come to your office pleading for help"

"I said almost never," Hunter whispered back, his lips brushing Morgan's ear, and then he said to the woman, "Why don't you take a seat and tell me all about it?"

"I'll make some tea," said Morgan.

About the Author

HK Nightingale writes about people falling in love, staying in love and, quite often, fighting evil. It usually ends well.

New to the romance genre, she has published various other things here and there, and has served a decades-long apprenticeship as a fanfiction writer.

She lives in Yorkshire with two rather odd and fluffy cats, teaches creative writing to many lovely people and gets far too involved with video games. She listens to a lot of BBC Radio 4 and watches a lot of reality TV, which really confuses people's algorithms.

She's currently working on the next book in the Hunter and Morgan series, and putting the finishing touches on the first of an urban fantasy romance trilogy, *Moonside*, to be published at the end of 2019.

You can find out more at www.hknightingale.com and follow her on Twitter @hk_nightingale.

Acknowledgements

Thanks to Fragilespark for the art and cover design; to Emma and Kate for first reading and edits; to Mim for giving me wisdom and spoons when I ran out and catching some truly hilarious typos; and thank you to everyone who encouraged me along the way.

I have the best cheerleading squad ever.

Printed in Great Britain
by Amazon

54694738R00208